A Craftsman's Work
K.J. Dando

CAHILL DAVIS PUBLISHING

ISBN 978-1-915307-18-7 (eBook)

ISBN 978-1-915307-17-0 (Paperback)

Cahill Davis Publishing Limited

www.cahilldavispublishing.co.uk

For my potty mouth mother - Look! I only went and did it again!

CHAPTER ONE

Near the village of Almondsbury, in South Gloucestershire, England, a Tudor-style Victorian mansion stood proudly, surrounded by nine acres of land. It had been used as a naval training base during World War II, then later as a training school for prison officers until it eventually became derelict and finally suffered a large fire. However, over the last two decades, it had been vastly and skilfully restored and renovated into a truly breathtaking family home. The grounds boasted an outdoor heated swimming pool, a tennis court, orangery, and a large vegetable garden that provided fresh produce for the in-house chef to use during the summer months.

The interior was even more impressive than the exterior. There were several elegant reception rooms, a cinema, a library, and even a fully stocked bar room. The vast open foyer contained a grand staircase that led to seven substantial bedrooms, each with an en-suite bathroom.

The owner of this remarkable property was the business magnate and philanthropist Michael Brookes, who was sleeping soundly next to his fiancée, Lindsey, in their super-king-sized bed in the master bedroom. It was the end of September. A Thursday, to be precise. The time was approaching half seven, and although it was beginning to get lighter outside, the blackout curtains ensured that the room remained middle-of-the-night dark.

Thirty-six-year-old Lindsey, who was twelve years younger than Michael, was just beginning to stir. She was in that blissful place between consciousness and unconsciousness. She let out a sleepy groan, turned, and snuggled into Michael, resting her head on his chest. The movement temporarily brought Michael out of his deep slumber, and he used his left arm to pull her in even closer before drifting off again.

Michael and Lindsey dozed together like that for a few minutes until a woman's voice dragged them reluctantly to the land of the living. The voice belonged to their young Spanish au pair, Eva.

"*Jacob*," she called out.

At this time of the morning, Eva would be getting four-year-old Jacob, Michael and Lindsey's son, up and ready for school. However, she normally did this quietly so as not to disturb them.

Michael stretched and yawned. Lindsey let out a heavy sigh and pulled the duvet over her head. Eva continued to call Jacob's name. Her voice came from Jacob's bedroom next door and it increased in volume with every repetition. Michael switched the bedside light on and swung his legs out of the bed.

"What's going on?" Lindsey asked, her voice sounding sleepy and muffled from beneath the duvet.

"It sounds like Eva's struggling to wake up our little man," said Michael, rubbing sleep out of his eyes with the heels of his hands. "Either that or he's hiding from her again."

Lindsey pulled the duvet down to her chin and squinted at the light. "He's probably just tired from his first few weeks of school, bless him."

In the room next door, Eva's voice was not only getting louder, it was sounding as though she was edging closer to the verge of panic.

Michael pushed his slender five-foot-ten frame off the bed and padded across the master bedroom wearing only black boxer shorts. He grabbed his blue dressing gown off its hook on the back of the door and threw it around himself.

Lindsey flung the duvet off herself and jumped out of the bed. "Wait for me," she urged.

She followed Michael's lead and threw her pink dressing gown over her silk black nightie and quickly brushed her fingers through her long blonde hair. Michael opened the door, and they hurried along the landing before turning into the room next to theirs. Jacob's room. The room from where Eva was now sounding frantic.

"What? What is it?" Michael cried out as he entered the room. "What's going on?"

The room was huge. Not quite as big as the master bedroom, but it had more than enough space to double up as a bedroom and a playroom for little Jacob. Storage units filled with toys and games covered almost every wall. There was a large play rug on the floor covered with toy cars and a big ramp that was used to make the cars perform jumps. A space-themed play tent was in one corner, and in the other corner was Jacob's bed. However, his bed usually would have the duvet haphazardly strewn across it at this time of the morning. Sometimes, half of it would be on the bed and the other half would trail off onto the floor. Typically, it would stay that way until the housekeeper arrived at nine.

But this morning, there was no duvet. And there was no Jacob. The pillow was on the bed, at the top, exactly where and how it should be, but Jacob and the duvet were nowhere to be seen. Instead, two items had been placed at the centre of the mattress. Michael stepped past Eva to get a closer look.

Eva shook her head and spoke with a mild Spanish accent that was laced with fear, "I cannot find him anywhere."

Michael walked up to the bed, his eyes fixed on the two objects. On the right was a cheap black plastic phone with big rubber buttons. Not a smartphone. On the left was a charger, presumably for the phone.

"Whose phone is this?" Michael asked, turning to look at Eva.

Her eyes bulged and she shook her head and shrugged her shoulders animatedly.

He turned back to the bed and picked up the phone. The screen illuminated and displayed an icon of an envelope with a bubble in the top corner containing the number one: one unread text message. Michael pressed the biggest button at the top of the keypad, and the envelope opened. Black letters on a luminous green background filled the screen.

As Michael read the message, the blood running through his veins turned glacial and he suddenly felt lightheaded. Becoming unsteady on his feet, he sat down on the bed to stop himself falling, but his eyes remained fixed on the words written across the garish green screen. He didn't even notice that Lindsey had crossed the room and was now standing right in front of him.

"What... what is it, Michael?" Lindsey asked, becoming more and more perturbed. "What's wrong?" She had never seen the colour drain from someone so quickly before.

Unable to speak, he raised the phone and handed it to her without looking up. Lindsey took the phone from him and started to read the message. She took a sharp and audible intake of breath and raised a shaky hand to her mouth. The message read:

"If you ever want to see Jacob again, answer this phone when it rings and DO NOT call the police. Yours sincerely, The Craftsman."

CHAPTER TWO

At twenty-five past nine on the same morning, Tom Crane was walking into a modern office building in Cardiff city centre, Wales. His six-foot-two athletic frame was suited and booted in a navy-blue suit, dark brown brogues, and a crisp white shirt. Usually, he opted for comfort and practicality. He had drawn the line at wearing a tie though, and his collar was unbuttoned and open. His short dark hair was neatly trimmed, and although this wasn't his first choice of attire, he wore it well.

There's something about confidently wearing a suit that seems to enable you to walk in and around places unchallenged. Like you have a right to be there. Although, looking around at the people loitering in the foyer, Crane questioned whether he'd made the right call. Skinny jeans and loafers with no socks seemed to be the popular choice for most of the young men. He was relieved to see a man around his age, mid-thirties, wearing a suit and an open-collar shirt, albeit a light grey suit and pink shirt.

The building was home to the popular online news website Red Dragon N&S, the N&S standing for news and sport. Crane walked to the right and around the large circular reception desk in the centre of the foyer. He nodded at one of the two receptionists. She smiled back as he continued to head towards the lifts. She didn't ask him if he needed help or attempt to challenge him in any way; he looked as if he'd been here before and acted as though he knew exactly where he was going. In truth, it wouldn't have been a big problem if he had been challenged; there was already a contingency in place. But it certainly made things easier.

There were two lifts, side by side, with a call button between them. The button with an arrow pointing upwards was illuminated, a lift having already been summoned by the man in the grey suit and pink shirt. Pink-shirt man was a good five inches shorter than Crane, rotund, and had a dark designer goatee. He was standing in front of the lifts, head down, scrolling through his smartphone. He sensed Crane's presence and looked up. Crane gave him a polite nod, which the man reciprocated before returning his focus to his phone.

A couple of seconds later, there was a high-pitched *ping* and the doors to the lift on the left opened. Crane motioned to the man in the pink shirt to go first, and he followed. Pink-shirt man pressed the button for the fourth floor and then looked at Crane with raised brows as if to ask, "Which floor?".

"Five," said Crane. "Thanks."

The man pressed five and the doors closed. He looked at Crane as the lift began to ascend and said, "The top floor." It was a question masquerading as a statement. "Going up to see the editors?"

"Just one of them."

The man didn't seem to recognise Crane's bluntness and the fact he wasn't up for a conversation. "Which one are you here to see?" he asked. "I've not seen you around here before."

"You should consider yourself lucky," replied Crane sternly. "If you see me, it means you've done something wrong."

The man looked into Crane's icy blue eyes and wilted. He broke eye contact and averted his gaze to the lift doors. The lift continued on its journey up to the fourth floor in complete silence, and when the doors pinged open, the man kept his head lowered, shuffled out of the lift, and walked away without glancing back.

The doors closed, and as the lift began to rise to the fifth and final floor, Crane's phone started to vibrate and ring in his trouser pocket. He pulled it out and looked at the screen. The call was coming from a private number. He rejected it and slipped the phone back into his pocket. He never answered calls from private numbers. If it was important, they could leave a message.

The lift doors pinged open once more, and Crane stepped out into an empty corridor and turned left. He had never been in the building before, but after spending ten minutes studying the blueprints last night, he had a good idea of where he needed to go. He was heading for the largest corner office. That was where he was expecting to find the senior editor.

Crane navigated his way through a couple of corridors, past several office doors and two glass-walled conference rooms. The two people he passed in the corridor and the four who were sitting in one of the conference rooms paid no attention to him.

Eventually, he reached an open area. On the left were four black leather sofas surrounding a large coffee table. On the right was a large desk with two black armchairs facing the person currently occupying the desk. A middle-aged lady with a mousy bob cut and black-framed glasses. A large plaque on her desk declared that she was the secretary. She was the gatekeeper.

She looked up and gave Crane a welcoming smile. "Can I help you?"

He returned the smile and approached the desk. "I'm here to see Trevor Awbrey."

Her smile remained, but her brow furrowed slightly. "I don't recall seeing an early appointment in the diary for Mr Awbrey. What's your name, please?" She looked down at the laptop in front of her and ran her index finger over the touchpad.

Crane gave her his name. she double tapped the keypad and raised her eyebrows.

"Oh, you're right," she said, surprised and confused. "There you are. Nine-thirty appointment to see Mr Awbrey."

To be fair, her reaction was completely warranted. The appointment hadn't been in the diary until late last night when Crane's best friend and business partner Ricky had hacked into the company's intranet and put it there.

She pushed her chair back and stood up. "If you'd like to take a seat, I'll let him know you're here."

Crane thanked her but remained standing as she scuttled off up the corridor behind her desk. This part of the building was notably quiet. He could clearly hear her lightly knocking on a door at the end of the corridor followed by the low rumble of a man's voice instructing her to enter. She went into the office and closed the door behind her, but even with the door closed, Crane could hear their voices going back and forth for a minute or so. He couldn't hear any specific words, but from the tones, he figured they were debating who had arranged the appointment.

Eventually, the secretary emerged from the office looking a little flushed and flustered, but she forced a smile when she reached Crane. He found himself hoping that his actions hadn't got her into too much trouble.

"You can head straight down," she said. "It's the last door on the left."

Crane thanked her and headed up the corridor. The last door on the left had been left wide open. He walked straight in without knocking and closed the door behind him. The office was just as big as he'd expected it to be from the blueprints. Large windows covered two of the walls and offered panoramic views of the city. There were two black leather sofas with a small coffee table in the middle for informal meetings, and a large desk at the back with two armchairs facing it.

Behind the desk stood a tall, slim man, probably mid-forties, with medium-length brown hair styled into a side parting. He wore a dark pinstripe suit with a light blue shirt and no tie. He was clean-shaven and smiled broadly as Crane approached the desk.

"Trevor Awbrey," the man said, confidently offering his hand. "And it's Tom Crane, isn't it?"

Crane shook his hand. "Just Crane is fine."

"Okay... Crane." For a second, Trevor seemed a little taken aback about only using Crane's surname, but he quickly recovered and gestured to one of the armchairs. "Please, take a seat."

They both sat down.

"Are you police? Or were you? Isn't that a police thing to go by your surname?"

"Ex-forces."

Trevor grinned smugly. "I knew it was something like that. Which branch?"

"Army."

Trevor nodded as if he'd guessed correctly in his head again. "And which regiment?"

"The Special Reconnaissance Regiment."

Trevor stopped nodding and frowned. "I've not heard of that one."

"Not many people have," replied Crane matter-of-factly, making no offer to elaborate.

"So," said Trevor after a few seconds of awkward silence. "I have an apology to give and a confession to make: I have no recollection of arranging this appointment, and to be completely honest, I have no idea what it's in reference to. Would you be able to enlighten me?"

"Of course." Crane sat back and placed his right ankle on top of his left knee. "I'm here representing my client, Lloyd Price."

This wasn't strictly true. Lloyd Price was a young Welsh boxer and the current British and Commonwealth lightweight champion, and although Crane was there to represent his interests, technically it was Lloyd Price's manager who had contacted Crane and asked for his help.

Trevor peered at him through narrow eyes. "Why would a representative of Lloyd Price need to speak to me?"

"Because you're planning on publishing a big story about him this weekend."

Trevor's brow furrowed. "If that's right, and I'm not saying that it is. But *if* it was right, how do you know?"

"Because the source who provided you with the story, and apparently a few photographs, called Lloyd when he was drunk a couple of nights ago and told him all about selling the story to you."

The source was Lloyd's ex-boyfriend Jamie. They had been together for just over a year. Both the relationship and Lloyd's sexuality had so far been hidden from the public eye.

"So you're a lawyer here to warn us off publishing the story?"

"No, I'm not a lawyer, I'm a—" Crane stopped himself from saying *fixer*. "I'm a consultant. And no, I'm not here to warn you off publishing the story. Well, not exactly."

Trevor was listening intently, his lips slightly pursed.

"We want you to delay publishing anything about Lloyd for one week," Crane continued. "*And* we want a slightly different story to be told."

"A slightly different story?" Trevor's face scrunched up in confusion. "Why? There's nothing to be ashamed of; it's completely natural. I'm sure Lloyd coming out as gay will be celebrated. It'll raise his profile."

"None of that is being disputed," replied Crane calmly, "but understandably, Lloyd wants to come out on his terms, not yours or Jamie's. How about instead of running with a vulgar story with some crude pictures from his bitter ex-lover, you get the exclusive *coming-out* interview with Lloyd himself? It might even give your website some credibility—publishing a *real* story straight from the horse's mouth rather than some sensationalist clickbait bullshit."

Trevor took a deep breath. "The problem is sensationalist clickbait bullshit is what sells, and unfortunately for you and Lloyd, that's what this business is all about. It's the reason why we're waiting until the weekend to put it out—that's when most of our subscribers and followers will be active on social media." Trevor raised a hand and rubbed his thumb across the tips of his middle and index fingers. "More clicks equals more money. Simple as that. It's the way of the world nowadays."

Sadly, Crane knew he was right; humans were their own worst enemy. Negative news always spreads further and faster than positive news, and as with all businesses, journalism provides a service based on supply and demand. The more people click and share negativity, the more journalists are happy to pump it out for us all to consume.

"And that's exactly what's wrong with the world nowadays," Crane retorted. "Morals and principles no longer seem to matter. In fact, the truth doesn't even matter anymore. It's all about being first and creating as much hype as possible, regardless of who you hurt or how much damage you cause in the process."

"Don't hate the player..." Trevor gave a one-shoulder shrug and an arrogant smirk. "Look, an exclusive interview with Lloyd would be good, but what we already have is huge. We're projecting it's going to go viral instantly and the amount of revenue it'll bring in from clicks alone will be tremendous. Not to mention, we've already paid good money to Jamie for his story and the photographs. If we don't use them, it'll be a complete waste."

"We could reimburse you." Crane said, upturning a hand. "Whatever you paid Jamie, we'll cover it, and then you can run the exclusive with Lloyd next weekend free of charge."

"Why next weekend?"

"Because Lloyd's team has been negotiating for a shot at the world title for months. Everything's been agreed in principle and the contracts are due to be signed on Monday."

"How would Lloyd *coming out* affect that?"

Crane raised a brow. "Come on, I'm sure a man in your position has been involved in negotiations before. If there's anything that the champ's team can use to try and squeeze an even higher percentage of the purse, they're going to use it. Lloyd's team can't afford to risk negotiations starting all over again and the fight being delayed."

Trevor leaned forward and placed his elbows on the desk. He steepled his fingers and placed them in front of his pursed lips. He stayed like that for almost thirty seconds before giving a little shake of his head. "I'm sorry," he said without a hint of sincerity in his voice. "I'm going to run with what we have. It'll generate more interest and more revenue than an exclusive with Lloyd. Plus, I've already told the shareholders that we've got something big being released this weekend."

Crane sighed and got up from his armchair. "Okay."

"What? That's it?" Asked Trevor, looking around the room as if he were searching for an invisible audience. "You're not going to threaten to sue us or anything?"

"Sue you?" Crane chuckled. "That's really not my style."

He turned and walked away, stopped after only a few steps, then turned back as though he'd just remembered something. "Just one last thing—why did you email that video to me last night?"

Trevor frowned. "What video? What are you talking about?"

Crane casually walked up to the desk. Trevor looked up at him, his frown deepening with frustration and even a bit of fear. He pushed himself backwards so that he sank deeper into his chair, as if worried Crane was approaching for a physical confrontation.

"The video of you masturbating in your study," said Crane. "I must say, it makes for pretty grim viewing. But I suppose it's the kind of thing that could go viral and get lots of clicks. Although, I'm not sure your wife will be too pleased when she finds out what you really get up to when you're *working late*." Crane used his hands to put the last two words in air quotes.

Trevor's panic-stricken eyes popped and his mouth opened and closed wordlessly a couple of times. Eventually, he uttered, "What... What the hell are you talking about?"

"You tell me. You're the one who emailed the video to me."

Trevor grabbed his phone off the desk to check his emails.

The truth was, Crane and Ricky had gotten lucky last night. While they were doing a little research on Red Dragon N&S and Trevor Awbrey, Ricky hacked into Trevor's personal devices and noticed that he'd been logging into an adult website at the same time almost every evening, last night being no exception.

Ricky had activated the camera on Trevor's laptop and they watched as he sat in his study working. Then at around ten, his wife came in, said goodnight to him, and told him not to stay up too late working. At ten fifteen, Trevor proceeded to log into the adult website, which connected people via their webcams so that they could pleasure themselves while watching each other online. Ricky was able to record the whole interaction, although neither Ricky nor Crane could stomach watching or listening to it. They had muted the computer and walked around Ricky's converted barn to avoid the visual and sporadically took turns risking glances until Trevor had... finished. Thankfully it, or rather he, hadn't lasted too long. Ricky then hacked into Trevor's personal email account and used it to email the video file to an address he'd created for Crane solely for this purpose.

Trevor had obviously found the email in his sent folder because he spat, "What the *fuck* is this?" There was a mixture of panic and venom in his tone. "How did you..."

"Don't worry," replied Crane. "It's nothing to be ashamed of; it's completely natural. You never know, it might even raise your profile."

If looks could kill, Crane would have been obliterated and plastered across the office wall by now.

Trevor hissed through gritted teeth, "What do you want?"

"I've already told you what we want. A one-week delay on anything being published about Lloyd. Jamie's story and pictures disappear, and as a gesture of goodwill, we'll still give you the exclusive with Lloyd free of charge, but his team has to sign off on the final edit before it goes public."

"And you'll reimburse us the money we paid to Jamie?"

Crane held back a laugh. "Don't push your luck. That offer expired when I stood up."

Trevor slumped back in his chair.

"Do we have a deal?"

Trevor sat in silence for a while, seemingly running the whole situation through in his mind, trying to think of another way out. Crane knew he would only be running into dead ends.

"Fine," Trevor conceded reluctantly. "But what am I going to tell the shareholders?"

"That sounds very much like a *you* problem."

CHAPTER THREE

After leaving Red Dragon N&S, Crane drove to Ricky's converted barn in north Cardiff. Crane and Ricky had been good friends for over seven years and became business partners around four years ago. Ricky was a technological genius with hacking abilities that not only astonished but even scared Crane at times. He was certainly grateful Ricky was his friend and not an enemy.

The only thing that Ricky struggled with was social interaction. He had always been painfully shy and awkward around new people, but over the last couple of years, he had been clearly suffering from severe social anxiety and even agoraphobia. He ordered everything online, including his groceries, and never visited anyone. Crane had been considering arranging a therapist to visit Ricky at home, but he knew deep down that for any kind of intervention to work, Ricky would need to admit that he had a problem in the first place, which he so far hadn't done.

Crane slowly turned his magna red Maserati GranTurismo Centennial Edition into the loose gravel driveway and parked a few yards from Ricky's front door. The Maserati wasn't Crane's usual mode of transport. It generally only came out of his garage on weekends, but Crane figured it would have looked unusual stepping out of his dark grey pickup truck dressed in a suit for his meeting with Trevor Awbrey.

Crane pushed himself up and out of the Maserati and heard an audible clunk as the electric motorised multipoint locks on

Ricky's front door disengaged. Ricky took the barn's security very seriously because of all the valuable computer equipment inside. Crane twisted the chunky steel handle and pushed the hefty reinforced steel door open.

Ricky's barn had been completely restored and renovated less than four years ago. It was modern, spacious, and entirely open plan. There was a kitchen and dining area on the left, and a sitting area with large leather sofas surrounding a giant TV on the right. Stretched across the entire rear wall was an array of monitors, big screens, and computer equipment that looked as if it were a set-up straight from GCHQ. Directly in the centre of the barn was a spiral staircase leading up to a balcony that held the sleeping quarters.

Ricky pushed his five-foot-eight and slightly overweight frame up from one of the sofas and walked towards Crane with a game controller in one hand and a headset with a microphone in the other. What appeared to be a car racing game was paused on the enormous screen behind him.

"Someone wants to say hi." Ricky held out the headset to Crane.

Crane gave a lopsided grin and took the headset. He put it on and adjusted the microphone. "Shouldn't you be in school, Chloe?"

"You know, Uncle Tom, conversations usually start with a hello."

"Hello, smart arse. Shouldn't you be in school?" he repeated. "I know you seem to think you're an adult, but you are only fourteen." He could already picture her rolling her eyes.

"I've got a free period. I don't need to go back in until after lunch."

"And you think using this time to play computer games with strange men online is a good idea?"

Ricky shook his head and placed his hands on his hips in feigned annoyance. Crane couldn't stop himself from laughing and neither could Chloe.

"*Uncle Tom*," Chloe scolded him in jest. "Ricky's not a strange man, he's lovely."

"I wouldn't go that far." Crane smirked. "He's okay, I suppose."

Ricky directed an explicit hand gesture at him, but although it was partially hidden by his bushy brown beard, there was a smile on his face.

"On a serious note, how is school going?"

Chloe hesitated for a split second. "Yeah, it's good."

"Remember, you need to knuckle down and get good grades if you want that car and those driving lessons I promised you."

"I will, I promise. And then when I'm driving, I'll be able to start my apprenticeship with Ricky."

Crane raised a brow and looked at Ricky. "Start your apprenticeship with Ricky?"

Ricky looked back at Crane, shaking his head and shrugging.

"Yeah, he's gonna teach me how to become a super hacker."

Crane laughed. "And what makes you think that Ricky's a *super hacker*."

"Because I've got eyes," Chloe quipped. "The back of his barn looks like something out of a sci-fi movie. Why else would he have so much high-tech computer equipment?"

"Maybe he's a web developer," offered Crane.

Chloe snorted in his ear. "Yeah, okay. I'll tell the jokes."

"You really are turning into a smart arse. Look, I need to borrow your buddy for ten minutes. He'll be back online playing with you soon."

"Okay. But before you go, are we still going for pizza on Saturday night?"

"Definitely."

Chloe's tone suddenly turned coy as she said, "Uncle Tom..."

Crane's eyes narrowed. "What?"

"You know when you pick me up..."

His eyes remained narrow, but the corners of his mouth began to turn up in a knowing grin. "Yeah."

"Could you pick me up in your Ferrari?"

"We'll see." He, and she, already knew that was a yes.

They said their goodbyes and then Crane handed the headset to Ricky.

"How did it go with Trevor Awbrey?" asked Ricky, once he'd fully disconnected and switched off the headset.

"It's done. Although, I did need to use the video to persuade him."

Ricky gave a thin smile. "I had a feeling that was going to happen."

"Lloyd's team needs to organise an interview with Trevor before next weekend, and they'll have the final say on the edit before anything goes public."

"What about reimbursing them for the money that they paid for Jamie's story?"

"Not required."

Crane's phone began to vibrate and ring in his pocket. He pulled it out, and the screen once again informed him that a private number was calling. He turned the screen around to show Ricky before rejecting the call.

"That's the second time this morning." Crane frowned, slipping the phone back into his pocket.

"Do you want me to see if I can trace the call?"

"No, don't bother. It's probably just telesales. If it's something important, they can leave a voicemail."

"Fair enough." Ricky turned as though he was about to head over to the kitchen area. "Are you staying for lunch?"

"No thanks, I'm meeting up with Ella for lunch." Crane glanced at his watch. "In fact, I should probably head off; I'm meant to be meeting her soon."

"Again?" Ricky's eyebrows shot up. "It sounds like things are getting serious between you two."

Crane hesitated, not quite sure how to respond. They had only been officially dating for a month. He settled with honesty. "It's going well, I really like her."

"It seems like you've been seeing each other almost every day this past couple of weeks."

A wry grin spread across Crane's face. "Awww... are you getting jealous?"

"No, not at all," Ricky said dismissively.

"Really? Because it sounds like you're getting a little jealous."

"Shut up."

"Come here." Crane grabbed Ricky and wrapped him up in a bear hug. "Don't you worry, I'll always have time for my bestie." He laughed heartily as Ricky struggled to wriggle free and push him away.

"Get off," Ricky cried out, but he was laughing just as hard as Crane.

CHAPTER FOUR

Ideally, Crane would have preferred to have popped home, got changed, and swapped vehicles before meeting up with Ella, but he didn't want to risk being late. Punctuality was one of his bugbears. It had been instilled in him to always be five minutes early for everything when he joined the army at age sixteen. Plus, it was Ella's lunch break from work, so he couldn't afford to be late.

Ella was employed by a local charity that supported families with sick and often terminal children. Sometimes, she helped the families to research and raise funds for special treatments; other times, she helped them raise funds to fulfil the child's final wishes, then supported them during their loss. Crane truly admired the work she did and was fascinated by her strength of character. How she was able to help families during the most heartbreaking of circumstances yet maintain such a positive and happy-go-lucky attitude was beyond his comprehension.

The charity's head office was in Rhiwbina, a peaceful suburb of north Cardiff that was fortunately not far from Ricky's barn. It took him less than fifteen minutes to drive there, then another five minutes to find somewhere suitable to park. He eventually found a scarce non-permit-only space just around the corner, in front of a residential property.

As soon as Crane got out of the Maserati, he sensed several pairs of eyes on him. Externally, he remained composed, but internally he was cringing. He only had himself to blame. If he didn't want to stand out, he shouldn't be driving around in a bright red sports car. *That's it. I'm selling the Maserati and getting something a bit more low-key.*

Crane set off, turned left onto the high street, and inhaled the homely aroma of freshly baked bread as he passed a bakery. Ella's head office was only a few doors up, nestled between a florist and a barber. The ground floor was a shop run by volunteers and the first floor, where Ella worked, was office space. Crane pushed the glass door of the shop open, and an unnecessarily loud electronic beep notified the shop assistant that someone had entered. At first, he thought the place was empty of people, then a head suddenly popped up from behind a shelving unit towards the back of the shop.

A lady with short white hair and thick red-framed glasses beamed and waved enthusiastically. "Hello."

Crane raised a hand and smiled back, then navigated his way between clothes racks and shelving units to reach her. The shop predominantly sold second-hand clothes, books, and knick-knacks that had been donated by generous locals. When Crane reached her, he noticed a half-empty box of books at her feet and a half-full shelf of books in front of her. She was wearing a red cardigan and a big white name badge that declared she was a volunteer and her name was Maggie.

"Can I help you?" asked Maggie, still smiling broadly.

"I'm meant to be meeting Ella for lunch."

"Oh, yes." Maggie's eyebrows went up so high and so fast they almost flew off her head. "Ella did mention her new man was coming to take her out for lunch." She looked him up and down. "You're a strapping young man, aren't you?"

Crane laughed. "Thank you. Although, I'm not sure I can be described as young anymore."

"Well, compared to me, dear, you're a baby."

It was difficult to put an exact age on Maggie, but it was probably fair to say she had been collecting her pension for more than a few years. Crane glanced down to check the time on his watch, and Maggie's smile fell away. A troubled expression overcame her.

"Ella might be a little late coming down for lunch, dear. They had some bad news this morning."

"Really? What's happened?"

"One of the children Ella has been helping had some results back from the consultants this morning."

Oh no. "Not Megan?"

Ella had told Crane all about a nine-year-old girl called Megan she'd started supporting this week. Megan had been a happy and healthy young girl until just a few weeks ago when she began suffering from headaches. At first, they were mild and sporadic, but they very quickly became frequent and more severe. Her parents became increasingly worried and took her to their local surgery, but the GP they saw didn't seem concerned and just put them down to childhood stress. Tragically, he was wrong. A couple of days later, she had a seizure in school. She was rushed to hospital in an ambulance, where she was immediately admitted for tests. The last Crane knew was that the initial scans showed a growth inside her brain, but further tests were required to determine exactly what it was.

Maggie nodded solemnly. "It's growing fast and it's not in a good place."

"Is there anything they can do?"

"They've advised that it's inoperable. They don't think she'd survive any invasive interventions."

A heavy silence fell over them and Crane's heart sank. What that poor girl and her family must be going through was unimaginable.

"It's terrible," continued Maggie. "They're saying she only has three months, maybe six at the most."

"That's heartbreaking." Crane's voice was barely audible.

"Ella's setting up a fundraising page on our website as we speak. Megan's parents wanted to take her to that big Disney park in Florida, but the doctors advised that she shouldn't fly. I think it's got something to do with the air pressure during the flight; it could cause complications." Maggie gave an unsure shrug. "Anyhow, they're looking into taking her to the one in Paris instead. The thing is, time is of the essence. They need to raise as much money as they can as quickly as they can. The doctors are worried that she's going to deteriorate very quickly, so understandably, they want to take her now while she's still able to enjoy it."

"How much is Ella trying to raise for them?"

"I think she said she was going to set a target of around ten thousand pounds. I guess she just wants to make sure the family has more than enough to really spoil her while they can." Maggie hesitated and then lowered her gaze and her voice before adding, "And maybe to help towards the cost of the... you know..."

Crane knew exactly what word Maggie didn't want to say—funeral.

A crushing silence fell over them once more as they retreated inside themselves to reflect. Crane didn't have any children of his own so felt as if he couldn't fully comprehend what the family was going through. He just knew that he felt overwhelmed with sympathy for them.

"I'll just go and let Ella know you're here," said Maggie, breaking the silence.

She walked to the back of the shop and went through a door labelled *Staff Only,* leaving Crane all alone in the shop. He immediately pulled out his phone from his pocket and dialled Ricky.

Ricky answered on the second ring. "Is everything okay?"

"I need you to do me a favour," said Crane, then gave Ricky a brief rundown of what Maggie had just told him.

"That's awful. What do you need me to do?"

"The charity Ella works for is setting up a fundraising page on their website. They're looking to raise around ten grand so that her family can make her final few months as special as possible. Can you keep an eye on the website and as soon as the page goes live, pay it? Whatever the target amount is, just pay it all."

"Consider it done."

"And if it allows you to, do it anonymously."

There was only a slight hesitation from Ricky, but he said, "Will do."

Crane thanked him and ended the call just as the door at the back of the shop opened and Ella and Maggie walked through. Ella's long wavy blonde hair framed her delicate features. She smiled when she saw Crane, and even though there was sadness in her green eyes, they still sparkled.

"You're looking very smart. Very smart indeed. What's the special occasion?"

"Well, I thought I'd make an effort for our lunch date."

"Really?" asked Ella in a sceptical and jovial tone. "Or did you happen to have a formal meeting somewhere this morning?"

Crane couldn't stop a wry grin from spreading across his face. "Maybe."

Ella giggled and turned to Maggie. "See, I told you he wouldn't have made the effort for me."

"You did, dear." Maggie shook her head in mock disapproval, then cracked a smile. "Now go on, you two lovebirds, go and enjoy your lunch together."

Maggie shooed them away with her hands. Crane headed through the shop to the front door, then held it open for Ella, quickly realising she wasn't behind him. She was still with Maggie, who was holding her arm and whispering something in her ear. Ella burst out laughing, then shook her head. She was grinning like a mischievous schoolgirl as she walked away.

"What was that all about?" Crane asked as she reached him and stepped onto the pavement outside.

Ella chuckled to herself and said, "Nothing."

"Well, whatever she said seems to have really tickled you." He was just happy to see her smiling, especially after the morning she'd had. "So, where do you want to go for lunch?"

Ella's eyes lit up. "Ooh, there's a new deli that's just opened around the corner I'd like to try."

"Sounds good to me."

As they started walking, Ella reached out and held Crane's hand. They had known each other for years and had been dating for several weeks, and during that time, they had been as intimate as two people possibly can be. But holding hands, especially in public, still felt a little strange to Crane. This was his first relationship since his wife's death almost five years ago, so a lot of things he was experiencing with Ella still felt new and fresh and, in truth, a little alien. But it also felt good. *Really* good. He gave Ella's hand a little squeeze, and she gazed up at him and smiled.

CHAPTER FIVE

Beneath the aroma of cooked food and freshly brewed coffee, a hint of paint and varnished wood still lingered in the spacious deli. The walls were cream. The floorboards were light oak and laid in a herringbone pattern. The tables were rustic wood and the chairs were black steel. Rectangular iron light fixtures with stringy green plants draping down from them were suspended from the ceiling. A long glass deli counter fully stocked with various fresh foods ran across the back wall.

It was almost jam-packed inside. Crane and Ella were fortunate to get the last unoccupied table in the front corner looking out onto the street. Crane habitually took the seat with his back against the wall, facing across the front window to the entrance. Ella sat opposite. There were two menus standing upright next to the salt and pepper shakers. They both picked one up and started to peruse their options. Crane decided on an all-day breakfast and Ella opted for the falafel salad.

Crane went up to the counter and placed their order, then miraculously sidestepped his way through the hustle and bustle back to the table without spilling a single drop of their drinks. He placed a steaming mug of green tea in front of Ella and kept the coffee for himself. A metal tin the server had given him, which he had tucked under his forearm, went between them. The tin was filled with cutlery, napkins, and a wooden spoon with their order number painted on the back of its head in black.

"So," said Crane, sitting back down opposite Ella. "What did Maggie say to you before we left the shop?"

Ella stifled a giggle. "She just said that you're a good-looking man."

"No, she didn't."

"Yes, she did."

"Well, that can't be all that she said." He narrowed his eyes in feigned suspicion. "Come on, what did she say that was so funny?"

"Nothing." Ella appeared to be battling to prevent herself from laughing again. "She was just being silly to make me laugh."

Crane continued to peer at her through narrowed eyes.

"Okay, okay. She said that you're a good-looking man and... if she was thirty years younger, she would destroy you."

Crane snorted and almost spat a mouthful of coffee across the table. Ella finally gave in to her laughter. They started to get looks from the people sitting on the tables closest to them. Most of the people around them smiled, but there were one or two fun sponges that appeared to be irritated by their laughter.

"Bless her, she was just trying to cheer me up." A sadness suddenly returned to Ella's eyes. "I haven't had a great morning, to be honest."

Crane reached out and placed his hand on top of Ella's. "Maggie told me about Megan. It's awful, I'm so sorry."

"Thank you."

Ella's phone beeped and vibrated on the table. She glanced down and caught the message preview. "*What?*" she exclaimed, picking up her phone and opening the message.

"Is everything okay?"

Ella's mouth was open in shock and she instinctively raised a hand to cover it. "Oh my god." Her words were muffled behind her hand.

"What's wrong?"

"Nothing." Ella lowered her hand from her mouth and breathed out in disbelief. "Nothing at all. In fact, it's the opposite. Someone has just donated all the money for Megan's fund."

Crane's brows shot up in feigned surprise, "That's great." *Thank you, Ricky.*

Ella nodded. "It is. The page has only just gone live and an anonymous donor just paid the full ten thousand pounds we were hoping for." She looked up from her phone and her eyes met Crane's. "Wait... was this you?"

"I've been with you the whole time."

It wasn't a full-on denial, but it certainly wasn't an admission. He hadn't lied. Ella continued to look into his eyes. He could tell she still had her suspicions, but she chose not to push him on it.

Crane had made many donations to the charity Ella worked for in the past, but it had been a while since he'd done so anonymously. He didn't want praise for doing it, he wasn't looking for a pat on the back from anyone, and he certainly didn't want people, especially Ella, thinking he was doing it to impress her. He simply wanted to help, and he was in a fortunate financial position to be able to do so.

Even though it was nowhere near the ideal outcome for Megan and her family, Ella seemed to brighten a little. She would soon be able to inform the family that they could start packing their bags and get ready to spoil Megan rotten.

The same young male server who had given Crane the drinks approached the table carrying two large white plates. After confirming who'd ordered the salad, the server placed the plates on the table, smiled politely, and left them to tuck in. The food was good. Crane hadn't realised how hungry he was until he started eating, and Ella must have felt the same, as they devoured their meals in near silence.

The brightness from outside dimmed a little, and Crane's eyes flitted to the window. A tall, slim man, probably mid-forties, with a neatly trimmed beard was looking through the deli window as if searching for someone, blocking out some of the natural light.

Ella placed her cutlery down and slid her plate away a few inches, then she glanced down at the time on her phone. "I need to head back to the office soon."

Crane didn't respond or even look her way. The man's eyes met Crane's and widened. He hastily looked at his phone. Ella's voice snapped Crane's attention back to the table.

"You're not even listening to me." She said it with a smile, but there was definitely a hint of annoyance in her tone.

"Sorry," said Crane, "I was somewhere else. What were you saying?"

"I asked if you fancy coming to mine for dinner tonight?"

"Sure." Crane nodded. "Sounds good."

Crane glanced out the window. The man was still there, head down, eyes on his phone. Suddenly, Crane's phone began to vibrate and ring in his pocket. He pulled it out and emitted a frustrated sigh when he saw the screen. He turned it around to show Ella before rejecting the call and shoving it back into his pocket.

"Don't they know you never answer private numbers?" Ella quipped, tongue firmly in cheek.

"Exactly. And that's the third time today."

In his peripheral vision, Crane spotted the man outside make a move towards the entrance. He watched as the man pushed the door open with one hand and walked into the deli, using his other hand to hold the phone against his ear. He headed straight towards their table. Ella was about to say something but stopped when the man came to a halt about a yard from their table and looked down at Crane. He was dressed in running trainers, blue jeans, and a khaki-coloured jacket. His hair was short and black, like his beard, but now that he was closer, Crane could see speckles of grey in both. He had a sheen of perspiration across his forehead.

"Can I help you?" asked Crane.

The man lowered the phone and held it out for Crane to take from him. "He wants to speak to you."

Crane looked at the phone, but he didn't take it. "Who wants to speak to me?"

There was an intense urgency radiating from the man's eyes. "Please." He thrust the phone towards Crane as though holding it was causing him physical pain.

Crane glanced around and noticed customers were starting to take notice of them—the couple who clearly looked confused, a nervous man hovering over them. Not wanting to draw any more attention to them, he sighed, took the phone from the bearded man, and held it against his ear. "Who's this?" he asked without attempting to hide his irritation.

"Hello, Mr Crane, I've been trying to call you." The voice was gravelly, with a slight Cockney twang.

Chief.

"I never answer calls from private numbers. What do you want?"

"Didn't you get my message?" Chief answered slowly and methodically. "I want to call in the favour you owe me. You know, since you killed one of my employees."

He did know. It had been six weeks since the incident, during Crane's hunt to find the person responsible for his wife's death. Although Chief's identity was a mystery, judging by the criminal activities his employee had been involved in, Crane figured Chief fancied himself as some sort of hot-shot crime lord.

"I did get your message," replied Crane, "but you used a private number that time too and you didn't leave any contact details for me to respond to you."

"I wasn't aware that my message required a response."

"Well, I certainly wanted to respond to it."

"Go on, then, Mr Crane. Enlighten me. How did you want to respond to it?"

Maintaining a calm and composed demeanour, Crane said, "I simply wanted to tell you to go fuck yourself. As far as I'm concerned, I owe you nothing." He didn't appreciate having his lunch rudely interrupted by some so-called crime lord.

Ella raised her brows in surprise and the man with the beard standing next to them dropped his mouth open in shock. Chief, however, didn't react at all as Crane had anticipated—he laughed. A low guttural chuckle that sounded genuine but also conveyed a sinister edge to it.

"I understand, Mr Crane. You see, I know a great deal about you. You have a formidable reputation and that's why I have a lot of respect for you. But, admittedly, you don't know who I am or anything about me, and for obvious reasons, I would like to keep it that way. However, it seems I need to show you exactly what I'm all about before you'll be open to having a real conversation with me." There was a slight pause as Chief, Crane presumed, was considering his next move. "I tell you what, I'll call you back from a number that ends in two-zero-six shortly. In the meantime, can you pass the phone back to the man who gave it to you?"

"There's no need to call me back; I've got nothing more to say to you."

"We'll see."

Crane held the phone out for the man with the beard. He reluctantly took it from Crane with a shaky hand and tentatively raised it to his ear.

"H-hello," he stammered. He remained standing next to their table, quietly listening to Chief. "Y-yes, I understand."

He ended the call and shoved the phone into his jeans pocket. His breathing was short and shallow, and the sheen of perspiration on his forehead was beginning to form beads. He sucked in a deep breath and slowly exhaled through pursed lips in an attempt to try and steady himself, then he stared directly into Crane's eyes and slowly and clearly said, "Nobody says no to him."

He took two big steps back, almost bumping into the table behind him. The two middle-aged ladies who were eating their lunch on it looked up at him questioningly. With his eyes still focused on Crane, he slipped his right hand into his jacket pocket and hastily pulled something out. Crane immediately spotted the glint of forged steel. He pushed his chair back and jumped to his feet, but it was too late. The man tilted his head up slightly, pushed the barrel of the snub-nosed revolver into the soft spot under his chin, and pulled the trigger. Even though the *pop* of the gunshot was slightly dampened by the man's flesh, it was still loud enough to startle everyone in the deli. For a split second, there was complete silence as every pair of eyes looked to where the sound had come from. Then the man's lifeless body tipped backwards like a felled tree and slammed onto the table behind him, knocking over a glass of water and sending a salad bowl tumbling to the floor. His arm dropped and the revolver slipped out of his grasp, landing with a dull thud on the oak floorboards. The two women were the first to scream, but soon the whole deli erupted with panicked cries.

Crane stepped in front of Ella to try to block her view of the man's body. He held out his hand calmly. "Come on, we should go."

Ella didn't move. Her eyes were glazed over, and although Crane was standing in front of her, she could still see the expanding pool of blood forming on the floor beneath where the bearded man's head was lolling off the edge of the table.

Crane took hold of her hand gently. She looked up at him, and he repeated softly, "Come on, we should go."

Ella nodded languidly and pushed herself up onto unsteady legs. Several people had already rushed out and more were following suit. Crane grabbed Ella's phone off the table and guided her outside. A crowd was forming and increasing in size by the second. Most were talking amongst themselves, some were being comforted and hugging each other, a few were on their mobile phones. Crane weaved through the horde with Ella in tow.

CHAPTER SIX

Crane and Ella walked together in complete silence, processing what had happened back in the deli. Questions were spinning around inside Crane's head, and one in particular truly concerned him—how had they found him? Ricky had encrypted his phone; it was meant to be impossible to trace.

Understandably, Ella was in a state of shock, but thankfully she did seem to improve the further they walked away from the scene. By the time they reached the bakery a few doors down from the charity shop, her gait had become more assured and some colour had returned to her cheeks.

Crane stopped on the pavement a few yards short of the entrance to the charity shop and turned to face her. "I know this is probably a stupid question, but are you okay?"

Ella went to speak, but no sound came out. She tried again. "I don't know." Her voice was weak and barely audible.

"Do you want me to take you home? I don't think you should go back to work after that."

Ella shook her head firmly. "I need to call Megan's family."

"Are you—"

"Tom, what was that all about?"

"What do you mean?"

"In the deli," said Ella, frowning. "I don't understand what happened. I mean, I was there, I saw what happened." She nibbled on her bottom lip and lowered her gaze. "But I don't understand it."

"To be honest, at the moment, neither do I."

"But who were you speaking to on the phone?"

Crane hesitated. "I don't exactly know that either."

She turned her head slightly to the side and looked at him through narrow, sceptical eyes. "Well, what did he say to you?"

"He said that I owe him a favour and he's going to call me back later."

"What favour?"

"He didn't say." Crane upturned a hand. "I didn't give him a chance to tell me."

"Why does he think you owe him a favour?"

"Look, I'm not sure what's going on or why this has happened, but trust me, I intend to find out." He hadn't meant for it to come across so abrupt, but Ella's reaction made it obvious that it had. She physically recoiled away from him and took a half step back. "I'm sorry. I didn't mean to—"

Ella raised a hand to cut him off. "It's fine. You don't have to share anything with me if you don't want to."

Her words were cutting and her tone was sharp. She didn't wait for him to respond. She brusquely walked away and pushed through the door to enter the charity shop, leaving a stunned Crane standing alone on the pavement outside.

He had never seen Ella like that before and he didn't want to leave things like that between them. He began to follow her, but as he looked through the window, he could see that Maggie was already talking to her. Even though he could only see Ella's back, he could tell by the stuttering shake of her shoulders that she was beginning to cry. Maggie approached her with open arms and embraced her in a sympathetic hug.

Maybe it's best to let her cool down. After all, he wasn't great at handling people when they were outwardly expressing their emotions; in fact, the mere sight of tears made him feel awkward and uncomfortable. He could never tell what the right thing to do or say was, which often meant he said or did the wrong thing. They could talk things through over dinner tonight... if his invitation still stood, of course.

Crane walked to his car and jumped inside, but he didn't start the engine. Instead, he pulled out his phone and called Ricky.

Once he'd briefly described to Ricky what had happened in the deli, he said, "I need you to run a check on my phone."

"What do you mean?"

"I mean, they tracked me to the deli and I want to know how. I was watching the bloke when he arrived outside and it looked to me like he was following directions on his phone."

"That's impossible. Your phone's fully encrypted. There's just no way."

"Are you sure?"

"One million per cent."

Crane was silent for several seconds, then he said, "If that's the case, it means they were tracking Ella's phone. It's the only plausible explanation. How else could they have found me?"

"All I can tell you is, your phone's secure. There's no way they could have traced it. I'll run a remote check on it now, just to see if I can find any evidence of an attempted breach. I'll let you know if I find anything."

Crane ended the call and tossed his phone onto the passenger seat. He started the four-point-seven-litre V8 engine, and it instantly released a thunderous roar before settling down to a deep rhythmical purr. He glanced at the road in his wing mirror to check it was clear before pulling out and tearing up the street.

CHAPTER SEVEN

Less than eight minutes later, Crane pressed a button on his key fob, and although he couldn't see them yet, he trusted that his electrically operated front gates were beginning to open. He eased his foot off the accelerator and allowed the Maserati to slow slightly before making the sharp left turn into his driveway. The gates weren't even close to being fully open, but Crane sped through the gap, leaving only a few inches of clearance on either side.

Crane lived near the summit of Caerphilly Mountain, which separated the city of Cardiff and the town of Caerphilly. His home was an impressive four-bed property. It was contemporary in style, built with light grey stone and complemented with sections of dark grey wood and broad windows. At over 3500 square feet, it was far too big for Crane to be living there on his own, but he wasn't planning on downsizing anytime soon. He had spent the best part of three years planning, designing, and building it. It was his pride and joy. His nest.

His driveway led to a substantial parking area and a double garage. Sitting in front of the right-hand garage door was his dark grey pickup truck. It was his workhorse and his preferred mode of transport for day-to-day use. As he approached the garage, he pushed another button on his key fob, and the left-hand garage door began to open smoothly. He turned the Maserati around and reversed it into the garage alongside his Ferrari F8 Spider. He had bought the Ferrari as a treat a few years ago, but the Maserati had been a gift from one of his previous clients.

Crane allowed the engine to idle for a minute or so before shutting it down. The familiar ticking sound of cooling metal came from beneath the bonnet as the fan continued to work overtime to force cool air through the radiator. Crane reached across to the passenger seat to grab his phone just as it began to ring. A number ending in two-zero-six came up on the screen.

Crane sighed as he stared at it, debating whether or not he should answer. Despite not believing he owed Chief anything, he didn't want to be the reason countless more people ended up dead, plus it was clear Chief wasn't going to leave him alone. It rang five times and then on the sixth, just before it was due to go to voicemail, he tapped the green icon to answer the call and tapped another icon to activate the speakerphone.

Chief's distinct, gravelly voice asked, "Are you ready to listen to me now, Mr Crane?"

Crane didn't respond.

"Are you upset about the man who blew his brains out in front of you and your lady friend? Don't feel bad for him," Chief continued. "The bloke was a nonce."

"What?" blurted Crane.

"That's right. He was a nonce, Mr Crane. A convicted paedophile. He was a football coach who groomed and abused young boys, and he was always going to die today, one way or another, so don't feel bad for him."

Crane slowly exhaled and noticed how this information seemed to ease some of the tension that had built up within him.

"I'm an opportunist, Mr Crane. And like I told you earlier, I know a lot about you. I know you're not happy that I made a man commit suicide in front of you and all those people. You think it was a sick and twisted way of getting your attention and, to be fair, it was." He let out a brief chuckle. "But I also know that finding out that he was a paedophile changes things for you.

Not much, but you feel a little bit better now that you know he was a filthy nonce, don't ya?"

Crane kept silent, not wanting to give him the satisfaction of agreeing with him.

"You see, I know that you have a strong moral compass and that you like to live by certain principles," Chief continued, seemingly unfazed by Crane's lack of response. "You'll be glad to know that the favour I want to ask of you doesn't conflict with any of them." Chief cleared his throat, but the gravel in his voice didn't wane. "Last night, a little boy was kidnapped. He was taken from his home while his parents slept in the next room. He's only four years old, bless him. I want you to help get him back home to his family. That's it. That's the favour. When you think about it, all I'm asking you to do is a good deed."

Crane replied with a single word: "Bollocks."

"What do you mean?" Chief sounded genuinely surprised by Crane's response.

"I mean, that's not it. The deed may be good, but your intentions won't be. Someone like you wouldn't do a good deed unless you're getting something out of it for yourself. So, what is it? What's in it for you?"

"You're right." Chief let out a deep breath. "I suppose this isn't entirely a selfless good deed on my part. But for you it is, and surely that's all that matters?"

Crane waited for an explanation.

"The boy's father is a very wealthy businessman called Michael Brookes, and I'm sure you'll be glad to know that all of Michael's business interests are legitimate and above board. Apparently, he's as straight as they come, a proper law-abiding citizen. I'm saying apparently because I don't know Michael personally, and before you start getting any ideas, he certainly doesn't know me or have any idea who I am.

"We do, however, share a mutual friend. Now, this mutual friend has asked me to help Michael. If I do, or should I say if *you* do, this mutual friend will owe me a favour. You see, that's what this game is all about when you reach my level. Networking and reciprocity. I scratch their backs and then they're indebted to me, and I like it when people are indebted to me."

Crane leaned a little closer to the phone. "So, who is this mutual friend?"

"Nice try." Chief laughed. "Now, the real question is, are you going to help this little boy and his family, Mr Crane?"

Under normal circumstances, there would have been no hesitation from Crane, but these weren't normal circumstances. "I'll think about it."

There was a moment of silence on the line before Chief said, "I know I don't need to explain this to you, but I'm going to say it anyway. This situation is obviously time-sensitive. He was taken last night, and the last I heard, the parents still haven't been contacted by the kidnappers. I'm going to message you their address now, and I'll trust that you'll go and meet Michael Brookes as soon as possible."

"And if I don't?"

"You will. I know you're a man of principle, Mr Crane. And I know that your desire to help an innocent four-year-old boy far outweighs any animosity you may hold towards me. You may think these are just words, but I do genuinely hope you're able to get this little boy back home to his family. Good luck." And with that, the line went dead.

Crane sat in the car for a couple of minutes replaying everything that Chief had said over and over in his head. Sure, he felt uncomfortable that Chief seemed to know so much about him yet he knew nothing about Chief. He also resented the feeling that he was being manipulated. But what pissed him off most of all was that Chief was right. Regardless of how he had been forced into this situation, there was a scared little boy at the end of it all and Crane couldn't walk away from that. It just wasn't in his DNA.

Crane's phone buzzed with a new notification. It was a text message from the number ending in two-zero-six. The message was short and only consisted of an address. Crane quickly typed out a message to Ricky asking him to find out whatever he could about the businessman Michael Brookes. He also asked Ricky to try to trace the phone that Chief had been using to contact him. He wasn't holding his breath; he fully expected it to be either a burner phone or encrypted.

Crane climbed out of the car, locked up the garage, and went inside the house to change out of his suit. He threw on a pair of dark blue chinos, a burgundy T-shirt, and a pair of navy blue walking shoes. He wasn't necessarily rushing, but he certainly wasn't dawdling. He reset the alarm, locked up, and jumped into his pickup truck. The electric front gates opened smoothly and silently. Crane drove through them, and thirty seconds later, just as they were programmed to, they smoothly and silently closed behind him.

CHAPTER EIGHT

Around half an hour into the forty-five-minute drive, Crane's phone rang through the speakers of the truck via Bluetooth. Ricky's name appeared on the infotainment system, and Crane pushed a button on the steering wheel to answer the call.

"What have you found out?"

Ricky's voice came through the speakers loud and clear. "Well, firstly, that phone number is a no-go. They're using an encryption app similar to the one I created for our phones where it bounces the signal all across Europe. There's no chance of tracing it."

Crane sighed. "I thought that might be the case."

"On a similar note, I ran a check on your phone and I couldn't find any evidence of an attempted breach. It's clean. I also..."

"You also what?" pressed Crane.

"I also accessed Ella's phone. I know you didn't ask me to, and don't worry, I didn't invade her privacy in any way. I didn't go anywhere near her messages or pictures; I only ran a quick check."

"And?"

"And it looks like she normally keeps the location services turned off, but it was activated this morning a little after half ten. Then, coincidentally, it was turned off again around the same time that you called me after lunch."

Crane's grip tightened on the steering wheel. "So they did trace Ella's phone to find me," he said through gritted teeth.

"It certainly looks that way."

Crane's knuckles had turned white and his forearms bulged. He felt a rage building inside him, and a voice in his conscious mind snapped, *How dare they*. But another voice, the more experienced and composed voice of his subconscious, instructed him to remain calm. Nothing good ever came from thinking or acting out of anger. His time would come, sooner or later. He inhaled deeply, eased his grip on the steering wheel, and asked, "What about Michael Brookes? What have you found out?"

"He's an extremely wealthy businessman," replied Ricky. "He started out selling used cars in his late teens and early twenties. By his late twenties, he owned several car dealerships before branching out into other areas of business, primarily land and commercial properties. When he hit forty, he sold off the majority of his businesses, but he remains on the board of a handful. He now classes himself as a full-time philanthropist. He's even set up a foundation that funds projects helping low-income communities in and around the Bristol area."

"So what are the bad bits?"

"The bad bits?" repeated Ricky, pronouncing each word slowly as though he was confused by the question.

"What skeletons does he have in his closet? Is he, or has he ever been involved in any illicit activities? Has he ripped anyone off to get where he is today?"

"I haven't found any bad bits so far. I mean, from everything that I can see, he seems like a decent bloke. Why have you asked me to look into him anyway? What exactly are you looking for?"

Crane gave him a brief rundown of what Chief had told him. "Can you make a list of his friends? Specifically, friends who are influential, or even if he is clean himself, does he have any friends with links to criminal activities?"

Ricky snorted. "Where do I start?"

"What do you mean?"

"Well, I haven't seen anyone with links to crime, but in terms of influential friends, the guy's a popular multi-millionaire. In the last couple of years alone, I've seen pictures of him at different events rubbing shoulders with dozens of celebrities and politicians."

Crane's brows raised. He liked to stay up to date with current affairs and found it strange that he'd never heard of Michael Brookes. "Where did you find all these pictures?"

"Mostly Instagram. And there's some bits on Twitter and Facebook, too."

"So, he's big into his social media?" *Well, that explains why I haven't heard of him.* Crane tried to avoid the world of social media like a bad smell.

"A bit, but I think it's more his fiancée Lindsey. I get the impression she enjoys the high life and likes to show it."

Crane flicked the indicator stalk down to signal before moving across into the left-hand lane. His junction was coming up soon. "What can you tell me about her?"

The sound of computer keyboard keys being rapidly tapped came through the speakers. "She's thirty-six. She went to the University of Bristol and got a degree in geography before spending most of her twenties working for numerous companies in administrative roles. Then, when she turned thirty, she hit the jackpot, literally. She landed a role in Michael's foundation and, looking at the timeline, it appears they very quickly began an affair."

"An affair? Michael was married?"

"He still is. From what I can gather, Michael and Lindsey became pregnant within just a few months of her joining the foundation. Michael separated from his wife, she moved out of their main residence, and then Lindsey almost immediately moved in with him."

Crane inhaled sharply. "Ouch."

"Ouch indeed," agreed Ricky. "Understandably, it looks like his wife didn't take too kindly to him upgrading to a younger model. I obviously don't know all the details, but it looks like Michael has been trying to divorce her since the separation, but she's been digging her heels in."

"How'd you mean?"

"Well, I imagine reaching a divorce settlement is complicated, especially since there's so much money and so many properties involved. But *five years.*" Ricky stretched out the words to emphasise the length of time. "It looks as though she's rejected every settlement proposal that Michael's solicitor has put forward so far. Although, saying that, one was put forward recently that is still awaiting a response. So, maybe they are getting close to reaching an agreement."

Crane appreciated the information Ricky had already found out about Michael, although he wasn't sure how useful any of it was. At least it was a start. He would be able to build more of a picture once he met Michael and Lindsey himself.

"Can you try to dig a little deeper?" asked Crane as he approached a roundabout and took the first exit on the left. "Specifically, does he have any enemies? Any business rivals that he's clashed with? Or maybe a disgruntled ex-employee? Is there anyone at all that he's pissed off recently?"

"I'm on it," replied Ricky, and the familiar sound of keyboard keys being tapped rapidly filled the truck.

Crane thanked him and ended the call.

CHAPTER NINE

A few minutes later, Crane took a left at a mini roundabout and entered a wide country lane. Tall hedgerows and dense bushes flanked both sides of the road. The trees above were beginning to speckle with shades of brown and red. Less than half a mile later, the satnav announced that he'd reached his destination. He eased his foot off the accelerator, and without the two-point-eight-litre diesel engine pushing it along, the truck gradually began to slow down. He coasted for about a hundred yards and then a gap in the foliage appeared up ahead on the left. Crane feathered the brake to slow the truck even further as he prepared to make the turn, if it was the one he was looking for.

A low grey stone wall came into view as he approached the gap. The wall was curved and led to a tall pillar made of the same grey stones. On the pillar was a wooden sign with the words "Woodlands Lodge" carved into it in a bold and swirly font. Crane applied even more pressure on the brake pedal and began to turn the steering wheel to the left. A matching stone wall and pillar came into view on the opposite side of the entrance. The pillars supported two broad Scandinavian redwood gates that were closed tight. He came to a stop at the intercom and lowered the driver's window. It was a simple chrome unit, similar to the one he had at home. He reached out and briefly pressed the call button, then waited. The best part of thirty seconds went by, then Crane's impatient side made him reach out and press the button again. This time, he kept his finger pushing down on the button.

"Hello? Hello?" a woman's voice came through the speaker a few seconds later. She sounded flustered and maybe even a little out of breath.

Crane released the button. "I'm here to see Michael Brookes."

The intercom went silent. A few seconds ticked by without a response and then suddenly the wooden gates began to open inwards. Crane waited for the gap to open wide enough before easing his truck through.

The driveway was long—well over a hundred yards. It ran alongside what would technically be the front lawn, but it was more of a neatly trimmed field. As impressive as the driveway and grounds were, it was the property at the end of it that made Crane involuntarily utter the words "holy shit" under his breath. In his line of work, he was accustomed to being around expensive and luxurious properties, and this one was up there with the most remarkable he'd seen. It was difficult to believe it was a family home; it looked more like a grand country hotel and spa.

Crane made his way down the shingle-covered driveway. The small stones crunched and complained beneath the truck's all-weather tyres. The driveway widened and opened up in front of the property, but there were no vehicles parked there. To the right was a detached garage building with four double doors spaced evenly apart. They looked to have been made from the same Scandinavian redwood as the front gates. Parked in front of the garage doors were three cars: an ancient black Land Rover Defender, a little red three-door hatchback, and an old grey Honda saloon. They weren't the kind of vehicles Crane had expected to see outside a property like this, but he guessed they must be owned by the household staff; a property like this would definitely require staff to manage and maintain it.

Crane headed straight towards the front door and stopped just a few feet shy of the steps leading up to it. He cut the engine but didn't make a move to get out of the truck. It had crossed his mind that this whole thing could be a setup. But then again, if Chief wanted him harmed or dead, he could've ordered the guy in the cafe to shoot him before turning the gun on himself. No, he wasn't being set up. *But still, it's always better to be safe than sorry.*

He leaned over, popped open the glove compartment, and pressed up firmly. There was an audible click and then a hidden compartment slowly and silently lowered. The handle of a robust, black plastic case came into view. Crane's fingers hovered in front of the handle, but he didn't touch it, wondering if he was overreacting. Inside the case was a loaded Heckler & Koch VP9 Match 9mm pistol and two spare magazines. His hand was still hovering in front of the handle when movement caught his attention.

The oversized front door of the property opened and a portly woman with short grey hair and thick-rimmed glasses stood in the doorway looking down at him. She wore blue jeans and a sage green jumper with the sleeves rolled up to her elbows. If Crane had to guess, he'd have said she was in her mid-to-late fifties. She waved at him, then used the same hand to beckon him. Crane raised his right hand in reply and quickly used his left hand to lift the hidden compartment back up until it clicked securely back into place, then he pushed the glove compartment shut before getting out of the truck.

"You must be Mr Crane," the woman called out in a thick Bristolian accent, now standing on the threshold with her hands resting on her ample hips.

So, they were expecting me.

"Just Crane is fine." He shut the truck door and headed up the four steps.

"I'm Carol." She held out her hand for Crane to shake. "The housekeeper and general dogsbody."

Now that Crane was closer, he noticed that it wasn't just the frame of her glasses that were broad. The lenses were just as thick and magnified her eyes, giving her an owl-like appearance. He briefly shook her hand and smiled politely.

Worry lines covered Carol's brow and a nervous energy radiated from her magnified eyes. Her words came quickly, almost as though they were spoken in a panic. "I hear you're going to help us get our little Jacob back home safe?"

"That's certainly my intention," said Crane, aiming for a reassuring tone but knowing that he sounded more matter-of-factly.

"Come on, then." She gestured for him to follow her with a wave of her hand and turned away. "There's no time to waste; I'll take you to see Michael."

Crane stepped into the vast foyer and closed the door behind him. Even inside, it was difficult to comprehend that this was a home and not a hotel. Crane could almost picture where the reception desk could be—right next to the spacious seating area, where two burgundy Chesterfield sofas and two matching armchairs surrounded a glass-topped coffee table. The walls were painted a shade of cream and each one was adorned with expensive-looking artwork.

Carol hurried on ahead, and Crane had to quicken his pace to keep up. She ignored the grand staircase on their right and headed towards the back of the foyer. They went through an archway and entered an area that could only be described as a mini foyer. There were two doorways—one on the left and one on the right. Carol took the one on the left, and they walked into an elegant sitting room full of golds and reds and creams. But it wasn't their destination; the room was empty and Carol didn't slow down. They passed two giant windows that looked out onto the rear grounds and an outdoor swimming pool. Crane found himself wondering if this was Carol's standard walking pace or if she was walking quickly out of a sense of urgency. It was likely the latter, but Carol did seem to give off a natural skittish vibe.

At the other end of the sitting room was another set of double doors. Carol barely stopped when she reached them. She knocked twice, and without waiting for a response, she turned the handle of the right-hand door and walked through.

Crane followed her inside. Two green Chesterfield sofas were facing each other dead ahead. One on the left, one on the right. A long mahogany coffee table sat between them. At the back of the room, between the sofas, stood a grandiose fireplace consisting of intricately carved wood, stained the same shade of mahogany as the bookshelves that covered every wall from the floor to the ceiling. The aroma emanating from the myriad of leather-bound books permeated the air—it was pungent yet pleasant and somewhat homely. Only one source of natural light entered the cavernous library, from a lonesome window up on the right-hand wall.

A man stood up from the sofa on the left at the sound of the door opening and turned to face them. He was a good four or five inches shorter than Crane, with neatly trimmed grey hair styled in a side parting. He was wearing beige corduroy trousers and a light blue polo shirt that his wiry frame struggled to fill.

Carol stepped to the right and turned so that she could see them both before declaring, "Crane, this is Michael." She made a sweeping hand gesture in Michael's direction, then she immediately repeated the gesture with her other hand towards Crane. "Michael, this is Crane." Without waiting for any kind of response from either of them, she turned on her heel and headed for the door. "I'll leave you two boys to chat."

When the door closed behind her, Michael drew his lips into a thin line. "Sorry, she can be a little... highly strung even at the best of times, which this obviously isn't." He stepped forward and raised his hand for Crane to shake. "Thank you for coming."

Crane shook Michael's hand and looked into his eyes. Part of him believed in the old adage—the eyes are the windows to the soul—the soul being a person's moral and emotional state, not the spiritual or immortal interpretation of the word. It was dim in the library, but Crane could see Michael's eyes were slightly bloodshot and the area around them inflamed, as though he'd recently rubbed them or had maybe been shedding tears. They were the eyes of a desperate man brimming with anguish and barely holding himself together.

"You'll have to forgive me," said Michael, releasing Crane's hand. "I've never been in a situation like this before. How do we even get started?"

"Before we even think about getting started, I need you to tell me the name of your friend. The one who organised for me to be here."

"He said you might ask me that."

"Well, now I have."

Michael raised both hands, palms facing forward in a gesture of surrender. "Look, Crane... all I know is my little boy has been taken. I called a friend for some advice, and he said he might know someone who could help. Then a few hours later, he informed me that you were on your way." Michael paused and then his mouth opened and closed wordlessly, as though he was having an internal battle of whether or not to say something. Eventually, he added, "He made me swear that I wouldn't give you his name. I'm guessing you haven't come here voluntarily, then?"

Crane considered the question for a second before responding. Technically he was willing to come, he wanted to help, but he certainly didn't appreciate Chief's method of getting him here. "It's complicated. Anyway, all that really matters is I'm here and I've come to help you get your boy back, but first, I want you to tell me who your friend is."

Michael clamped his lips shut; it was evident he didn't want to give up his friend's name. "I'm sorry," he said, grimacing. "I gave him my word."

"Okay," said Crane, with a one-shoulder shrug. "Good luck getting your boy back."

Michael's eyes went wide and his voice went up an octave. "Wait. You're not going to help us?"

"If you're not going to help me with what I want, why should I help you with what you want?"

"But... it's not that I don't want to help you. It's a matter of... loyalty. You seem like a man of principles. Surely you understand the importance of giving someone your word?"

Crane more than understood the importance of principles, but agreeing with Michael wouldn't have helped his cause. He decided to allow the silence to do the legwork for him, and it didn't take long for Michael to break.

"Look, how about I pay you double the standard fee you would normally charge for this kind of thing?"

Crane shook his head. "I'm not motivated by money."

"Ten times your standard fee?"

"Good luck." Crane turned around and headed for the door.

He wasn't really going to walk away from Michael and his little boy, but he was willing to bluff to try to get what he wanted. The door was only five steps away, and he'd already taken three of them. He'd expected Michael to have said something by now, but the room remained silent behind him. Crane deliberately slowed his pace for the last two steps. *Is he really going to call my bluff?* Crane grabbed hold of the brass door handle. Nothing. He pushed it down and pulled the door towards him. Still nothing. He moved to take a step out of the library and into the adjoining sitting room.

"Wait."

Crane stopped and looked back over his shoulder.

Michael sighed and lowered his head, defeated. When he spoke, the words came low and slow. "When my boy's back home safe, I'll give you his name."

Crane stepped back and pushed the door closed until the latch clicked into place, then he turned around to face Michael, his head still lowered, eyes fixed somewhere on the carpet in front of his feet. He looked as though he was still in a battle with his conscience. Crane didn't hang around. He didn't want to give Michael an opportunity to change his mind. The five steps he had taken to reach the door turned into three strides to return to where he had previously stood in front of Michael, then he raised his hand to offer another handshake. A prehistoric gesture between two men to symbolise a mutual commitment to an oath or a promise. Michael looked down at Crane's hand and, after a brief hesitation, he reached out and their hands firmly clasped together to represent the sealing of a bond.

CHAPTER TEN

"Does the name 'The Craftsman' mean anything to you?" Crane asked Michael, sitting on the opposite sofa, still in the library. He was sitting back, his right ankle resting on top of his left knee, his head tilted down, eyes fixed on the phone in his hand that the kidnapper had left behind.

The corners of Michael's lips downturned, and he shook his head. He'd already described the morning's events to Crane and was now perched on the edge of his seat, his spine tall and tense. "No, not at all."

"Have you pissed anyone off recently?"

Michael frowned. "What?"

"Have you pissed anyone off?" Crane repeated, looking up from the phone. "Either personally or professionally?"

Michael's frown deepened. "You think this could be someone looking for revenge?"

"I'm keeping an open mind to all possibilities, but most abductions are committed by a parent due to a custody dispute. When that's taken out of the equation, you're only really left with three other motives, and given your level of wealth, the odds would point to the first two—money or revenge."

"What's the third motive?"

Crane took a second to consider which words would be the most appropriate to use to the father of an abducted child. The best he could come up with was, "Someone who's unhinged and has sinister intentions."

Michael recoiled slightly. "You mean a paedophile?"

Crane ignored the question. He didn't believe it required an answer. Michael was an intelligent man with the ability to read between the lines. Instead, Crane raised the phone in his hand to emphasise his next point. "This definitely makes it look as though the motive is either money or revenge, maybe even a bit of both. So, I'll ask you again, have you pissed anyone off recently?"

Michael's eyebrows pinched together in deep concentration. "No... at least, no one that would do something like this."

"So you have pissed somebody off, then?"

Michael winced and tilted his head to the side slightly. "Not intentionally."

"Who are they? And what did you do?"

"I just outbid him for a piece of land."

Crane looked at Michael and waited for him to elaborate. It didn't take long for Michael to get the message.

"His name's Steve Flockton, and he's the owner of Flockton Contractors Limited. It's a mid-sized construction company, but apparently he's trying to expand and start some of his own projects. A plot of land came up for sale in the centre of Bristol a couple of months ago. We both went in for it and"—Michael upturned both of his hands and shrugged—"I outbid him."

Crane gave Michael a sideways glance. "That's it?"

"Not quite." Michael sighed. "A couple of days after my bid was accepted, Steve found out what my plans were for the site and approached me. You see, I'm looking to build a high-end six-storey apartment block with commercial lets on the ground floor. He asked me to give him the contract to build it." Michael paused for a second. "No. Let me rephrase that, he *demanded* to have the contract to build it. The thing is, from what I've heard, Steve's a very slippery character. I wouldn't trust him or his company to build me a garden shed, never mind a high-end block of apartments.

"Anyway, at first, I was trying to be amicable and polite. I told him that I'd already agreed to give the contract to a firm I'd been using for the last twenty years and I didn't want to jeopardise my relationship with them." Michael appeared to tense up and a flash of anger crossed his face as he recalled his interaction with Steve Flockton. "But he wouldn't take no for an answer and started getting aggressive and raising his voice, telling me that I owed him. That I stole the plot off him and the least I could do was give him the building contract. I was out for lunch with Lindsey in one of our favourite restaurants at the time. It was hugely embarrassing. He caused such a scene. As you can imagine, I really didn't appreciate the threatening behaviour he displayed, especially in front of Lindsey. In the end, I had to tell him to leave using short, sharp words."

"And did he?"

"Thankfully, yes. Although, not before threatening me."

"What did he say?"

Michael waved a dismissive hand to show he wasn't worried about the threat. "I can't remember his exact words, but it was something childish like, 'you're going to regret this' or 'I'll make sure you end up regretting this'."

Crane made a mental note of Steve Flockton's name. "Is there anyone else?"

"No," replied Michael, his tone firm and assured. "That's the only significant confrontation I've had in years."

Michael naturally had an amiable demeanour, but at times, there were glimpses of tenacity, almost a harshness. Crane hadn't been in his presence for long, but he could easily see how Michael would have been a shrewd operator in the boardroom.

Crane lowered his right foot to the floor and shifted his weight forward, resting his elbows on his knees. "So, going back to last night, do you know how the kidnapper got in and out without you knowing? What kind of security do you have here?"

Michael hesitated and flushed slightly, seemingly embarrassed to answer the question. "The house is fitted with a decent alarm system. There's contact sensors on all the windows and doors, and there's motion sensors throughout the ground floor. When the alarm is triggered, our home security company is alerted and they try to call us. If we don't answer within two minutes, they contact the police."

"I'm guessing it wasn't set last night?"

Michael clamped his lips together. It seemed to be a habit of his whenever he wanted to refrain from saying something. "The truth is, we hardly ever set it."

Crane's eyebrows went up and his forehead wrinkled in surprise.

"I know," said Michael, looking down at the coffee table to avoid Crane's eyes. "The thing is, I've lived in this house for almost twenty years and I've not had a single issue in that time. To be completely honest, I only agreed to upgrade the security system a few years ago because the insurance company insisted on it. I've always felt so safe and secure here. How wrong was I?"

"Do you have any cameras?" Crane hadn't noticed any outside or when he'd walked through the house to the library.

"Yes, but only one." Michael leaned to the side and reached into his pocket, pulling out a smartphone and using his thumbprint to unlock it. "I absolutely despise the idea of having cameras all over the place, like bloody *Big Brother*. However, we do have one of those doorbell camera thingies." He swiped and tapped at the screen on his phone. "I've always argued that if someone was going to break in, they would cover themselves up so that they couldn't be recognised by a camera anyway. So why bother?" He stood up and leaned over the coffee table to hand his smartphone to Crane. "Here you go. This goes to prove my point."

Crane took the phone from Michael. The screen was filled with a still image of the steps leading down from the main entrance of the property. They appeared to be illuminated by lights coming from somewhere out of shot. Crane thought back to when he'd pulled up to the house and remembered there were two colonial-style wall lanterns either side of the front door. The light must have been coming from them. Beyond the steps was black. Complete darkness.

The time and date were displayed across the bottom of the screen and there was a play symbol at the centre. The footage was paused at twenty-three minutes past two this morning. Crane tapped the play icon, and apart from the seconds ticking away at the bottom of the screen, the image remained unchanged.

Around half a minute into the footage, a figure entered the shot from the right, dressed in black jogging bottoms and a black hoodie with the hood up. They had their back to the camera and it looked as if they were hugging something in their arms. The corner of a duvet was visible over their left shoulder and another big lump of duvet was visible by their right hip. It was difficult from the footage to tell exactly how tall they were or to even accurately judge their build.

Whoever it was, they knew exactly where the camera was. Without looking around and running the risk of their face getting caught in the camera's shot, they reached back with a gloved right hand—a glove that was also black. It disappeared out of the frame followed by most of their right arm. Judging from their movement, Crane figured they were closing the front door behind them. Once that was done, their right arm returned around their front to hug the duvet. To hug little Jacob, who would have been wrapped up tight inside and sleeping soundly.

They took their time, painstakingly lowering themselves down each step, being mindful not to make any sudden movements that could have woken the sleeping four-year-old in their arms. By the time they reached the part where the shingle-covered driveway narrowed, they were barely visible, and after only a few more steps in the direction of the front gate, their outline had blended into the surrounding darkness.

Crane couldn't help but think about poor little Jacob, all warm and snug in the duvet, completely unaware that he was being ripped away from his parents and his home. There was no doubt he would have awoken disoriented and scared. In a strange place, with a strange person. Or people. After all, it was likely The so-called Craftsman wasn't working on his own.

Crane tapped the screen to pause the video and handed the phone back to Michael, who was still standing opposite him. "Were your windows and doors locked?" He tried not to sound too judgemental, but he could tell by the way Michael flinched at the question he had failed miserably.

"Of course they were. I may not be consistent with setting the alarm, but I always check that all the windows and doors are locked before heading up to bed every night."

Crane had no idea how many windows and doors the property had, but he found it hard to believe Michael's claim. "*All* of them?"

"Well... obviously not all of them." Michael waved his arms around to emphasise the size of the property. "The thing is, it doesn't matter how big your home is or how many rooms you have. You still end up living in the same handful of rooms that you would in a smaller house. There are rooms in this place I haven't set foot in for months." Michael took a steadying breath, but it didn't completely expel his defensive tone. "So, in answer to your question, no. I didn't check *every single* window and door, but I did check all the ones that we frequently use."

"Maybe—"

"And this morning, I did a full walk-through to try and find out how he'd gotten in, and every single window and door was locked tight. Except the front door, of course. As you can see in the video, he left it unlocked. But anyway, my point is, I have no idea how he got into the house."

"Maybe," Crane started again, "a window or a door was left unlocked, and after getting inside, he locked it behind him to cover his tracks. Or maybe he was already inside the house before you locked up and went to bed. I'm sure there's plenty of places to hide in here."

Michael's eyes flashed wide with fear. "You really think he could have been hiding inside the house?"

"It's certainly a possibility, but without an active alarm system or any cameras, we'll probably never know."

"Christ, you're right." Michael seemed to go a little unsteady on his feet and dropped himself back down on the sofa. "I should have been more security conscious. This is all my fault." He buried his face in his hands, and his shoulders shuddered as he began to sob.

Crane returned his attention to the phone that had been left behind by the kidnapper, leaving Michael with his emotions. It was black, made of cheap plastic, with a small screen sitting above the chunky push buttons. Crane opened the menu and looked through the features. There was no data connection and no GPS. It was the most basic of basic phones. Crane hadn't seen one like it since the early noughties. He went into the settings to look up the phone's number and pulled out his own phone from his pocket.

He quickly typed out a brief message to Ricky simply saying, "This is the phone left by the kidnapper", followed by the eleven-digit number.

There were no numbers saved in the phone's address book and there was only one text message—the one he'd already read. He opened it to get the number of the phone that had sent it, but the message had been sent to and received by itself.

Crane stood up, pocketed his own phone, and looked down at Michael, who rubbed his face, sniffed twice, and sat upright, attempting to compose himself.

"Look, I wasn't trying to insinuate that it's your fault. It's not."

Michael looked up at Crane, his eyes red and inflamed.

"It's just, the more information we have, the better chance we have of finding out who has him."

Michael rubbed his eyes with the back of his hand. "I understand."

"How many staff do you have working here today?"

"Why? Do you think one of them could be involved?"

"Do *you* think one of them could be involved?"

Michael shook his head. "No, of course not. They wouldn't be here if I thought they were capable of something like this."

"Good. But I still want to talk with all of them. How many are there?"

"Only three. You've already met Carol, our housekeeper. Then there's Eva, our au pair, and George, our chef."

Crane pulled his wallet out of his pocket, opened it, and slipped out a business card. It was plain white, with just his surname and phone number printed on it in small but bold black lettering. He leaned over the coffee table and held it out for Michael. "Text me their full names, addresses, and phone numbers."

Michael took the card.

Crane then handed him the phone the kidnapper had left. "Keep this with you at all times. If I'm not with you when it rings, put it on loudspeaker and use your phone to video or record the call. I want to hear everything he has to say when he calls." Crane held up three fingers. "There's three objectives I need you to focus on during the call. Get him to talk as much and for as long as possible. Insist on speaking with Jacob; we need proof of life before we consider listening to any of his demands. Try and remain calm. At the moment, we have little to no control over the situation, but let's not give him any satisfaction by sounding helpless or desperate."

Michael nodded resolutely.

Crane turned to head for the door, but he stopped when a thought popped in his head. "Where's Lindsey?"

Michael pointed towards the ceiling. "She's in Jacob's room. "She's really struggling with all this."

"It's understandable. But can you ask her to come and find me for a quick chat?" Crane realised his request sounded a little cold, so he added, "When she feels up to it, of course."

"Of course. Do you want me to come with you to introduce you to the staff?"

"No, you go check on Lindsey." Crane wanted the staff to speak freely, without the pressure of their boss listening in.

As he left the library and closed the door behind him, one question was burrowing itself deep into his brain: *Why did the kidnapper leave via the main entrance?* It was where the only camera for the whole property was located. It was as though he was taunting them, as if he was saying, "Look, I'm taking your little boy."

CHAPTER ELEVEN

Crane retraced his steps through the sitting room adjacent to the library. He planned to just wander around and get a feel for the place. He'd speak to whomever he happened to come across first. He took a right out of the sitting room but was forced to come to an abrupt halt. He hadn't been expecting to bump into anyone so soon, but especially not almost literally. A petite blonde lady wrapped in a fluffy pink dressing gown was padding barefoot towards him, her head down, eyes on the floor, seemingly lost to her thoughts. She must have sensed his presence because she looked up at the very last moment. Her eyes popped and she gasped audibly as she stopped, avoiding a head-on collision with him by mere centimetres.

Crane immediately stepped back. "Sorry."

"No. It's my fault," said the lady, quickly regaining her composure. "I was miles away."

Her face looked drawn and the area surrounding her eyes was blotchy and red, hinting that she'd recently been crying. Although he had a good idea who the lady could be, Crane didn't want to make any assumptions. "Lindsey?"

She nodded.

"I'm Crane."

"I know." Her voice was flat and almost lethargic. As though she'd had every last drop of emotion squeezed out of her and she was running on empty. "I was actually coming to find you.

Please, come with me. I want to show you something." Without waiting for a response, she turned her back on him and started walking away.

Crane followed her. They went into the foyer and started up the grand staircase. They walked in silence; Lindsey didn't seem to have the energy to walk and talk at the same time. Each of her steps were slow and laborious. Crane patiently stayed just off her left shoulder all the way up to the top landing, then Lindsey ambled across and entered a spacious hallway.

Crane's phone vibrated and beeped in his pocket. He quickly pulled it out. It was a text message with names, addresses, and phone numbers from Michael. Crane sent it on to Ricky and slipped his phone back into his pocket just as Lindsey stopped in front of a closed door. It was a traditional Victorian four-panel door made of solid oak. There was a plaque, painted blue with swirly silvery writing stuck on the centre mullion of the door. The plaque declared that the room belonged to Jacob.

Lindsey pushed the door open and entered the room. Crane followed her inside. The room was enormous and evidently doubled as a playroom and a bedroom. Even with the bed in one corner and a space-themed play tent in the other, there was still ample space left over. In fact, they still had enough room to fit a full-sized bouncy castle in the middle if they so wished.

Lindsey made her way directly to Jacob's bed. The pillow was where you'd expect to see it and the mattress was covered with a cream-coloured fitted sheet, but the duvet was missing.

Lindsey turned and sat down on the bed near the top, next to the pillow. She looked up at Crane, her eyes glistening with fresh tears. She tapped the mattress next to her. "Please," her voice choked a little. "Sit with me."

Crane hesitated for a second, but his curiosity to find out what Lindsey wanted to show him surpassed his uneasiness of sitting on the missing boy's bed. He stepped forward, and as he turned to take a seat alongside Lindsey, she fished out her smartphone from her dressing gown pocket. She shuffled closer so that their thighs were almost touching and then, without saying a word, leaned forward and held the phone out between them so that they both had a good view of the screen. She then tapped the centre of the screen with her index finger.

Soft background music began to play, and a still image of Lindsey wearing a patient gown and sitting up in a hospital bed filled the screen. She was gazing down adoringly at the newborn baby swaddled up tight in a fluffy white blanket cradled in her arms.

Five seconds later, the image faded and was replaced with another photograph. This one was black and white and looked like a professional shot. Little Jacob was still a tiny newborn. He was being held between Michael and Lindsey, who were embracing around him. Their foreheads were touching and they were smiling down at their baby boy.

A couple more baby pictures followed and then suddenly the music stopped and a video clip of Jacob cut in. He was probably around six months old, on his back on a padded playmat and rocking side to side. Lindsey, who must have been the one recording the video, could be heard saying, "Here he goes." A couple more side-to-side rocks and then Jacob flipped over onto his front. The camera followed him and caught the proud gummy smile that spread across his face.

The music kicked back in and more pictures appeared and faded at five-second intervals. Jacob looked a little bigger and slightly more grown up in each one. The next video to briefly pause the music was of Jacob crawling up to a coffee table, then using it to haul himself up to his feet. This time, Michael was the camera operator. He could be heard saying, "Is he going to do it? Is this going to be Jacob's first step?" Lindsey was on her knees a couple of yards from the coffee table, beaming. Her arms were outstretched towards Jacob and she was frantically opening and closing her hands in an attempt to entice Jacob to take a step towards her. Jacob reached out with his hand, but he couldn't quite reach her. His wobbly legs edged him closer, but she was still just out of reach.

"Come on," Lindsey beckoned. "You can do it, Jacob."

Reluctantly, he released his grip on the table and staggered towards her. One step. Two. Then he dived into his mummy's open arms for a big cuddle. Michael and Lindsey both cheered.

Once again, the music returned and more pictures began to fade in and out. The whole video lasted almost five minutes; it was a brilliant ensemble documenting Jacob's first four years.

As a baby, Crane could see a lot of Michael in Jacob, but as he grew and developed, he started to look more and more like his mother with his blonde hair and blue eyes.

The final video clip appeared to have been taken recently. Michael and Jacob were playing football on some neatly trimmed grass, probably in the back garden. Michael was doing the typical dad thing of keeping the ball from Jacob and having him chase after it. Jacob, being a boisterous four-year-old boy, soon got tired of this and decided to turn the kickabout into a rugby match instead. He wrapped his arms around his dad's leg and, although he could have stayed on his feet if he wanted to, Michael played along and allowed himself to be tackled to the ground. Michael was laughing, and Lindsey, who must have been the one filming the video, could be heard laughing in the background, too. Jacob stood up and then flopped on top of his daddy in a sort of wrestling move, then he spotted that he was being filmed.

Jacob screeched, *"Mummy, Mummy, no."* He jumped up, started to giggle, and ran up to the camera. He grabbed it, pulled it close to his face, and with a mischievous glint in his eye, he blew a raspberry into it.

The video stopped and the screen went blank. Crane looked at Lindsey. Tears were streaming down her face. She slipped the phone back into her dressing gown pocket and then folded forward and used the gown's long sleeves to cover her face. Her shoulders heaved with each sob.

Crane stood up and walked around to a door just a few feet from the bottom of the bed. He pushed it open, expecting to find an en suite. He'd guessed right. The bathroom was very white, but the toys in and around the bathtub and a *Minions* electric toothbrush standing next to the sink added a little bit of colour.

Crane grabbed a roll of toilet tissue from the holder and returned to Lindsey. She was still snivelling into her sleeves but caught sight of the roll when he held it out for her.

"Thank you," she spluttered, taking it from him.

Crane sat back down on the bed as Lindsey unwound and tore off a big wad of tissue. She dabbed at her eyes and cheeks before finally using it to blow her nose.

When he sensed that she was beginning to regain some composure, he turned towards her, raising his knee up and onto the bed at an angle. "Why did you want to show me that?"

"Because..." Lindsey sniffed and cleared her throat. "Because you're here to help us get Jacob back home and..." She sniffed again and used the now scrunched-up tissue to wipe her nose. "I just need you to know that he isn't some kind of package or a parcel. He isn't some faceless little boy. You're helping us to get our little Jacob back. The kindest, sweetest, most adorable little boy in the whole world. You're helping to get him back home to his mummy and daddy, who both love and adore him more than anything in the whole world."

Crane understood Lindsey was trying to get him emotionally invested. She was trying to intensify his desire to help them get Jacob home. It was working.

Lindsey took a steadying breath, her eyes remaining focused on Crane's. She clasped her hands together just below her chin. When she spoke again, her voice was barely audible. "Please promise me you're going to get my little boy back home safely."

A big part of Crane wanted to be the reassuring guy. The guy who said the right thing to help comfort a desperate mother whose child had been taken. But no matter how much he wanted to console Lindsey and tell her what she wanted to hear, he could never be the guy who made promises he didn't know if he could keep. There were too many variables, too many things that were outside of his direct control; he was in no position to guarantee any outcomes.

Without breaking eye contact with Lindsey, he said, "I can promise you I'll do everything in my power to get Jacob back home safe to you."

A moment of silence passed between them. It was impossible for Crane to tell exactly what was going on behind Lindsey's eyes, but the slightest of vertical head movements told him she appreciated his honesty and response.

The sound of a man clearing his throat dragged them out of the moment and demanded their attention. Crane peered over his shoulder and found Michael standing in the doorway with his hands on his hips.

"Sorry, I hope I'm not interrupting anything," said Michael in a way that made it obvious he wasn't really sorry for the interruption. He walked into the room and directed his next words to Lindsey. "I was just coming up to check on you and see if you were feeling up to speaking to Crane, but it looks like he beat me to it."

"Actually, I went downstairs to find Crane and asked him to come up here with me."

"Oh, right." Michael flushed, likely embarrassed by his initial tone being somewhat defensive.

"I was just showing him the video of Jacob."

"I see." Michael gently bit down on his bottom lip.

Lindsey turned her attention back to Crane. "So, you wanted to speak to me?"

"I only want to ask you one question."

"Please do."

"Don't think too hard about it, just trust any gut feeling that you may have." Crane paused briefly to give the question some weight, fully aware that what he was about to do could backfire. "Who do you think is involved in Jacob's kidnapping?"

Without a moment's hesitation, Lindsey said, "Christine."

Michael groaned and rolled his eyes.

Lindsey's gaze snapped to the sound. "Look, I know you think I'm being silly, but that woman has spent the last five years trying to do whatever she can to make our lives a misery."

"Don't you think you're being a little dramatic?" asked Michael in a way that sounded more like a gentle plea than condescending. "I mean, yes, she dragged her feet with the divorce—"

"And tried to take as much as she possibly could from you."

"But it's all sorted now; we've agreed on everything in principle."

"But she still hasn't signed the papers."

"Even so, I don't believe for one second she has anything to do with this."

"How can you be so sure?" asked Lindsey, a hint of frustration creeping into her tone. "You said it yourself, she's turned into a psycho."

Michael gave an awkward glance in Crane's direction. Evidently, he was becoming uncomfortable having the back and forth with Lindsey in front of him. "She's certainly changed a lot from the person I knew, but kidnapping Jacob..." Michael shook his head, then held his arms out wide and shrugged. "Why? What would be her motivation? We just rolled over and gave her everything she wanted to get the divorce over the line."

"Exactly," Lindsey retorted. "Now that we've succumbed to all of her ridiculous demands, she's lost all of her power over us. Maybe this is her final hurrah to hurt us."

"Do you really believe that?"

Lindsey opened her mouth to reply, but no sound came out. She tried again. "I don't know." Her voice choked and the tears began to flow again. "I just... I just want our baby boy home."

"I know, sweetheart, me too," said Michael softly as he took a step towards her.

Crane stood up and moved aside to allow Michael to take his place on the bed. Michael opened his arms, and Lindsey leaned into him, burying her distraught face into his shoulder. He wrapped his arms around her in a loving embrace and gently stroked her hair as she wept.

Still facing them, Crane started to edge back towards the open door. In a voice that was close to being a whisper, he said, "I'm gonna go downstairs and speak with the staff."

Michael looked up at Crane and blinked back tears of his own. He went to open his mouth to speak, but his bottom lip quivered and no sound came out. Instead, he just gave a single nod before turning and planting a tender kiss on top of Lindsey's head.

CHAPTER TWELVE

When Crane reached the top of the stairs, he could hear a vacuum cleaner being pushed around somewhere down in the foyer. He walked down and found Carol vacuuming the already spotlessly clean carpet near the front door. She hadn't spotted him coming down the stairs. Possibly because she was engrossed in her task, or maybe because her spectacles didn't provide good peripheral visibility.

She eventually caught sight of his feet as he approached her, and she looked up. Her eyes went wide, or maybe they didn't—it was difficult to tell from the magnification of her thick lenses. She used her foot to depress a button on the base of the vacuum cleaner and the sound of the motor gradually faded away.

"Oh, hello," she said, still radiating a nervous energy, although it seemed to have dialled down a notch from earlier. "Can I get you anything? A drink, perhaps?"

"No, thank you." Crane waved away her offer. "Actually, I'd like to have a quick chat with you, if that's okay?"

"What?" Carol furrowed her brow. "You want to speak to me? But I'm just the housekeeper."

Crane appreciated humility, but sometimes he felt there was a fine line between humility and self-deprecation. "No, you're not *just* the housekeeper, you're *the* housekeeper, which means you know more about this house and the people in it than anyone else."

Carol's brow unfurled and the corners of her mouth upturned slightly. "Yes," she said, pushing her shoulders back like a proud peacock. "I suppose you could say that."

One corner of Crane's mouth went up into a half-grin. "Which is exactly why I want to speak to you." Crane gave a nod in the direction of the seating area. "Come on, let's sit down."

He walked across and took a seat on one of the burgundy armchairs. Carol followed and hesitantly sat on the sofa diagonal to him, perching herself on the edge of the seat as though she were prepared to get up and continue cleaning at a moment's notice. Crane, hoping that Carol might mirror his body language and relax a little, sat back, spread his arms out wide, and folded his left ankle over the top of his right knee. Carol didn't follow his lead. She remained rigid and unmoved, watching and waiting for him to speak.

"So, Carol, how long have you been working here?"

Carol glanced up and to the left, as if the answer were scribbled somewhere on the ceiling. "Oh, it must be coming up to nine years now."

Crane's eyes widened slightly. It was longer than he'd expected. "Nine years. So you were here when Michael's ex-wife lived here?"

"Yes, Christine. Although, she's not his ex-wife yet." Carol leaned a little closer and lowered her voice slightly, not that she needed to, as there was no one around to hear them. "Apparently, she's not making life easy for them with the divorce."

"So I've heard. Why do you think that is?"

Carol tilted her head down and looked at him over the top of her spectacles. "Hell hath no fury like a woman scorned."

Crane was familiar with the idiom. It had been adapted from a line in William Congreve's play, *The Mourning Bride*. The original line was: "Heaven has no rage like love to hatred turned, nor hell a fury like a woman scorned." It basically meant that there is no greater anger than that of a woman who has been rejected in love.

"Five years is a long time to hold a grudge; he must've really hurt her. Has she always been the type to hold a grudge?"

Carol snorted. "Darlin', I'll let you in on a little secret," she said in her thick Bristolian accent. "Us women, we bloody love to hold a grudge." She eased back on the sofa, finally relaxing a little. "Even if sometimes we don't deserve to hold a grudge."

"Are you talking about Christine? You don't think she deserves to hold a grudge?"

Carol tilted her head from side to side a couple of times as though she were weighing up which way to answer. "Yes and no. I mean, technically Michael did do the dirty on her, but their marriage was dead long before he met our Lindsey."

"Really?" Crane shifted his weight forward in his seat.

"Oh yes. They were more like housemates than a married couple during the last couple of years before they separated. I got the feeling that Michael kept trying to make it work, but Christine was happy to let their marriage fizzle out and turn into more of a friendship. I think she assumed that Michael would always be there. Like all she'd have to do is click her fingers and he'd come running to her." Carol snapped her fingers to emphasise her point. "To be fair, she was probably right. Well, that was until he met Lindsey, of course. She gave him the confidence to finally call it a day with Christine."

"Do you think Christine could be involved in Jacob's kidnapping?"

"What?" Carol flinched. "No."

"Are you sure?"

"Yes. You can probably tell I don't think very highly of the woman, but she wouldn't harm a child. No way."

"Okay." Crane eased back in the armchair. "So, who *do* you think took Jacob?"

"How would I know?"

"Because, as we've already established, you know more about this house and the people in it than anyone else. So, I'd like to know your best guess. Who do you think could be involved in taking him?"

"Wait." Carol squinted at him. "You think someone within the household, like a member of staff, could be involved in Jacob's kidnapping?"

Crane narrowed his eyes. He hadn't mentioned anything about the staff. "Do you?"

"No, not at all." Said Carol, waving an open palm at Crane vehemently. "But I asked you first, do *you* think one of the staff could be involved?"

"I don't know, but the kidnapper certainly knew his way around. He also seemed to know what security the property has, or should I say the lack thereof. So, I think he either gathered this information firsthand or it's been fed to him by someone who knows the property well."

Carol looked at him blankly, as though she wasn't completely following his thought process.

"Essentially, anyone who knows the property well or has been inside the property over the last few months is a person of interest."

Carol winced.

"What is it?"

"It's just... I think your list of suspects may be bigger than you think. Michael and Lindsey are very sociable people and enjoy hosting. They're constantly having family and friends over for dinner parties and gatherings. In fact, it was only a couple of weeks ago they had a load of clients and business associates over for a barbeque and pool party. There must've been at least fifty of 'em."

Bollocks. The extremely difficult challenge he faced had just become nigh on impossible.

CHAPTER THIRTEEN

Crane left Carol to finish vacuuming the foyer, feeling a little deflated after their conversation.

He followed the directions Carol had given him to get to the kitchen, where apparently he would find George and Eva. After walking through the archway, instead of turning left towards the sitting room and library, he turned right. The first double doors he walked through opened into an elegant dining room. Two crystal chandeliers hung above a long rectangular dining table, the rich mahogany complemented by the fourteen cream-coloured leather chairs surrounding it. A strip of neatly spaced tealight candles in crystal holders ran down the centre of the table, and there was a huge vase bursting with fresh white and pink lilies where a middle tealight should have been. On the left, two huge windows provided a view of the patio and barbeque area. On the right was a grand fireplace, similar to the one in the library. At the end of the dining room was another set of double doors, identical to the ones he'd just walked through.

Crane pushed one of the doors open and stepped off the soft cream carpet of the dining room and onto the hard slate tiles of the kitchen. On the left, in front of a set of bifold doors that stretched across the full width of the kitchen, was another dining table, but this one was smaller and made from solid oak, with chalky white legs. The main kitchen area was on the right. White cupboards and light oak worktops followed the walls around in a giant U-shape, split in half by a huge farmhouse-style range cooker. Directly in front of Crane was an island with matching cupboards and worktop, featuring a double stainless-steel sink.

George and Eva were sitting on the opposite side of the island, facing Crane. Both jumped up from their stools at the sound of the door opening. Eva was petite, with long brunette hair tied back in a loose ponytail and flawless olive skin. George was only a couple of inches taller and looked to be only a couple of years older than Eva, maybe five-foot-six and early-to-mid-twenties. He was slim verging on skinny, black, and had his hair styled into neat cornrows. He wore a black apron with the words "An apron is just a cape on backwards" written across it in a bold white font.

"Sorry. I didn't mean to intrude."

George waved away his apology. "You're not intruding at all. It's Crane, isn't it?" He walked around the island and offered his hand to Crane. "I'm George, and this is Eva."

Crane shook George's hand and gave a polite nod to Eva, who stayed on the other side of the island. She waved back at him timidly before sitting back down on her stool.

"I was just about to make a start on dinner," declared George, "but can I get you anything first? Tea? Coffee?"

"A coffee would be great, thanks."

"How do you take it?"

"Black, one sugar, please."

George gave a thumbs up and then turned away to make a start on the coffee. Crane took a seat on one of the wooden stools at the island opposite Eva. She looked up at him with a deep worry crease between her brows.

"Has there been any news on Jacob?" she asked in a doleful voice with only a hint of a Spanish accent.

"Nothing yet." Crane slowly shook his head before fixing her gaze. "You were the first to notice Jacob was missing, weren't you?"

Eva swallowed the lump in her throat. "I was meant to be waking him up and getting him ready for school, but..." Her voice trailed off and she paused to take a breath before continuing. "At first, I thought he was just hiding. I looked everywhere but... but he was gone." She looked down at her hands, which were resting on the worktop, and began fidgeting with a silver ring on her right ring finger as she fought back tears.

Crane gave her a few seconds respite and watched George load an aluminium pod in a black and chrome coffee machine. He knew the next question ran the risk of sounding like an accusation and could upset Eva, but it was a question he wanted to know the answer to, and at this stage, finding out the facts took priority over hurting feelings.

"Michael said you spent around fifteen minutes searching for Jacob before you finally started to panic and raised the alarm."

Eva, still looking down at her hands, gave the faintest of nods.

"How come you didn't panic or raise the alarm sooner? Didn't you notice Jacob's duvet was missing and a phone had been left on his bed?"

She looked up at Crane with teary eyes that were full of concern and not in the slightest bit offended. "I did notice, but Jacob loves playing hide and seek. He often hides from me in the mornings when I go to get him ready for school. I just assumed this time he was hiding somewhere with his duvet. And as for the phone"—she shrugged—"I assumed it was some kind of toy. I've never seen a phone like it before."

Crane figured she was around nineteen, maybe twenty. It was completely plausible. At her age, the chances were she'd have grown up around smartphones. The one the kidnapper left behind looked archaic in comparison and the push buttons did make it look a bit like a toy.

"Here you go," said George, placing a double-walled glass mug in front of him.

Crane thanked him, but George didn't move to step away. Crane raised his brows to invite him to speak.

"We've been told you're here to help get Jacob back."

"That's right."

"Do you have any idea who took him, then?"

"Funnily enough, I was about to ask you the same question."

George took a half step back. "Me? How would I know?"

Crane raised his mug and inhaled the aroma. The coffee smelled good—nutty and smoky with a hint of sweetness. "How long have you worked here, George?"

"Just over two years."

"Well, I've only been here for just over two hours. So, out of the two of us, you're more likely to know who took him than I am."

"But..." George tilted his head to the side and peered at Crane, "Does that mean you think it's someone we know?"

"It could be." Crane took a sip of his coffee. "Does anyone spring to mind?" He alternated his gaze between Eva and George. "Have either of you noticed anyone acting suspiciously recently?"

George and Eva took a second to think.

"Can you think of anyone who may want to hurt Michael or Lindsey?" pushed Crane.

"No way," George said definitively and without hesitation. "They're good people; everyone loves 'em."

Crane looked at Eva to gauge her reaction.

She hesitated for a split second before agreeing with George. "Yeah, they're lovely."

Holding Eva's gaze, Crane said, "You hesitated."

Eva flinched. "No, I didn't."

"Yes, you did." Crane took another sip of his coffee before placing the mug down on the island in front of him. "What are you not saying?"

"Nothing."

Crane looked into her eyes and waited.

It only took a few seconds of uncomfortable silence for Eva to break. "I... I shouldn't say anything."

"Why not?"

"Because I don't really know anything. I just overheard them talking a few weeks ago."

"Who?" asked Crane, leaning forward and resting his elbows on the worktop. "Michael and Lindsey?"

"Yes."

"What did you hear them talking about?"

Eva chewed on her bottom lip and glanced at George.

"Go on, Eva," encouraged George. "It's okay. Tell him what you told me."

She took a breath, then said, "I overheard them talking to their friends about an argument they'd had. It had something to do with buying some land that some other guy wanted. Apparently, this guy was really angry with Michael and threatened him over it. I can't remember his name, but I think I heard them saying he had his own building company or something."

"Steve Flockton."

Eva's eyes flashed with recognition. "Yes, that was his name."

"I know all about it." Crane picked up his coffee and took another sip.

Eva sighed and sagged with relief. "I wasn't sure if I should have said anything."

"Is there anything else either of you want to tell me? It doesn't matter how small or insignificant you may think it is. At this stage, any little thing could help."

Crane drained the last of his coffee as George and Eva shook their heads.

"Okay." Crane stood up from his stool and pulled out his wallet. "If you do think of anything or if something new comes to light, call me." He handed them both a business card, then asked a question that had been on his mind since he'd watched the footage of the kidnapper leaving via the front door. "How many exits does this place have?" Crane pointed towards the bifold doors at the other end of the kitchen. "I can see the doors here and there's obviously the front door. What other ways can you get out?"

"There's another set of bifolds in the bar and games room on the other side of the house, next door to the library," said Eva.

"Yeah, and there's a side door in the utility room," added George, pointing at the door behind Eva where the kitchen worktop came to an end. "Why?"

"Just curious."

Crane walked around the island and headed over to the door George had just pointed at. He pushed it open and stepped into the utility room. The floor was covered with the same slate tiles as the kitchen, and the units and worktop that stretched across the full length of the left-hand wall also matched the kitchen. On the right-hand wall was an overflow chest freezer, a couple of tall cupboards, and a tumble dryer. At the far end was a window on the left and a door on the right.

Crane made his way over to the door. It was brown composite with four squares of obscure glass running down its centre and a chrome handle. Beneath the handle was a chunky thumbturn lock; no key was required to unlock it from the inside. Crane twisted it, and after one full turn, there was an audible click as the lock disengaged. He pushed down on the handle and pulled the door open with ease. A small step led down to some grey paving slabs. Beyond the paving was around twenty feet of neatly trimmed lawn before what appeared to be the edge of some dense woodland.

Crane stepped outside and looked left. Apart from the path leading to the back of the house and the lush green lawn running alongside it, there was nothing to see. He turned to the right and was greeted with more paving and lawn, but a little further on, towards the front of the house, a cobbled stone border brought the lawn to an abrupt end. Beyond the border, the ground was covered with shingle, which seemed to lead around to the front of the house and up to the side of the garages. From where Crane stood, he could see the front bumpers of the three cars that were parked in front of the garages. There was no fence. In fact, you could walk from the front to the back of the property completely unimpeded.

This only served to amplify the question that had been echoing inside Crane's mind: *Why did the kidnapper use the front door?* There was only one logical reason Crane could think of—the kidnapper wanted to be on camera taking Jacob. He wanted to be seen. *Why?*

Crane went back into the utility room and locked the side door behind him. As he headed back towards the kitchen, he checked his watch and stopped a couple of steps short of the doorway. It was almost five. *Shit.*

He pulled out his phone and quickly typed out a message for Ella to say he was tied up with work and wouldn't be able to make it to dinner. He ended the message by telling her that he'd call her as soon as he could, then slipped the phone back into his pocket. He was about to take a step forward when something caused him to freeze. A sudden overwhelming feeling that he was being watched.

In a single rapid motion, he turned his head and upper body around to look behind him. A man's face was tucked into the bottom left corner of the window, watching him. The man's eyes flashed wide and he ducked below the windowsill, disappearing from view. Crane had only vaguely caught sight of the pale face and dark hair, but he didn't get a chance to register any facial details.

"*Hey*," Crane called out impulsively.

A shot of adrenaline burst into his system as he bounded back to the side door. He started to twist the thumbturn lock and caught sight of the man through the window, sprinting across the lawn towards the cover of the trees. He was dressed in khaki cargo trousers and a dark grey sweatshirt. Crane yanked the door open and jumped outside to give chase.

The man had a decent head start and he was quick. But Crane was quicker. He immediately started eating up the distance between them. The man reached the area of woodland and began to weave between the trees. Crane momentarily lost sight of him.

A man's voice called out from somewhere behind them, but Crane was too fixated in his pursuit to care who it was or what they were shouting. He reached the edge of the lawn and hurdled stinging nettles to enter the woodland close to where he'd seen the man go in. He dodged the trunk of a huge sycamore and then spotted the man's flailing arms up ahead grasping at the tree trunks in a frantic effort to help him quickly change direction and lose Crane. But his efforts were futile; Crane was closing in on him fast. He could even hear his panicked breaths up ahead now.

The man attempted to jump over a felled tree, but his take-off was lackadaisical and his leading foot got caught on the remnants of a snapped branch. He landed heavily on his front with a thud, hands outstretched in front of him in an effort to break his fall. He slid forward like he was impersonating Jürgen Klinsmann's goal celebration before desperately scrambling to get back up to his feet. But Crane was already over him.

With the adrenaline still coursing through his veins, Crane practically picked the man up from the ground by the scruff of his neck and slammed him against the trunk of a nearby oak tree. The man was either disoriented or smart enough to know not to resist and fight back. Crane spun him around so that he was now facing him, then he pinned him to the tree using his left forearm across the top of the man's chest, just a few inches below his neck and only a small movement away from choking him. Crane turned so that he was standing side-on; he didn't fancy catching a stray knee where it hurt.

The man was a couple of inches shorter than Crane and slight in build. He looked to be maybe mid-twenties. His hair was greasy and his fringe was long, sticking to his forehead and almost reaching his eyebrows. His lower jaw protruded forward creating a pronounced underbite, and his eyes were fixed on an area of ground behind Crane.

He kept repeating the same three words over and over in a high-pitched voice between gasps: "I do nuffin'... I do nuffin'."

"Who are you?" demanded Crane.

"I do nuffin'," the man cried once again, still staring at the ground.

Crane could hear someone else approaching from the same direction they had just come from. Maybe the man wasn't alone. Maybe he had a friend. An accomplice. Crane looked over his left shoulder towards the oncoming sound and braced himself, his right hand clenched into a tight fist. He would put the man he was restraining to sleep first to neutralise the immediate threat, then deal with the next one.

An older man stumbled into view and came to a halt about ten feet from them. He bent over, placed his hands on his knees, and sucked in deep, desperate breaths. He appeared to be in his late fifties or maybe even early sixties. He was wearing brown trousers, a blue checked shirt with the sleeves rolled up, and a brown tweed flat cap. His grey hair poked out from under the cap, the colour of which matched his bushy eyebrows and three days' worth of stubble.

"Who are you?" asked Crane.

"Who am I?" snapped the old man before gulping another breath. "Who the *fuck* are you?"

As if on cue, George burst into the clearing behind the old man, closely followed by Michael.

"Crane." Michael raised both hands in a calming gesture before placing a hand on the older man's shoulder. "This is

Geoff, our gardener." He nodded towards the man Crane was restraining against the tree. "And that's his apprentice, Toby."

"Well, young Toby here was watching me through the utility room window."

Geoff huffed and raised a frustrated hand. "I told him to check for weeds in the gaps of the paving slabs around the house. You probably just caught sight of each other at the wrong time."

"If that's the case, why run?"

"Probably because you scared the shit out of the poor lad." Geoff pointed towards Toby's groin. "Look."

Crane glanced down and saw a small dark patch on Toby's khaki trousers begin to expand and spread down his right leg.

Geoff's face had already been red from the physical exertion, but it had now developed into an incensed shade of crimson. "He's got... learning difficulties, you bloody pillock," he seethed through gritted teeth.

"*Shit.*" Crane released the pressure from Toby's chest.

Toby swayed a little but remained on his feet. "I do nuffin'," he mumbled one last time before moving away from Crane on wobbly legs.

"Come on, lad." Geoff stepped forward and put a supportive arm around Toby's shoulders to guide him back the way they'd come. "I think I've got a spare pair of trousers in the orangery."

"Sorry, Toby." Crane was embarrassed by the outcome, but he didn't regret his actions. The day he failed to remain alert and reactive to all potential threats would likely be the day he would draw his final breath.

Before disappearing amongst the trees, Geoff glanced back over his shoulder to give Crane one final filthy look followed by an exasperated shake of the head.

Crane turned to Michael. "You said there were only three members of staff working today."

Michael, unaccustomed to having any of his errors pointed out, immediately went on the defence. "Yes, that's right, inside the house."

Crane's glare said everything he didn't. "Send me their details, too."

CHAPTER FOURTEEN

The earthy aroma of fresh coffee hit Crane's nose well before the first drop left the whirring machine. A steady black stream began to flow into his cup as he pulled out his phone to check his messages. Surprisingly, there was still no word from Ricky. Unsurprisingly, the presence of two blue ticks told him that Ella had read his message from earlier but hadn't replied. He pocketed his phone and stifled a sigh knowing full well that he was in the doghouse.

The coffee machine fell silent and released its final drops. Crane grabbed his cup and returned to the kitchen dining table, retaking his seat opposite Michael and Lindsey. There were only the three of them left now.

They'd sent George home after dinner. He'd cooked a delicious homemade lasagne with garlic and rosemary focaccia bread, and triple-cooked chips. Crane had demolished his portion, but understandably, Michael and Lindsey had barely picked at theirs. Eva hadn't fared much better either before she excused herself and headed up to her room. Crane didn't blame her for making herself scarce; the tension had been gradually building as more and more time passed by without any contact from the kidnapper.

It was now approaching seven and the phone the kidnapper had left behind sat silent and unmoving at the centre of the dining table.

Lindsey, still wearing her pink dressing gown, had spent most of the last fifteen minutes staring at it, yearning for it to ring. "What if it's broken?" she asked with an edge of panic in her tone. "What if he's been trying to call us, but it's not connecting for some reason?"

Michael placed a reassuring hand on top of Lindsey's. "It's got four bars of signal, sweetheart."

"But it could still be broken. I mean, just look at it, it's ancient. Do you think we should try calling it ourselves to check if it even works?"

Michael shrugged and looked to Crane for some guidance.

"If it'll put your mind at ease, go ahead," Crane said to Lindsey. "Just be quick because we need to keep the line open."

Lindsey slipped her phone out of her dressing gown pocket. "I need to get the number from it."

"I've got it." Crane pulled out his own phone.

He scrolled through the messages he'd sent Ricky earlier until he found the one he was looking for, then he read the number out for Lindsey while she tapped it into her phone. All of a sudden, the phone in the centre of the table started to vibrate and emit a high-pitched ringing.

Lindsey gasped. "That's not me." She turned her phone around to show them she hadn't pressed the call button yet.

Crane sat up and grabbed the phone off the table. The incoming number had been blocked by the caller. He reached over the table to hand the phone to Michael but didn't release his grasp when Michael went to take it from him.

"Try to keep him talking," instructed Crane quickly but clearly. "Use Jacob's name as often as you can and insist on getting proof of life before listening to any demands."

Michael's eyes were wide and anxious, but he gave Crane a determined nod before taking the phone and placing it on the table in front of him. He pressed a button on the phone to answer the call, then immediately pressed another button to activate the speakerphone. Meanwhile, Crane opened his phone's camera feature and started recording.

"H-hello..." Michael stammered. He was hunched over the phone, both elbows on the table. Lindsey leaned across and held on to his upper arm to listen in.

A few seconds of silence passed before The Craftsman spoke. When he did, his voice was low and flat and every word was pronounced slowly and clearly. "Michael, if you want to see your boy again, you need to listen to my instructions very carefully."

"Not until I speak to Jacob."

"I'm not letting you speak to him."

"Then I'm not listening to your instructions." Michael's voice went from hesitant and unsure to resolute and assured. It was as if he were in the boardroom negotiating a deal. "I want proof of life before we go any further."

The line fell silent, then ten painfully slow seconds ticked by until The Craftsman finally huffed, "Fine."

The sound of a car door being opened from the inside came through the speaker followed by crunching footsteps. It sounded as though he was walking across a patch of gravel. Crane counted thirteen steps in total, then they heard two loud bangs that were dull, metallic, and hollow. It sounded to Crane like he was slamming the base of his fist against corrugated steel. *Probably the side of a shipping container or maybe a metal shed of some sort.*

"Say hello, Jacob," The Craftsman hollered.

Jacob's voice came through the phone sounding distant and muffled, "*Mummy. Mummy.*"

Lindsey immediately cried out, "*Jacob, Jacob,* it's mummy. Mummy's here." She raised a trembling hand to cover her mouth as the tears began to flow.

Another two hollow bangs came through the phone followed by The Craftsman shouting at Jacob to, "*Shut up.*" Then thirteen crunching footsteps and the sound of a car door closing.

"Now then, Mummy and Daddy, if you want to see your little boy again, all you need to do is follow these very simple instructions. Firstly, you need to download an app called EAPA. You can get it from the app store on your phone. Then, once you have the app downloaded onto your phone, you'll need to create an account. When you've done that, I want you to preload your account with one hundred thousand pounds. You've got twenty-four hours to get this done."

"And then what?" asked Michael. "You'll bring Jacob back to us?"

"No, I won't be bringing him back to you." The Craftsman chuckled. "But when I have the money, I'll tell you where you can find him."

"Please." Lindsey leaned closer to the phone. Tears were running down her cheeks and her voice was choked and desperate. "P-please don't hurt our little boy."

"I'll call you at the same time tomorrow with further instructions," The Craftsman replied coldly, then the line went dead.

Crane stopped recording and placed his phone down on the table.

Michael looked up at him with furrowed brows. "One hundred thousand pounds. I thought he would have asked for more."

"He still might."

"But he said we'd get Jacob back once he got the money."

"He did, but technically he said, 'the money'. He didn't specify the amount at that point. There's still a chance he could ask for more."

Michael's forehead crinkled. "So, you don't think we're going to get Jacob back tomorrow?"

Crane took a sip of his coffee. "Look, the truth is, I don't know. I would love to sit here and tell you that everything's gonna be fine and we'll have Jacob home tomorrow, but at this moment in time, he's in complete control. He's got Jacob and we don't know who he is or where he's holding him." Crane placed his mug down on the table next to his phone.

"Now, there are always anomalies to this, but typically it'll go one of two ways tomorrow. One..." Crane raised the thumb on his right hand. "He's a pro. He wants to be in and out for a quick payday and disappear. In which case, a hundred grand makes complete sense. It's easy to split, transfer, and hide without raising any red flags. Two..." Crane raised his index finger. "Tomorrow's payment is just a test run. If the money goes through fine, he'll get greedy and demand more."

"So, what should we do?" Lindsey sniffed, her eyes still watery and bloodshot.

"Just so we're clear," said Crane, shifting his weight to sit a little more upright, "it's not my place to *tell* you what to do. I'm happy to advise you, but at the end of the day, it's your son being held captive. Ultimately, you need to be the ones to make the decision."

"I understand," said Michael. "So, what do you *advise* we do?"

Crane suppressed the urge to smirk at the rewording of the same question. "Well, we don't exactly have a lot of options at the moment, so we need to follow his instructions for now."

"Okay, so first I need to download this app. EAPA, isn't it? Do you know what it is?"

"No," said Crane, "but I know someone who will." He grabbed his phone from the table, pushed his chair back, and stood up. "Before you do anything, let me just make a quick call."

Crane made his way into the utility room for some privacy before dialling out. Within two rings, Ricky answered with, "I got nothing." No "hello", just straight to business. "Those names you sent through, from what I can see, they're clean. In fact, they're more than clean; they all seem like really decent people."

"They are," agreed Crane, casually pacing around the utility room. "At least, that's the feeling I've got from first impressions.

Although, let's not write anyone off just yet, as it's still early days, and as we know, first impressions can be deceiving. I've got another two for you to look into."

"Go ahead."

"A guy called Steve Flockton. He owns a construction firm called Flockton Contractors Limited."

Ricky mmhmmed and tapped away on his computer keyboard.

"And look into Christine for me. Michael's ex."

"Okay, will do."

Crane stopped pacing and leaned back against the chest freezer. "Have you ever heard of an app called EAPA?"

"Yeah, why?"

"The Craftsman instructed them to download it, create an account, and prepay a hundred grand onto it."

"To be fair, it's quite clever. It alleviates the risks involved with organising a cash drop, and a hundred grand can easily be moved around and hidden."

"I had the same thought. But what exactly is it? How does it work?"

"It stands for Encrypted Anonymous Payments App, and it pretty much does what it says on the tin. It's an app that allows people to anonymously transfer cash or cryptocurrency to each other. Instead of users displaying any of their personal details, they create an account, usually using a nickname, but essentially, they can use any combination of letters, numbers, or symbols to hide their true identity. As the name implies, all personal data and transaction records are encrypted to ensure users have complete anonymity when using the app."

"It sounds impressive, but I'm sure a technological genius like yourself can get in and trace a payment?"

Crane's tone had an air of jest, but only because he fully expected Ricky to come back with one of his usual wisecracks like, *Does the pope shit in the Vatican?* Or, *Do politicians overpromise and underdeliver?* However, no such remark materialised and Ricky went quiet. He was about to ask Ricky if he was okay when he heard him take a deep breath.

"I don't know. I mean, there's a small window of opportunity, but it's gonna be tight."

"How'd you mean?"

"Well, what's likely to happen when he calls tomorrow is he'll give Michael his username and tell him to transfer the money. Michael will just have to type in the username, enter the amount, and hit the transfer button. When he hits that button, the transfer will happen almost instantaneously, and that will be the window of opportunity closed. He'll be gone and so will the money."

Crane walked over to the window, but he could only see his reflection. Dusk was falling rapidly outside and the bright spotlights in the utility room made it impossible to see out. "So, what's the plan?"

"When he gives you his username, text it to me as quickly as you can and then delay the transfer for as long as possible. Obviously, don't put the boy in any danger by delaying for too long. He'll be expecting the transfer to be complete in less than a minute, so I imagine he'll start getting suspicious if you try and delay it for too long."

"How much time will you need?"

"I don't know."

"What's your best guess?"

Ricky hesitated for a couple of seconds and then said, "Two minutes if I get lucky, but don't hold me to that."

"Okay, well, we've got nothing else at the moment so at least it's a chance, albeit a slim one."

"A very, very slim one."

Crane ended the call by telling Ricky he would pop round and see him in the morning, then he went back into the kitchen. Michael and Lindsey were still sitting at the dining table, exactly how he'd left them. They looked up at him expectantly as he approached.

"It's an anonymous payments app," said Crane, still standing. "Go ahead and follow his instructions for now. If you have any issues setting up the account or preloading the funds, let me know and I'll get my colleague to assist you."

"Are you leaving?" asked Lindsey.

Crane nodded. "There's not much more I can do here until he calls back tomorrow night."

"So, that's it?" said Michael. "We just sit around and wait?"

"Not quite," replied Crane. "In the meantime, I'll be shaking some trees to see if I can get some fruit to drop. If you guys think of anything else that I should be aware of, call me." And with that, he turned and walked out.

CHAPTER FIFTEEN

The chunky all-weather tyres crunched over the shingle as Crane reversed his pickup truck away from Michael Brookes' front steps. He stopped to shove the transmission into drive, but before stepping on the accelerator, he tapped the phone symbol on the infotainment system. The screen filled with a list of his most recent contacts, and the one he was looking for was near the middle. He touched Ella's name, then swung the truck around and started to head up the driveway as a ringing tone sounded through the truck's speakers. Halfway through the third ring, it cut to the answerphone; she'd rejected his call. Crane, feeling the full force of Ella's cold shoulder, released a frustrated sigh as he hit the red icon on the touchscreen to end the connection before it beeped for him to leave a message.

The truck triggered a motion sensor as it reached the final third of the driveway, and the gates began to open inwards. By the time he reached them, he was able to drive straight through, but he slowed to turn right onto the dark country lane. As he did, the truck's headlights swept over the bushes and undergrowth opposite. Two bright yellow dots caught the edge of the sweeping light and then immediately disappeared in a flurry of leaves and branches. *Probably a startled rabbit or a cat, or maybe even a fox.*

He flicked the stalk to switch the headlights from dipped to the main beam and accelerated up the lane. The truck's speakers began to ring loudly for an incoming call. Crane's eyes shot to the infotainment system, half expecting to see Ella's name displayed on it. Maybe she'd rejected his call by accident, or maybe she'd been on the phone to someone else when he'd called, but it wasn't Ella. It was someone who Crane predominantly considered a friend, but someone who also happened to be a detective sergeant in the Police.

Crane tapped the green icon to answer the call. "Hi, Carter. Or should I be saying good evening, Detective Sergeant?"

Carter laughed. "Well, I guess the motivation for the call relates more to the latter. However, it's certainly an informal call and I'm using my personal phone, so read into that as you will."

"Fair enough. What can I do for you?"

"Did you hear about the man who committed suicide in Rhiwbina earlier today?"

Crane's eyes narrowed; Carter was testing him. There'd been CCTV cameras inside the deli and Carter must've recognised him from the footage, hence the call. "No, I didn't hear about it, Carter, I was there. But you already know that, don't you?"

"So, what happened?"

Crane spotted the faint glow of headlights approaching in the distance and began to slow down. He flicked the stalk to dip his headlights and pulled into an area on the left where the lane widened. "He just stood in the middle of the deli, put the barrel of the gun under his chin, and pulled the trigger."

"I mean before that," replied Carter. "Specifically, what happened when he stood at your table talking to you?"

"The guy just walked in and—"

"*The guy?*" Carter cut in. "So, you didn't know him?"

"No, never seen him before in my life."

"So, *you* didn't know *him*, but *he* knew *you*?"

"No, I don't think he did." The approaching car gave a quick flash of the headlights in thanks to Crane before it trundled past. "He didn't use my name or even say who was on the phone. He just handed it to me and said someone wanted to speak to me."

"Okay," said Carter with a hint of scepticism creeping into his tone. "So, who was on the phone, then?"

Crane pulled back out, flicked on his main beam, and accelerated up the lane. "I don't know."

"Come on, Crane. You gotta gimme something."

Crane took a second to consider his response. He didn't want to lie to Carter, but he also didn't want to reveal too much to him either. "Look, it was really busy in the deli and it was difficult to hear anything. All I can tell you is it sounded like he had a Cockney accent and I heard him say something about being owed."

"Owed?" repeated Carter. "Owed what? Money?"

"I didn't hear him say the word money, but like I said, it was loud in there and I may have missed it." Crane recognised that there was an opportunity to direct Carter and essentially the police in The Chief's direction. Committing or attempting to commit suicide isn't a criminal offence; however, encouraging or assisting suicide is. "Whatever it was, he didn't sound happy about it. He told me to give the phone back to the guy who'd given it to me, then a minute later, that guy shot himself in the head."

"Are you saying the man on the phone said something to cause the other guy to take his own life?"

"Well, I obviously don't know what was said, but it certainly looked to me like he was under duress. I mean, he seemed on edge as soon as he walked into the deli, but whatever the man said to him on the phone definitely tipped him over." Crane emerged from the country lane and went straight over a mini roundabout, heading into the hazy orange glow of a street-lit urban area. "I'd say it's definitely worth you finding out who it was on the phone to him. Did you recover the dead guy's phone from the scene?"

"That's the funny thing." Carter sighed. "We did recover the phone, but it's fried."

Crane raised a brow. "What do you mean it's fried?"

"Exactly that. The tech guys have been working on it for hours, but they think it was fitted with some sort of self-destruct mechanism. All the internal components have been burned. They're saying they've never seen anything like it before."

"That is odd," said Crane, although the revelation didn't really surprise him that much.

"It is," agreed Carter. "Look, would you be able to pop to the station and make a formal statement with what you've just told me?"

"Of course," said Crane, but then silently mouthed the word *shit*. He really didn't want to go to the police station and make a statement, but there was no way he could say no. Carter had been good to him and had never refused to help him in the past. In truth, it was the least he could do. "It's just, I've got quite a bit going on at the moment. Can you give me a couple of days?"

"Sure. Or I could send an officer around to your home if it's easier for you?"

"No, it's fine, I'll come to the station. Does Monday work for you?"

"Yep, Monday works for me."

"Great, I'll see you then."

"Before you go, I've just got one more question for you. Out of all the people that were in the deli at lunchtime, why do you think he approached you?"

Crane had been anticipating this question and tried to deflect it with humour. "I guess I've just got one of those friendly and welcoming faces."

Carter laughed, but Crane could tell he wasn't buying it. Even so, he didn't offer another explanation and Carter didn't push for one.

After saying their goodbyes, Crane tapped the red icon on the infotainment system to end the call, then his finger lingered in front of the screen as he toyed with the idea of trying to call Ella again. No, he'd go around and see her. It was harder to reject a knock at the door than it was to reject a phone call. And he was eager to check that she was okay after what had happened at lunchtime.

Crane returned his left hand to the steering wheel and was about to sit back and get comfortable for the drive ahead when something caught his attention in the left wing mirror. What looked like a small white van was speeding up the road behind him. It was difficult to judge distances through the mirror and under the artificial glare of the streetlights, but it looked like he was about a hundred yards back and closing in on him fast. He checked the road ahead and glanced at his other mirrors to gain full awareness of his surroundings. The roads were quiet. There was only his truck and the van on this side of the road. A small black hatchback passed him on the other side followed by an old red estate.

As the van got closer, he could hear its engine squealing and not just because it was revving high; the fan belt didn't sound healthy at all and it was letting everyone within earshot know. Crane watched in the rearview mirror as it kept coming without even attempting to slow down. The headlights disappeared from view below the rear window of the hardtop canopy and he half expected to be rear-ended, but nothing happened. The van must've hit the brake just at the last moment before contact. Crane hadn't been too worried either way; the van would have come off much worse than his truck if it had driven into him.

There was a T-junction around seventy yards ahead with a set of traffic lights that were currently on green. The road began to gradually widen and split into three lanes for the junction. According to the road markings, the left-hand lane was for turning left only and the other two lanes were for turning right. Crane was going right, so he took the middle lane. It would give the driver of the van a choice between the left-hand lane to turn left or the right-hand lane to overtake him. A younger Crane may have taken the right-hand lane and slowed down just to piss the van driver off for driving so erratically, but with age and experience, he was becoming more empathic. He had no idea who was driving the van or what reason they had for driving the way they were. It could be an absolute idiot, but it could just as easily be someone with a legitimate reason to be in a rush. Maybe it was a soon-to-be father taking his partner to hospital to give birth. Either way, he was trying to choose his battles more wisely.

When the road had widened enough, the van swerved to the right and sped up to get past Crane's truck. The engine screeched as though a dozen cats were being strangled beneath the bonnet. Crane glanced across as it went past and noticed the passenger seat was empty. There was no pregnant partner currently in labour there. Maybe the guy was just an idiot after all.

"*What the fuck,*" Crane involuntarily cursed as the van suddenly cut across into his lane and slammed on the brakes. Thankfully, Crane's foot had been hovering over the brake pedal in preparation to slow down for the right turn. He stamped on the pedal and yanked the steering wheel to the right. The front left side of his truck's bumper only missed hitting the rear right corner of the van by the width of a gnat's shaft.

Both vehicles jolted to an abrupt stop, with the van ending up a little further ahead and partially over the solid white stop line. The traffic lights next to it switched from green to amber. Crane could hear a horn blaring as he rocked back in his seat. It took him half a second to realise it was his horn. He'd automatically palmed it during the emergency stop. He released the pressure, and the sound died just as the driver's door of the van popped open.

There are three ways of responding to a threat: fight, flight, or freeze. People are capable of all three responses depending on the situation and the level of threat, but most people tend to have a natural or predisposed response to most threats. Crane's natural response was to fight.

As soon as he saw the van door start to open, Crane released his seatbelt and jumped out of his truck, all the while keeping an eye on the man getting out of the van. Specifically, he was looking at the man's hands to ensure he wasn't carrying a weapon. His hands were empty.

The man appeared to be in his late twenties, around five-eleven, and skinny. He wore black workman trousers and a dark green T-shirt. His face was twisted into a menacing scowl beneath a mop of ginger hair. "Who the fuck do you think you're beeping at?" the man spat, swinging his scrawny, tattoo-covered arms excessively as he swaggered towards Crane.

Crane was planning to use his nonverbal communication skills to respond to the question. He took a step towards the oncoming guy and braced himself, getting ready to throw a punch that would knock this mouthy arsehole into next week. But as he took another step forward, he suddenly felt a strange scratching sensation at the back of his brain. His subconscious was trying to warn him that something wasn't right about the situation. He almost ignored it. Partly because *nothing* was right about the situation and partly because he really wanted to punch the guy in the face. He stopped by the front right corner of his truck and stood his ground. A flash of surprise seemed to cross the guy's face, but then the scowl quickly returned as he came to a stop just over a yard away from Crane. They were now within swinging distance of each other, but they kept their arms by their sides.

"What's your problem?" snarled the guy.

"You're my problem," replied Crane, sounding a lot calmer than he felt. "Why did you stop the van like you'd just found out your sister's been cheating on you?"

The guy either ignored the insult or it had gone right over his head. Crane was inclined to believe it was the latter. He turned to the side and pointed back towards the traffic light. "It was red."

"Bollocks," said Crane. "No, it wasn't."

"Are you calling me a liar?"

"Yeah, that's exactly what I'm calling you."

The guy squared up to him again, but Crane wasn't even looking at him anymore. This person clearly wasn't a threat. He looked around. A few cars had stopped around the junction, even the ones whose traffic lights were on green, but no car doors were opening and no pedestrians were in sight. He couldn't see any other threats in the immediate vicinity. *What am I missing?*

"I should fuck you up," the guy growled.

And that was when Crane spotted it across the road, two-thirds of the way up one of the lampposts—a grey traffic camera pointing directly towards them.

Crane looked directly into the guy's eyes. "Go on, then, fella. Take a swing."

The guy tried his best not to react, but his eyes failed him. They widened ever so slightly before he could quickly deepen his frown to disguise it. "No, you first, *fella*."

Crane smirked. "Who got you to set me up?"

"What?" The guy's eyes failed him again. "I don't know what you're on about, pal."

Right on cue, a siren could be heard in the distance, reinforcing Crane's suspicions. He smiled to himself and pulled his phone out of his pocket. After unlocking it with his thumbprint, he opened the camera, held it up, and took a picture of the guy.

"Hey, what the fuck are you doing?" The guy raised a hand to block the shot, but he was too late.

Crane ignored him and walked towards the front of the van. It was in terrible shape; every panel was dented or scratched or both. There were patches of rust on the wheel arches and along the front edge of the bonnet. The front bumper was patched up in multiple places using silver duct tape and appeared to be hanging on by a thread. Crane took a picture of the front of the van, ensuring he captured the number plate clearly. Using the digits on the plate, he deciphered that the van was eighteen years old, and by the looks of it, each one of those years had been tough.

The guy stepped in front of his van. "Hey, stop taking pictures of my van."

Crane gave a single-shoulder shrug. "Make me." Then he took another picture. Not because he needed another one, he just wanted to piss off the van driver a little more and see how he would react. But as expected, he just stood where he was and glowered at him.

"What's wrong? Can't you risk looking like the aggressor in front of the camera?" He pointed up to the lamppost with the camera attached to it.

"No, not at all," the guy snapped like a petulant child. "I just want to give you a fair chance by letting you take the first shot."

Crane was unable to hide his amusement and snorted, "Yeah, okay."

Now he was certain he'd read the situation correctly. He pocketed his phone and started to head back to his truck. The sirens were getting louder and he didn't want to be there when they arrived. He hadn't done anything wrong, but he couldn't be bothered to waste the rest of his evening answering the police's questions and having to explain to them how much of a tool the guy was.

"What are you, some kinda pussy?" The van driver called after him.

"I guess we'll have to wait and see."

Crane opened the door to his truck, jumped inside, and put the transmission into drive. The traffic lights had just changed to green. He lightly pressed on the accelerator and steadily drove forward into the junction, then he turned right just as he'd always intended to. A glance in the wing mirror showed him that the guy was still standing in front of his van, watching him drive away, arms extended out to the sides as if to say, "Where are you going?"

CHAPTER SIXTEEN

Crane pulled up outside a neat two-up, two-down semi-detached house in a quiet suburb in North Cardiff. Before getting out of his truck, he sent the pictures of the ginger guy and the van to Ricky, with an accompanying message asking him to try to find out who he was. If he was the real owner of the van, it would be child's play for Ricky, but Crane wasn't holding his breath; he knew the van was far more likely to have been stolen.

He then sent a text message to Ella that simply read, *I'm outside*. It was the right thing to do. He didn't want to scare her by knocking on the door completely unannounced, even if it meant she could now choose to ignore him.

Crane opened the truck door and stepped out into the fresh evening air. Autumn was truly beginning to set in. The temperature had dropped to a cool twelve degrees and he could feel the odd spot of rain in the air. He glanced up and down the well-lit street before closing the truck door behind him. It was only twenty to nine, but it could have easily been two in the morning; the street was deserted and deathly quiet.

He walked past Ella's small white hatchback, which was parked on the driveway, and stopped at her front door. She didn't have a doorbell, so he gave two gentle taps with the chrome knocker to get her attention. He took a step back and noticed a soft glow around the edges of the curtains in the front room. It wasn't bright enough to be coming from the main light, so it was probably coming from a lamp or the TV. Maybe both.

What felt like two minutes but was probably more like twenty seconds ticked by before Crane heard a click as the door was unlocked from the inside. The chrome handle turned down and the door slowly opened. Ella was dressed in pink fleece pyjama bottoms and a matching hooded jumper. Her blonde hair was tied back in a loose ponytail, revealing an impassive facial expression.

Crane fought the urge to say something humorous in an attempt to shatter the ice, but when he looked into Ella's eyes, he knew it wouldn't land the way he'd want it to. Even Rocko, Ella's beige pug, must have sensed the atmosphere on the doorstep. Usually, he would have jumped out and greeted Crane by pawing at his leg; instead, he stood between Ella's bare feet and stared up at Crane with his permanently sad-looking face.

"Hi," said Crane, ending the silent standoff.

"Hi." Ella's tone was as reticent as her facial expression.

Another moment or two of awkward silence passed before Crane asked, "Can we talk?"

Ella moved aside to give him room to pass. Crane stepped inside and bent down to greet Rocko with a scratch behind his ears. Like with all pugs, Rocko's tail was curled, and couldn't wag on its own. Instead, his entire hind quarter began to wiggle from side to side in appreciation, which Crane had always found a little amusing. He knew he'd won Rocko over when he tried to give his wrist a grateful lick. After a couple more scratches, Crane stood up and looked at Ella. She turned and wordlessly walked away. Crane and Rocko looked on as she went down the hallway and turned left into the living room. Evidently, she wasn't going to be won over so easily.

Rocko looked up at Crane with eyes that he could have sworn were saying, *What have you done?* and then he trotted off to catch up to Ella, his claws clickety-clacking on the laminate flooring.

Crane closed the front door behind him, removed his shoes, and placed them at the bottom of the stairs next to the front door before heading into the living room.

The laminate in the hallway flowed into the living room, but a large teal-coloured shaggy rug filled the centre of the floor space. A flat-screen TV sitting on a black glass stand in the corner of the room was paused on a still image of an albatross feeding its chicks. *Probably the latest Attenborough documentary.*

There was a light grey armchair beneath the window and a matching sofa against the left-hand wall adjacent to the hallway. Both were complemented with teal-coloured cushions. Ella had already taken the armchair and was hugging her cushion tightly across her tummy. She looked forlorn and vulnerable. Rocko sat on the floor next to her feet.

Crane approached and took the closest seat on the sofa diagonal to her. He leaned forward, rested his elbows on his knees, and started with the easiest and most obvious question, "How are you doing?"

"I... I honestly don't know how to answer that." Ella's eyes focused somewhere down on the rug. "I still don't feel like I've even begun to process what happened today."

"I understand."

Ella's gaze snapped up from the rug to meet his. "Do you?"

Crane's brow furrowed. He was more taken aback by her accusatory tone than the question itself. "Of course I do."

"Are you sure? Because from where I'm sitting, I don't feel like you do."

Crane struggled to keep his voice calm and level as his defences rose. "What is that even supposed to mean?"

"It means a man put a gun to his head right in front of us and he..." She clamped her eyes shut and briefly shook her head, as if trying to erase the image from behind her eyes. "You know what he did."

"Yeah, I do know what he did. I was there with you."

"Exactly," Ella exclaimed. "You were there, yet it hardly seemed to affect you."

Crane raised a brow. "What?"

"While the rest of us were in a state of utter shock, you seemed completely unfazed and got me to walk away with you as though nothing happened."

"I just wanted to get you away from there and keep you safe."

Ella sat up and gripped the cushion even more tightly into her tummy. "But we should have stayed and spoken to the police. We should have told them what happened."

"I've already spoken to the police. I'm going to the station to give them a formal statement on Monday." Crane chose to leave out the fact that he wasn't exactly doing it voluntarily.

"Really?" Ella exhaled and her grip on the cushion appeared to ease slightly.

"Yes, really. And with regards to how I reacted, you know my background. I've had years of training and conditioning so that I can still perform and get things done in moments of crisis. It doesn't mean I'm not affected by things, it just means I may not show it."

Ella's eyes were glistening with approaching tears.

"Look, what is this really about?" asked Crane, his voice softer now.

Ella picked up the remote control from the arm of her chair and turned off the TV. Crane was glad she did, as he'd been finding the still image of an albatross regurgitating squid into its chicks' expectant beaks a little off-putting. Although, he got the impression she only did it to give herself a moment to gather her thoughts.

"The thing is, I don't really know who you are." Ella placed the remote control back on the arm of her chair before focusing her attention fully on him. "Like, I know you, but I don't *know* you."

Crane leaned forward and he asked, "What do you mean?" Deep down, he knew exactly what she meant.

Ella took a breath and seemed to hug the cushion a little tighter. "I mean... it feels like there's so much I still don't know about you. So much that you don't share with me."

"Like what?"

"Okay, let's start with something easy." She pressed her lips together for a second or two while she decided on her question. "How about, what exactly do you do for a living?"

"You already know what I do, I'm a con—"

"Consultant. But what does that even mean? Who do you consult? And what do you consult them about?"

Crane found himself questioning how much he wanted to tell Ella, or more precisely, how much of himself did he want to reveal to her?

"I want to be with you, Tom. But I need to know who you are."

"Okay." Crane sat back on the sofa to get comfortable. He knew what he was about to say would only raise more questions. "I suppose a more accurate title for the work I do would be a fixer. People come to me with problems and I make their problems go away."

Ella's nose crinkled. "What kind of problems?"

The corners of Crane's mouth downturned and he shrugged. "All sorts of things."

"Well, give me an example, then."

"Okay. I'm currently helping a couple whose four-year-old son was kidnapped last night."

"*What?*" blurted Ella, raising a hand to cover her mouth.

"The kidnapper took him from his bed in the middle of the night while his parents were asleep in the next room."

"Oh my god, that's awful."

Pre-empting her next question, Crane added, "The kidnapper left a phone on the boy's bed for the parents to find this morning.

It had a message on it instructing them not to call the police if they ever wanted to see their son again."

Ella lowered her hand. "So, that's why they called you?"

Crane hesitated. "In a roundabout way, yeah."

Ella's eyebrows pinched together. "What do you mean 'in a roundabout way'?"

"I mean, I usually get a call, but this particular job was brought to my attention using... an unorthodox method."

"The deli?"

Crane nodded.

Ella opened her mouth to say something, but no words came out. She tried again. "So, the parents sent that man to get you to help them?"

"No, not at all. The parents are good people. That was someone else."

"Who?"

Crane hesitated again. The conversation was heading in a direction he didn't feel comfortable with. "It's complicated."

"Which really means you don't want to tell me, doesn't it?" There wasn't an ounce of anger in her tone, only disappointment.

Crane's brain was throwing out suggestions of how he could respond, like a bonus round on a pinball machine. He knew he could lie or manipulate the truth, but there was one thought that overruled all the others and pushed itself to the forefront of his mind—relationships were built on trust.

"You're right," said Crane. "I don't want to tell you."

Ella sank back into her armchair.

"Look, I know it's not what you want to hear," Crane continued, "but it's the truth. There's often times in my line of work when I'm forced to cross paths with some very dangerous people. For your safety, there's things I won't be able to share with you." He leaned forward and shifted his weight to the front edge of the sofa. "However, I'm not going to sit here and lie to you or insult your intelligence by claiming that's the only reason for not sharing. Yes, it plays a big part, but the truth is, there's a part of me that I don't want you to know."

"But... I don't understand." Ella's shoulders sagged with disappointment and her voice was barely more than a whisper. "What part?"

"The dark part." Crane was beginning to think that maybe the person he was now might not be capable of having a serious relationship, especially with someone who was so inherently kind-hearted and gentle as Ella. "The part that's willing to do whatever it takes to get justice."

"You mean violence?"

"Sometimes. If the situation requires it."

Ella broke eye contact and focused her gaze somewhere down on the rug, just as she had at the start of the conversation.

"I want to be with you," said Crane, edging even closer to her. "But if what I can offer you isn't enough, or if who I am isn't what you want, I understand."

Ella's eyes were glazed and tearful, but she wasn't yet crying. Crane took her reaction, or lack thereof, as his cue to leave. He reluctantly stood up and walked out of the living room. At the front door, he bent down to put his shoes on and heard Rocko's clickety-clacking claws heading his way. He turned and looked over his shoulder, expecting to see Rocko trotting towards him, hankering for one final ear scratch before he left, but was surprised to see Ella also standing in the hallway.

He straightened up and turned to face her. They both stood there looking at each other for a few moments, neither of them saying a word or even moving a muscle. Little Rocko sat in the middle and alternated between looking at them both, like a spectator at a tennis match. His big bug eyes appeared to be wondering what was going on. Then Ella stepped forward. A slow, tentative step at first, but it was swiftly followed by three big strides, then she wrapped her arms tightly around Crane. He reciprocated without hesitation and pulled her in close.

"Don't go," she whispered into his chest.

He gave her a squeeze and then leaned back slightly. Ella tilted her head up to look at him. Her luminous green eyes sparkled like emeralds. A single tear had escaped and was gradually making its way down her left cheek. Crane brought his hand up and tenderly cradled the side of her face, then used his thumb to gently wipe the tear away. Now that he was this close, he could smell her. Floral and sweet. Intoxicating. His hand slid around to the nape of her neck and he began to bend down. Ella's lips parted expectantly and her breath seemed to catch in her throat.

They kissed. A soft and delicate kiss at first, then Crane slowly slid his other hand up Ella's back, beneath her fleecy top. Her skin felt silky smooth and warm, hot even. He pulled her in even closer as his hand slowly travelled up to the space between her shoulder blades. They paused and looked into each other's eyes, as though they were in sync and just wanted a second to enjoy this moment together. Then they kissed again, but this time with much more intensity. Crane's nails were cut short, but he lightly dragged what he had down Ella's spine. Her whole body shuddered and she let out a satisfied groan as she melted into him. She pulled his hips into her and kissed him even harder, craving him.

Then suddenly, she stopped and broke away. At first, Crane thought something was wrong, but when he looked into her eyes, he saw an alluring glint that told him the opposite was true.

Ella took hold of his hand, then turned around and started heading up the stairs. Crane was more than willing for her to take the lead and followed her up to the landing. She padded across the cream-coloured carpet with Crane in tow and led him into her bedroom. She stopped at the foot of the bed and turned to face him. Raising herself onto her tiptoes, she kissed him before playfully pushing him backwards. Crane fell back onto the soft duvet and Ella climbed on top, straddling him.

She leaned down to kiss him again, but something caught his eye. He held up a hand and whispered, "Hold that thought."

Crane picked Ella up by her backside as he stood up, then spun around and placed her gently back down onto the bed. Even in the dim lighting of the bedroom, there was a clear look of confusion on her face, but he didn't say anything, he just turned around and looked down at Rocko, who was standing just inside the bedroom doorway, watching them.

"Sorry, little buddy." Crane walked over and scooped him up in one hand. "You haven't got a ticket for this show."

Ella stifled a giggle behind him as he placed little Rocko down on the landing. Feeling a slight pang of guilt, he gave Rocko a quick scratch behind his ear before closing the bedroom door on his sad-looking face.

CHAPTER SEVENTEEN

As always, Crane's body clock woke him up at six. It was still dark outside, which meant it was near pitch black inside Ella's bedroom. Crane rolled onto his back and slid his hand across the mattress in search of Ella but found her side of the bed cold and empty. A hazy memory of her getting up around an hour ago came back to him. He'd assumed she was heading to the toilet and he had fallen back to sleep; evidently, she hadn't returned.

He sat up and swung his legs out of the bed, his bare feet sinking into the soft carpet as he reached out and switched on the bedside lamp. After a quick yawn and stretch, he stood up and began collecting his clothes, which were strewn around the bedroom floor. Once he was fully dressed, he made his way downstairs.

The house was so quiet you could've heard a spider cough, and the only source of light came from a lamp in the living room, which was where he found Ella, sitting in the armchair and nursing a white mug in her lap. Little Rocko was lying on the floor, resting his head on her bare feet. He raised his head when Crane walked in but immediately dropped it back down with an audible *harrumph* when he recognised Crane. He obviously hadn't been forgiven for shutting him out of the bedroom last night.

"Hey," said Crane softly as he approached.

Ella looked up at him and gave a thin smile in reply.

Crane stopped abruptly, sensing a palpable shift in Ella's demeanour. "Is everything okay?"

Ella nodded, but her eyes told him a different story.

Crane hesitantly approached the sofa and sat down in the same spot as the previous night. He noticed her mug was filled with some sort of purple-coloured fruit tea that she'd barely touched. The bag was still floating at the top and all the steam had long since dissipated.

"What's wrong?"

Ella clamped her lips shut and shook her head.

Crane leaned forward and rested his elbows on his knees in an attempt to catch her eye and to alleviate the sinking feeling that had suddenly materialised in his gut. "Come on," he coaxed. "Tell me what's on your mind."

She took a breath before she spoke. "I just woke up and couldn't get back to sleep."

"Okay. And that's something that typically happens when there's something on your mind. So, what is it? What's bothering you?"

Again, she didn't respond.

"Has it got to do with what we were talking about last night?"

She nodded, the movement small and almost imperceptible.

"Please," said Crane, shifting his weight even further forward to get closer to her. "Talk to me."

She turned to look at him. "I woke up thinking about what happened in the deli yesterday. My mind keeps playing it over and over, and it's so vivid. I can see everything. I can see his face and the way he looked at you before he..."

"I'm sorry." Crane reached out and placed a reassuring hand on her knee. "You never should have experienced that."

"But I did, and it showed me..." Her voice choked. She swallowed hard and tried again. "It showed me a glimpse of your world. I keep thinking about what you said last night—that there's a side of you that you don't want to share with me. Well, yesterday, I wanted to share everything with you and I wanted you to share everything with me. I wanted our worlds to become one." The tears began to fall and she used the back of her hand to paw them away. "But..."

"But now you're not so sure."

Ella bit down gently on her bottom lip to stop it from quivering. "I just... I just don't know how far apart our worlds are."

Crane did. Crane knew exactly how far apart their worlds were. And although it pained him to admit it, he knew she was too good for someone like him and his world.

"Are you ashamed of what you do? Is that why you don't want to share it with me?"

"No." Crane surprised himself with how quickly he answered and how adamant he sounded. "I only help good people and I make sure their cause is worthy before I do."

"But you said you often use violence."

"Not *often*. It's typically a last resort."

Ella's tears had stopped flowing and she fixed his gaze. "Would you give it up?"

"What? Violence?"

"All of it. Your job—fixing, or whatever it is you call it."

For Crane, what he did wasn't a job. Yes, he was remunerated for the work he did, often remunerated extremely well, but it was more than that. After everything he'd been through over the last five years, this was who he was now. It was his identity. Whether it was helping to fix peoples' problems or using the money he earned from it to help children and families in need. Helping people gave him purpose. Could he really give it all up for Ella?

Crane was usually decisive and direct, but looking into Ella's luminous green eyes, he became hesitant. "I... I don't know."

Ella couldn't stop the disappointment from showing on her face. The corners of her lips downturned and she looked away from him to avoid his eye contact.

"Often, the people I help have nowhere else to turn," said Crane. "I don't know if I could turn my back on them."

"Well, I don't know if I can be with someone who can't share their whole self with me." Ella's tears began to flow again, but she kept going, intent on getting her words out. "And I don't think I can be with someone who puts themselves in harm's way for a living."

There it was. Ella's line in the sand had been drawn and Crane's intrusive thoughts from the previous night were now becoming his reality. Who he was now wasn't compatible with Ella. Maybe he wasn't compatible with anyone. Maybe he never had been.

Crane—suddenly feeling claustrophobic—pushed himself up from the sofa. Ella used her sleeve to mop away yet more tears from her cheeks. It seemed as though she couldn't even bear to look at him.

Crane approached her, bent down, and gently kissed the top of her head. "I need some time," he whispered, then turned and left the room.

When he reached the front door and bent down to put on his shoes, the sound of Rocko's clickety-clacking claws could be heard heading his way, but this time, when he turned to look over his shoulder, he only found Rocko standing in the hallway. Rocko trotted over to Crane and pawed at his leg, hankering for one final ear scratch. Crane willingly obliged before he stood up, opened the front door, and stepped out into a dull and unremarkable dawn that was just beginning to break over Cardiff. It wasn't raining outside, but the ground was still saturated from the rain that had evidently fallen during the night and the dark overcast sky certainly threatened that there would be more to come throughout the day.

Crane closed Ella's front door behind him and strode to his truck. He jumped inside and tried to squeeze and massage the tension out of the back of his neck. In truth, he was fighting the urge to shout and curse and punch the steering wheel; however, instead of allowing his emotions to rise to the surface, he did what a lot of men do—he pushed them down. Deep down. The inner turmoil, the frustration, the feeling of rejection. It was all compressed, forced down, and bottled up tight.

Crane drove home, parked in front of the double garage, then headed inside and up the stairs to the master bedroom. He changed into a pair of training shorts and a T-shirt, then went down to his gym room. Using an app on his phone, he tapped on a playlist, which immediately blasted out of the speakers that were mounted on the walls around the room. The bass reverberated through his bones and threatened to rock the house from its foundations.

Normally, Crane would have started with some dynamic stretches, but this morning, he was in no mood to warm up. He wrapped his hands, slipped on some boxing gloves, and headed over to the heavy bag that hung from the centre of the reinforced ceiling. He paused to take one deep breath before unbottling his emotions and unleashing unholy hell onto the poor heavy bag.

CHAPTER EIGHTEEN

Crane took the final bite of his bacon and eggs on toast, then grabbed his pint glass and downed the rest of his water. His entire body ached. His knuckles, elbows, and shins were red and sore from the heavy bag, but his mind was now clear and focused on getting little Jacob back home safe to Michael and Lindsey. He took his mug to the sink, locked up the house, and jumped in his truck.

He drove to Ricky's first, wanting to make an itinerary for the day ahead. He parked in his usual spot, jumped out, and pushed down on the handle to open the front door, but nothing happened. He frowned as he tried the handle a second time, but surprisingly, it was locked. Normally, the cameras picked up any movement on the driveway and notified Ricky, who would then unlock the door for Crane, often before he'd even stepped a foot out of his truck. And being agoraphobic, Ricky was *always* home to unlock the door.

Crane pulled out his phone and opened an app that Ricky had installed on there for him. A couple of taps later and the electric motorised multipoint locks disengaged with a solid clunk. Crane pushed open the reinforced steel door expecting to find Ricky engrossed playing one of his computer games, but was surprised to find the lounge area deserted and the big screen switched off. He briefly scanned the kitchen area and the workstation at the back of the barn, but Ricky was nowhere to be seen.

It's nine o'clock, thought Crane. *Surely he isn't still sleeping.* He headed towards the spiral staircase with the intention of going up and giving Ricky a rude awakening, but as soon as his foot landed on the first step, he heard a noise coming from the downstairs bathroom. Crane stopped and listened, then he heard the flush. A few seconds later, the bathroom door opened and Ricky stepped out. He looked at Crane, puffed his cheeks, and let out a huge huff.

"Are you okay?"

"I'm not sure," said Ricky, closing the bathroom door behind him. "Have you ever taken a shit that was so bad you offended even yourself with it?"

Crane looked away and scrunched his face up in disgust. "That's grim, Rick."

"What?" Ricky held his arms out to the sides and shrugged. "I'm just being honest."

"No, you're oversharing," said Crane, signalling for Ricky to stop "Remember, we talked about this. We need to have boundaries."

Ricky's brows shot up, seemingly shocked by Crane's reaction. But it didn't last long. Crane snorted and Ricky burst out laughing.

"On a serious note," said Crane between chuckles, "that really is grim."

"I know." Ricky grinned without showing a single ounce of shame.

Ricky headed over to his workstation at the back of the barn and sat down in a black ergonomic office chair in front of a huge bank of computer monitors. Crane followed and stood next to him as he tapped the space bar on the keyboard. The main screen directly in front of Ricky came to life and prompted him for a password. His fingers danced over the keyboard in quick time as he typed out fourteen characters and then smacked the enter key. All six monitors in front of them woke up, but it was the one positioned top left that immediately caught Crane's eye. The screen was filled with a headshot of the ginger guy from the night before.

"That's him," exclaimed Crane, pointing at the monitor. "That was the guy in the van last night."

"I know," said Ricky, looking up at Crane with a raised brow, as though it was a daft statement. "You sent me a photo of him and his van yesterday."

"Wait." Crane looked down at Ricky. "So, it is his van?"

"Yeah," said Ricky, as one corner of his mouth went up in a lopsided grin. "Why wouldn't it be?"

Crane briefly described what had happened the previous evening. Ricky listened to him intently, then asked, "So, you think he was setting you up?"

"It's the only thing that makes sense to me. The way he cut in front of me and slammed his brakes on, then practically begged me to hit him right in front of the traffic camera."

"But why? What's the motive?"

"To stop me looking into Jacob's kidnapping," suggested Crane. He'd been confident in his theory at the time, but now, after sleeping on it, he was starting to second-guess himself. "Maybe I could be wrong and this guy could just be an absolute bellend who was looking for a fight, but the police sirens definitely sounded like they were heading our way. I think they were hoping I'd assault him and get myself locked up."

"They? So, you think he might be working with The Craftsman?"

"That's exactly what I want to find out." Crane pointed at the headshot. "And it's why he's first on the list of people I want to speak to today."

Ricky stroked his beard. "Just throwing this out there—have you considered that maybe *he* could be The Craftsman?"

"No," answered Crane instinctively, then internally cursed himself for not keeping an open mind. "I mean, I suppose we shouldn't completely rule it out as a possibility, but I really didn't get the impression that he could be the brains behind any of this. In fact, I didn't get the impression he could be the brains behind much at all."

Ricky gave a one-shoulder shrug. "For what it's worth, I think you're probably right from what I know about him so far."

"Go on, what have you found out?"

Ricky turned away from Crane to look at the far-left monitor, then he started reading out some notes he'd made on a virtual Post-it note. "His name's Darren Peterson, twenty-eight, he lives on his own in a one-bedroom flat in Bradley Stoke—which is just up the road from Michael Brookes' place—and he's a self-employed electrician. Although, not a very good one according to the reviews that got him booted off one of those trust-your-tradesman-type websites." Ricky swivelled on his chair to face Crane. "But that's about as deep as I went. I didn't know why you wanted me to look into him, so I didn't go digging."

"Okay," said Crane. "Ideally, I want to see him this morning. Do you think you can track his phone?"

Ricky scoffed with feigned offence. "Did Elvis wear blue suede shoes?" he asked, then swivelled back to face the monitors without waiting for a response.

His fingers danced over the keyboard once again and lots of windows began popping up all over the different monitors in front of them. One screen in particular grabbed Crane's attention—it was filled with a map of the UK and it was gradually zooming into South Gloucestershire. He watched as the map seemed to expand and the different place names came into focus, then suddenly a red dot appeared near the words Bradley Stoke.

"So, it looks like he's at home." Ricky pointed towards the map Crane was already looking at. "And judging by the inactivity on his phone, I'd say he's still asleep. Although, that isn't much of a surprise considering he was scrolling through his Instagram feed till gone two in the morning."

Ricky tapped a few more keys and then almost excitedly pointed to another screen. "Now that's interesting. He received a call from a blocked number just before six last night, and then a little after half seven he called nine-nine-nine."

"That's around the same time he cut me up," said Crane, staring at the call list Ricky was pointing at, with a steely gaze. "So, he *was* trying to set me up."

"It certainly looks that way."

"Send his location to my phone so I can track him," instructed Crane before turning to leave.

"Wait. You said he was the first on a list of people you wanted to speak to today. So, who else is on your shitlist?"

Crane stopped and turned back to face Ricky. "Christine, the soon-to-be ex-wife, and Steve Flockton. Although, this could change depending on what Darren has to say for himself."

Ricky gave a thumbs up, but as Crane was about to turn away again, he asked, "Are you okay?"

Crane gave him a sideways glance. "Yeah, why wouldn't I be?"

"I don't know, you just seem a little... not quite yourself."

"I'm fine. I just want to get Jacob home safe and then we can concentrate on finding out who The Chief is." He paused, then added, "Isn't it funny how we're suddenly dealing with these arseholes who like to give themselves nicknames? Like The Chief and The Craftsman."

"Yeah, it is," agreed Ricky before a wry grin spread across his face. "It reminds me of those other arseholes who only go by their surname."

"Sod off," replied Crane, somehow keeping a straight face. He walked out to the sound of Ricky laughing behind him, but he was smiling, too.

CHAPTER NINETEEN

Crane didn't want to risk spooking Darren by parking his truck outside the flat, so he left it in a street around the corner and walked the rest of the way. Darren lived in the middle of a generic housing estate and his flat was in what looked like a standard end-of-terrace house. What set it apart from the other houses on the street was the front porch—it had two doors, one on the side for the flat on the ground floor, and one on the front for the flat upstairs. A T-board belonging to a local estate agency was staked into the front lawn and advertised that the ground floor flat was up for let.

There were no pedestrians in view and only the occasional vehicle trundled past. Keeping a watchful eye on the upstairs windows, Crane crossed the road and walked past Darren's battered white van, which was parked on the street outside. He made his way up the short path and stopped at the white UPVC door at the front of the porch. He gave the doorbell button a short press and heard a shrill ringing deep within the property. As he lowered his hand, he glanced at his watch. It was a little after ten thirty on a Friday morning and Darren was still home. *Not only is he a bad electrician, he clearly isn't a very busy one either.*

It didn't take long for a shadow to appear on the other side of the obscure glass of the front door followed by the sound of a key being turned inside the lock. Crane took a half step forward with his left foot and clenched his right fist in anticipation. The door swung inwards, revealing Darren and his mop of greasy ginger hair. He was dressed in baggy black shorts and a white vest.

"Good morning, turd blossom." Crane's voice was cheerful, but his body language certainly wasn't.

It took a half-second for Darren's eyes to pop open with a mixture of recognition and panic, then his natural reflexes took over and forced him to clamp them shut as Crane's fist smashed into his face. Darren's nose audibly cracked and he went reeling back on wobbly legs before falling heavily onto his backside at the bottom of the stairs. Crane casually stepped inside as though nothing had happened and closed the front door behind him. Darren's hands instinctively shot up to hold his damaged nose as the blood began to flow and drip onto his vest. Crane took a step forward.

"Okay, okay." Darren raised one of his bloody palms towards Crane, his voice muffled behind his other hand. "I deserved that. I'm sorry, okay."

Crane stopped and frowned. It wasn't the response he'd been expecting. "So now you're admitting you were setting me up?"

Darren squinted at him through painful watery eyes. "Yeah."

Crane glared down at him. "Start talking."

"Can I at least get some tissue first?" Darren pleaded, briefly removing the hand from his face to show Crane just how much blood was pumping out of his wonky nose. It trickled over his chin and down his neck in rivulets, and what had started as a few spots of blood on his white vest had now become a rapidly expanding crimson patch.

Crane hesitated for a second or two, then reluctantly gave a curt flick of his head towards the top of the stairs. Darren quickly grabbed the hem of his vest and pulled it up and over the lower half of his face in an effort to help catch the fresh blood. He then struggled to get to his feet without using his hands, evidently not wanting to get any blood on the carpet. Crane stood and watched him struggle wondering why he was bothering—the beige carpet was filthy and already covered in countless stains; a few drops of blood wouldn't have made a blind bit of difference.

When Darren eventually got to his feet, he swayed side-to-side and had to take a second to steady himself before attempting to climb the stairs. Crane followed him up but remained alert and kept his distance just in case Darren got brave and decided to kick out. Not that he thought Darren was a threat, he was just experienced enough to know not to take any unnecessary risks.

At the top of the stairs, Darren took the first doorway on the left and went into the bathroom. He bent over the sink and let his nose drip into the basin as he turned the tap on and began washing the blood off his hands. While he cleaned himself up, Crane took the opportunity to have a quick look around.

There were three other doorways on the landing, all of them with wide-open doors. Opposite the bathroom was a small lounge. A black faux-leather sofa faced a coffee table that was covered with dirty dishes and an overflowing ashtray, the smell of which tainted the air. However, the air inside the flat was dense with more than just the aroma of cigarette smoke and ash. There was an underlying whiff of body odour combined with something stale and musty that didn't become obvious to Crane until he stepped into the bedroom. The bitter stench of clothes and bedding that were long overdue a wash caught the back of his throat and almost caused him to gag. Holding his breath, he stepped over a pile of dirty clothes on the floor at the end of the bed and opened the window to let in some fresh air. The window looked out onto the glass roof of a small conservatory below and the bland but well-kept rear garden. Crane sucked in a deep breath of clean air before turning around and heading to the final room.

The narrow galley kitchen held no surprises. The bin at the end was overflowing and more rubbish was stacked on the worktop next to it. Dirty dishes filled the sink along with every other horizontal surface. The laminate floor looked as though it hadn't seen a drop of bleach or a mop for months if not years. Crane thought he could even see mouse droppings on the floor along the edge of the cupboards; at least, he hoped they were from mice and not any of their bigger cousins. Looking around the place was beginning to make his skin feel itchy. He wasn't an obsessive cleaner, but he did hold personal hygiene and cleanliness in high regard—they were just some of the many habits that had been drummed into him from his army days.

Crane went back to the landing satisfied that they were alone in the flat and there was nowhere to hide a four-year-old boy. In the bathroom, Darren was still hunched over the sink, but he'd removed his vest and had dumped it on the floor between his bare feet. His hands and face appeared to be clean, but the bleeding from his nose had barely slowed.

Darren spotted Crane's reflection in the mirrored door of the medicine cabinet above the sink and huffed. "It won't stop fucking bleeding."

"Do you want me to nip out to get you some tampons?"

Darren rolled his eyes. "Ha ha, very funny."

Even though it had been said in jest—Crane had no intention of leaving to get anything to help Darren—a pair of tampons would have actually been quite useful to him right now.

Crane leaned against the door frame and folded his arms across his chest. "It's time for you to start talking."

Darren lowered his gaze to the sink. "I got a call last night."

"From who?"

"I've no idea," replied Darren, with a half-hearted shrug. "Some bloke calling from a private number."

"Do you always answer calls from private numbers?"

Darren looked up at Crane's reflection in the mirror and upturned a hand. "Well, I'm not inundated with work at the minute, so I can't really be choosy about which calls I answer. You know, just in case it's for a job."

Crane gave a single nod; it was a fair point. "So, what did the guy on the phone say to you?"

"He asked me if I wanted to earn some quick and easy cash." Darren reached up and tried to pinch the upper part of his nose in an effort to stem the flow of blood, but immediately sucked in a painful breath through gritted teeth and lowered his hand.

"Go on," urged Crane, a hint of impatience beginning to creep into his tone.

"Well, I'm pretty skint at the minute, so I obviously said yeah. Then he told me to go down and check the front door. At first, I thought it was some kinda windup or summin', but when I went down to have a look, there was an envelope on the floor. I asked him what it was, and he told me to open it. There were five hundred quid in it."

"What did he want you to do for it?"

"That's exactly what I asked him, but he said it was a, uh..." Darren snapped his fingers a few times, as if trying to remember the exact words that had been used, then on the fourth snap, his index finger shot up in the air. "*Down payment*. That's it. He said it was a down payment.

"He said that if I did one little thing for him, he'd give me another envelope, and the next one would have a grand in it. He told me I had to park up on Woodlands Lane and wait for a grey pickup truck to drive past. He even gave me your reg number and said you'd probably go past between seven and nine o'clock." Darren placed a hand on either side of the sink and leaned his weight forward. The blood still dripped relentlessly from his nose, and it was gradually turning the inside of the basin bright red. "He said I had to follow you to the junction turning onto Bradley Stoke Way before bumping into your truck with my van. Then he told me to call the police and tell them I was being attacked before getting out and trying to get you to hit me. He said if I did, he'd post the grand through my letterbox."

"And you believed him?"

"Like I said, I'm skint. There's not much I wouldn't do for the chance of getting a grand."

"So, I take it because I didn't hit you last night, you didn't get the extra money?"

"Nope," said Darren flatly, glaring at Crane's reflection. "You didn't lay a finger on me when it would have made me a grand, and instead, you turned up at my home this morning and broke my fucking nose for nuffin'."

Crane could hear Darren, but he'd stopped actively listening. A thought had crossed his mind and stolen his focus—either The Craftsman had eyes on the junction last night to know what had happened, or he'd never had any intention of paying Darren the extra thousand pounds.

"Have you heard from him since?" asked Crane.

"Nope."

"You said he told you to bump into my truck, so why didn't you?"

"I was trying to be clever." Darren snort-laughed at himself but then immediately winced at the pain it caused. "If I'd 'ave bumped into you, my insurance premium would have gone through the bloody roof next year. So, I tried to get you to bump into me, but you did some crazy ninja driving skills and missed me."

"Where's the five hundred pounds he gave you?"

Darren's eyes went wide in the mirror and he started to shake his head. "Please don't. I really need that money; I'm overdue on my rent."

"I'm not going to take it," said Crane. "I just want to see it."

Darren stared at Crane's reflection, his lips drawn into a thin line.

"It's the only piece of physical evidence you have that corroborates what you've told me, so where is it?"

"I've put it somewhere safe."

"Where?"

Darren clamped his lips shut.

"Look, you can either tell me where it is, or I can make you tell me."

Crane's tone had been calm and level, but Darren must've seen something in his eyes that let him know Crane wasn't the type of person who made empty threats. He sighed and lowered his head in defeat. "It's in the microwave."

Crane cocked his head to one side. "In the *microwave*?"

"Yeah. If someone were to break in looking for something valuable, the microwave would be the last place they'd look."

"If someone were looking for something valuable, they wouldn't break into this shithole in the first place."

Darren's eyebrows pinched together and he looked genuinely hurt by the comment. Crane was surprised to find himself feeling a little sorry for Darren.

"No offence to the flat itself, but you could do with giving the place a bit of a clean." He unfolded his arms and made a point of looking around, then added, "And maybe get it sterilised and fumigated while you're at it."

Darren tilted his head to the side as if to say, "Fair point". Crane turned around and went back into the kitchen. The microwave was a cheap white plastic model with two turn dials and a push button to open. It was on the kitchen worktop next to a four-ring gas hob that was caked in grease and grime. The acrid smell filled Crane's nostrils, and although it was unpleasant, it was somewhat of an improvement compared to the rest of the flat.

Crane pushed the button on the microwave and the door popped open. Sitting in the middle of the glass turntable was a small white envelope. He grabbed it and took a look inside. It was filled with twenty-four twenty-pound notes.

"There's four hundred and eighty pounds in here," he called out.

"Yeah, I know. I treated myself to a cheeky takeaway last night on the way home."

Crane tossed the envelope back inside the microwave and pushed the door closed with his knuckles, then made his way back to the bathroom. Without saying a word, he picked up the roll of toilet tissue that was sitting on top of the cistern and unravelled a big wad before replacing it.

Darren watched him out of the corner of his eye. "What are you doin'?"

"Hold still," ordered Crane, knowing full well Darren wouldn't be able to obey his instruction with what he was about to do.

Crane grabbed a handful of Darren's greasy hair at the back of his head, and with the wad of tissue, he clamped Darren's crooked nose between his thumb and first two fingers. Darren squealed like the fan belt on his van and tried to pull his head back, but Crane had a good hold on him and slowed down his movement. The nose crunched and cracked beneath Crane's grip as he forced rather than manipulated Darren's nose back to its rightful place. It was the kind of treatment and care you get from someone whose only medical experience came from battlefield first aid training.

"*Fuck*," Darren yelped, desperately trying to push him away.

Crane released his grip, and Darren staggered backwards a step before tripping and falling arse first into the bath.

"What the *fuck*, man," Darren cried out. His face was scrunched into a tight scowl and his eyes were watering profusely, but at least his nose was straight.

"You're welcome," said Crane nonchalantly as he dropped the bloody wad of tissue into the toilet. He then picked up what was left of the roll from the top of the cistern and tossed it to Darren. "I've just straightened it and saved you a trip to the hospital."

"Yeah, great. Thanks for that," replied Darren in a tone dripping with sarcasm. He made no effort to get out of the bath;

instead, he just sat there with his legs hanging over the side and unravelled a load of toilet tissue that he then used to mop the blood off his bare chest.

Crane pumped what appeared to be the final two squirts of liquid soap out of the dispenser on the sink's ledge into his hand. "Just so we're completely clear," he said, turning the tap on and washing Darren's hair grease off his hands, "if I find out you've lied to me about anything, or if you've withheld any information that could be useful to me…" Crane turned the tap off and looked at the towel hanging from the chrome ring holder on the wall next to the sink. What he assumed had once been a fluffy white hand towel had taken on more of a drab beige hue. He decided against using it and just shook the excess water off his hands as he turned to face Darren. "I'll come back and break more than just your nose."

Darren raised his right hand with three of his fingers extended in a Scout's honour salute. "I've told you everything, I swear."

Crane walked out of the bathroom, down the stairs, and out the front door. Outside, the street was just as quiet as it had been when he'd arrived and the murky sky was still threatening more rain to come. Before crossing the road, he pulled his phone out of his pocket and dialled Ricky. Crane gave him a brief rundown of what had happened with Darren as he walked back to his truck.

"So, what's the plan of action now?" asked Ricky when he'd finished.

"I think we should stick to the original plan for now, just in case Jacob's kidnapping isn't purely motivated by money." Crane unlocked the truck and jumped inside. "I still think it's worth speaking to Christine and Steve Flockton. They're the only two so far who may have other motives."

"I anticipated you might say that, which is why I've already arranged an appointment for you at one o'clock with Christine."

"Arranged an appointment?"

"Yeah. She's got a small marketing agency based in Bristol, which she started up shortly after her separation from Michael. Although, if the truth be told, it appears to be more of a status symbol than an actual business. They've only got a handful of regular clients and it's been haemorrhaging money since day one. Looking at the accounts, it should have closed down within the first six months, but Christine seems to be happy to keep pumping her own money into it to keep it going."

"But why?" The question wasn't necessarily aimed at Ricky, he was just thinking out loud. "I understand we all need to feel purpose in our lives or at least a sense of achievement, but it doesn't sound like she's gaining either and just wasting her money."

"You're right, she is. However, she's probably not overly bothered. Compared to how much money she already has to her name, and certainly compared to what she's expected to get from the divorce settlement, it's a drop in the ocean."

"Okay, well, send me the address and I'll head there now," said Crane, pushing the ignition button to start the truck's engine.

"It's a little early," said Ricky, his voice now coming through the speakers in the truck via Bluetooth. "You're only forty-five minutes away in current traffic."

"I'll grab a bite to eat before the meeting," Crane said before ending the call.

CHAPTER TWENTY

Christine's offices were on the ground floor of a converted grade II listed Georgian townhouse on Queen Square—an elegant park area in the heart of Bristol surrounded by trees and cobbled streets. Fortunately, Crane had found a space to park his truck nearby; unfortunately, he had to pay for the privilege. After tossing the pay and display parking ticket onto the dashboard, he pushed the door closed and headed across the cobbled street for his one o'clock appointment, which, as always, he was five minutes early for.

The ground was drenched from a recent downpour, but now a small gap between the dense grey clouds allowed the sun to make a brief appearance. The glare from it reflected off the ground and forced Crane to squint slightly as he walked up the short path leading to the property. When he reached the broad front door, which looked as though it had recently had its umpteenth coat of black paint applied to it, he noticed that Christine's marketing agency wasn't the only business based there. On the stone wall next to the door was a chrome intercom panel with three small plaques on it, each one engraved with a different company name sat alongside its own push button. Crane pressed the one at the bottom.

A few seconds later, a chirpy female voice came through the small speaker. "Original Marketing Solutions."

Crane leaned closer to the intercom. "I have a one o'clock appointment with Christine."

"One moment, please."

The speaker went silent and Crane counted twenty-seven seconds before the door was eventually pulled open, revealing a petite brunette dressed in a black pencil skirt and a crisp white blouse.

She gave him a welcoming smile. "Mr Crane?"

"That's right."

"Great." She beamed, offering her hand. "I'm Rachel. It's a pleasure to meet you."

"Likewise," said Crane, giving her hand a cursory shake.

Rachel moved aside. "Please, come in."

Crane entered the hallway and waited for Rachel to close the front door behind him. There was a wide staircase straight ahead and an open doorway on the left. Once Rachel was happy the door was closed properly, Crane followed her through the doorway and into what appeared to be a waiting room with a reception desk built into the corner. In stark contrast to the Georgian architecture on the exterior, the decor inside was ultra-modern—clinically light and white with sharp edges and minimal furniture. Rachel's impossibly high heels clacked on the parquet flooring as she went right, heading towards the glossy white reception desk.

"Please, take a seat. Christine won't be long." She glanced over her shoulder and gestured with a wave of her hand towards the seating area on the left. "Can I get you a tea or a coffee while you wait?"

"A coffee would be great, thanks."

Crane walked towards the seating area as Rachel busied herself with the coffee machine behind the reception desk. A pair of fancy-looking swivel chairs upholstered in bright yellow fabric flanked a little white coffee table, but Crane didn't sit down; instead, he went up to one of the two tall windows and looked out onto the cobbled street and the park beyond. Crane imagined that during drier spells and particularly during the summer months, it would be a popular spot for the local office workers to take a stroll during their lunch breaks. But not today. A fresh batch of raindrops began to fall from the sky, which meant the only movement out there came from the ripples in the ever-growing puddles on the ground. Rachel's voice brought him back into the room.

"Would you like milk and sugar?"

"Just one sugar, please." He turned around and headed over to the reception desk.

Rachel placed a white cup and saucer on the top counter. "There you go."

"Thank you. Have you been busy?" Crane asked, somehow stopping himself from cringing at his pointless question.

"Oh yeah, we've been flat out," Rachel replied enthusiastically. "We're pretty much at full capacity of how many clients we can take on."

Crane smiled. Not because he could hear the insincerity in her voice or the fact that Ricky had told him exactly how busy the company really was, but because he could see the reflection of Rachel's computer screen in the chrome letters on the company's signage behind her. She'd clearly been passing the time by playing solitaire.

Thankfully, he was saved from any more small talk by a loud chirping sound that came from the desk phone. Rachel jumped slightly, startled by the sudden noise, as though the sound of the phone ringing was a rarity. She snatched up the handset and answered it with an informal, "Hi". She then went quiet for a few beats while she listened to the caller. "Okay, will do. Thank you, Christine." She replaced the handset into its cradle and looked up at Crane. "She's ready to see you now."

"Great," said Crane, picking up his coffee from the counter.

Rachel led him down a narrow corridor and then gently knocked on the last door to the left before pushing it open. As she did, Crane noticed that Christine was still using her married name on the door plaque. He followed Rachel into an office that was smaller than he'd expected and looked almost like a replica of the reception area, with another two fancy yellow swivel chairs facing a glossy white desk. A pear-shaped lady with wavy jet-black hair stood up and stepped around the desk. She wore navy trousers with a matching blazer over a baby-blue blouse.

"Mr Crane, it's a pleasure to meet you," she said, smiling and extending a hand towards him. "I'm Christine."

Crane shook her hand while holding his coffee in the other. "Thank you for agreeing to meet me at such short notice."

"Don't mention it," she replied and then gestured to the yellow chairs with her free hand. "Please, have a seat."

"I'll leave you both to it," said Rachel, already heading for the door. "Just give me a shout if you need anything."

The door clicked shut behind Crane as he placed his coffee down on Christine's desk and took a seat on one of the yellow chairs, which, as he'd expected, was just as uncomfortable as it looked.

"So, Mr Crane," started Christine, sitting down opposite him, "your assistant informed us that you were looking to create a marketing campaign for your company that specialises in"—she turned her head to the left to read from her computer screen—"holistic penis enlargement therapies."

Crane had to use every ounce of his self-discipline to suppress a laugh while he made a mental note to get Ricky back for that one. "It seems my assistant thinks he's somewhat of a comedian."

"Oh, right, I see." Christine flushed slightly. "I'm sorry, we took him at his word and didn't get a chance to research you or your company before the appointment."

"Please, don't apologise; in fact, it's me who should be apologising to you."

Christine shook her head as if to say there was no need.

"Not just because my assistant has a very immature sense of humour," Crane went on, "but also because this isn't a business opportunity for you. The real reason for the appointment is to speak to you about something unrelated to your marketing services."

Christine's eyebrows pinched together with a mixture of confusion and curiosity. "And what might that be?"

Crane picked up his cup of coffee from the desk, took a sip, and sat back, folding his left ankle over his right knee. "I'd like to speak to you about your husband, Michael."

Christine's expression immediately darkened. "Oh, for fuck's sake." She huffed and rolled her eyes. "You can tell that prick I'll sign the divorce papers in the next few days; he didn't need to send over one of his bloody henchmen."

Crane took another sip of his coffee before calmly responding. "Firstly, I'm not one of his bloody henchmen. Secondly, I couldn't care less about when you're going to sign the divorce papers. And lastly, thank you for answering the first question I was going to ask you."

"What first question?"

"I was going to ask if you still hold much of a grudge against him, but your reaction to just hearing his name makes that crystal clear."

Christine scoffed. "He traded me in for a younger piece and ruined my life, so of course I still hold a grudge." Her face was twisted into a scowl. The friendly and welcoming lady he'd met just a few minutes ago seemed to be long gone. "Anyway, why are you even asking me that?"

"Because I want to determine whether your grudge against him could result in you seeking some sort of vengeance against him." Crane maintained eye contact and carefully observed Christine's reaction to his words.

Her expression softened slightly. "Something's happened, hasn't it?"

Crane didn't respond.

"What is it? What's happened?" The harshness in her tone was beginning to dissipate as she fired the questions at him; instead, it was replaced with something else, something that Crane struggled to decipher at first but became clear when she asked her final question. "Has something bad happened to Michael?" Her eyes flashed with excitement—she was actually excited at the prospect that something bad had happened to Michael.

Crane drained the last of his coffee and placed the cup back onto the saucer on Christine's desk. "Do you want something bad to have happened to Michael?"

Christine opened her mouth to answer but then demonstrated some restraint by clamping her lips shut before any sound could escape. "That... shithead," she seethed, "started screwing some young slutty gold digger from his foundation, got her knocked up, and then practically kicked me out of *our* home to move *her* in. On top of that, all of my so-called friends dropped me because their husbands were either doing or hoping to do business with him. In the space of a few weeks, I lost my husband, my home, and all my friends." She pursed her lips and frowned as though she'd tasted something bitter. "Or at least people I thought were my friends. And then, as a result of all this, I spiralled into a pit of depression that I am only just clawing my way out of now. So, in short, yes. I would like something bad to happen to Michael." She leaned forward and rested her elbows on the desk as though she were getting ready to hear some juicy gossip. "So, come on, what is it? What's happened?"

Crane cleared his throat. "I'm not at liberty to give details."

"Bor-ing." Christine rolled her eyes and pushed her bottom lip out.

Crane chose to ignore her rudeness. "Does the nickname 'The Craftsman' mean anything to you?"

"The Craftsman?"

Crane gave a single nod to confirm she'd heard him correctly.

"No, I've never heard of... The Craftsman. What kind of a nickname is that? It sounds like he's a carpenter or something." Christine pursed her lips and took a moment's consideration. "This is all very cryptic. I must admit, you've got me really intrigued now." She leaned even closer and a vindictive smirk spread across her lips. "Who is The Craftsman, and what has he done?"

"It's really not for me to say."

Christine let out a frustrated huff and sat back in her chair. "Well, if you're not going to tell me what's happened, you might as well piss off. This conversation is over."

She picked up her smartphone from the desk and started tapping away as though she were writing a message or making a note. Crane didn't move; he wasn't ready to leave just yet. Although, he wasn't quite sure why. Christine had been blatant about her desire for something bad to happen to Michael and seemed genuinely pleased to know that something bad had in fact happened. If she were involved in Jacob's kidnapping, would she really be quite so open and jubilant? Crane didn't think so. But something still wasn't sitting right with him. Yes, she had every right to feel bitter and betrayed, and maybe her rude and obnoxious behaviour towards him was warranted. But it just seemed to come too naturally to her, and Crane found himself questioning her integrity.

"Well, you're still here," said Christine, placing her phone back down on the desk. "Does this mean you want to tell me what's happened?" The corners of her mouth gradually upturned to form a conceited grin.

A part of Crane didn't want to tell her, but a bigger part wanted to wipe the smirk off her face and test her. "Michael's four-year-old son Jacob was kidnapped last night."

Christine's face dropped. "W-what?" she stammered and raised a hand to cover her mouth.

"He was taken from his bed in the middle of the night and he's currently being held to ransom."

"That's terrible," she muttered, lowering her gaze to the desk. "Really and truly awful. That poor, poor boy."

Crane studied her reaction carefully and had to admit it seemed genuine. Either that or it was a performance worthy of winning an Oscar.

"Wait," she said, looking up at him. "You think I have something to do with this?"

"Do you?"

Christine flinched and her mouth dropped open, but no words came out. It took her a few seconds to regain her composure and find her voice. "I... I can assure you, Mr Crane, as much as I would like to see Michael suffer, I would never want to harm his child... or any child, for that matter."

Crane stood up. He'd heard enough. Christine was an unsavoury character, but he believed her.

"You're going?" she asked, sounding a little surprised.

"Yeah. Unless you've got any information that could help me find Jacob?"

Christine's lips downturned and she slowly shook her head. "No."

"I'd appreciate it if you keep what we've discussed between us and these four walls." Crane turned away from her and headed for the door.

Crane got back in his truck just as another heavy downpour began. The rain thundered off the truck's thin metallic roof and cascaded down the windscreen in sheets, blurring his view of the park ahead. Crane started the engine but didn't make a move to pull out of the space or even switch on his windscreen wipers; instead, he waited for Bluetooth to connect to his phone and then used the infotainment system to dial out.

Ricky answered almost immediately with, "How did it go with Christine?"

Crane used the controls on the steering wheel to increase the volume on the call; he could barely hear Ricky's voice over the noise of the rain hammering down on the truck. "She's rude, she's obnoxious, and she definitely seems like the vindictive type."

"It sounds like there's a 'but' coming?"

"*But* I don't think she's behind the kidnapping. If something had happened to Michael directly, Christine would be my prime suspect, as she openly wants to see him suffer. But when I told her about Jacob..." Crane stared at but didn't take in the water running down the windscreen, he was replaying Christine's reaction in his mind's eye. "She seemed genuinely shocked. I really don't think she would do anything to harm Jacob."

"Okay. So we'll put her to one side for now and not spend too much time digging into—"

"On that note," interrupted Crane, "can you dig a little deeper into the household staff?"

"Really?" asked Ricky, his voice raised in pitch. "I thought we agreed they seemed clean."

"Yeah, we did, but something's been bothering me since speaking to Darren this morning. The Craftsman used him to try and set me up last night, so he obviously knows I've been at the house and I'm helping Michael. But how? At first, I thought maybe he'd been keeping an eye on the place himself, potentially spying on us from a distance. Then I thought maybe we should sweep the place for bugs in case he planted cameras or microphones somewhere in the house during the kidnapping." Crane's frown deepened. "But if that were the case, why go to the effort of paying Darren to set me up? He could've just told Michael that he knew I was there and demanded they get rid of me during the ransom call. But he didn't. Why?"

Ricky didn't respond, and Crane continued after a short pause.

"I can only think of one reason why not—he doesn't want us to know he has eyes and ears on the place. He doesn't want us to know how he's getting the information, or should I say who he's getting the information from."

"You really think one of the household staff is working with him?"

Crane hesitated. He hadn't spent long with any of them individually, but even so, none of them had stood out to him as a possible accomplice. On the other hand, if any of them were working with The Craftsman, they'd obviously be making every effort to hide the fact. "I don't know. Maybe," said Crane without much conviction. "Or maybe they could be inadvertently feeding him information."

"How'd you mean?"

"Maybe The Craftsman has befriended one of them recently and they're telling him what's going on at the house without realising who he really is."

"Okay, it's worth looking into," said Ricky, although he didn't sound overly convinced. "I'll get digging and let you know if I find anything."

"Great," said Crane. "In the meantime, where can I find Steve Flockton?"

"I've already sent the address he's at to the satnav in your truck." The smugness in Ricky's voice was amplified through the truck's speakers. "There should be a notification at the top of your screen. Just tap it and then press start."

Crane followed Ricky's instructions and the satnav informed him he should arrive at his destination in thirty-six minutes with current traffic conditions. Ricky added, "He works out of a large unit on the outskirts of Bristol. Let me know how it went once you've spoken to him."

"Will do." Crane ended the call, switched on the windscreen wipers, and reversed out of the parking space.

CHAPTER TWENTY-ONE

Thirty-three minutes later, Crane pulled up to a pair of galvanised steel gates just as a man wearing blue coveralls and a red beanie hat finished wrapping a heavy-duty steel chain around them. A large blue sign next to the gates with 'Flockton Contractors Limited' in bold white letters confirmed he was at the right place. The man looked over his shoulder at Crane's truck and gestured "one minute" to him by holding up an index finger. Smoke from a lit cigarette dangling precariously between his lips caused him to squint. They were in a period of respite from the rain, although the sky was still overcast with dark, menacing-looking clouds. Crane waited patiently for him to padlock the chain, then buzzed the window down as he approached the driver's side.

"I take it Steve's not here?" said Crane, making the assumption that the scrawny man in his forties with calloused hands and tobacco-stained teeth wasn't in fact Steve Flockton.

The man scoffed at the question and blew a cloud of cigarette smoke at Crane and into the truck's cabin. Crane's jaw tightened and he held his breath. He didn't enjoy inhaling cigarette smoke at the best of times, but even more so when it was secondhand.

The man raised his left wrist to make a show of checking the time on his non-existent watch. "It's Friday afternoon, mate. He'll be in the pub by now."

"Which pub?"

The man took a drag of his cigarette, then turned side-on and pointed up the road behind him. "The Shipyard. It's just up there, on the corner."

A hundred or so yards away, Crane could see a sign sticking out at the end of a row of terraced houses. He gave the man a quick thumbs up and a, "Cheers."

In response, the man gave a single nod, then took the final drag of his cigarette before flicking the butt on the ground and turning to walk away. He then strolled over to an estate car that Crane guessed had been red once upon a time, but the years had taken their toll and worn it down to a shade somewhere between light red and dark pink. As the man got in and fired up the diesel engine, an inevitable cloud of black smoke burst from the exhaust pipe. It was soon followed by the excruciating sound of grinding metal as he struggled to get it into first gear. When the teeth eventually lined up and it clunked into place, he pulled out without indicating and chugged up the road leaving a dense trail of dark fumes in his wake.

Crane reversed his truck away from the gate and then pulled into the space the man had just vacated. After getting out and locking up, he crossed the road and walked along the pavement in front of the row of terraced houses. The closer Crane got to The Shipyard, the more he suspected the man in the red beanie had been playing a prank on him. The place looked derelict, with peeling exterior walls that looked as though they hadn't seen a fresh lick of paint in years, possibly even decades. All the signage was weathered and hanging on by a thread. The only window he walked past was boarded up with plywood and it had been vandalised by an amateur graffiti artist with the most basic depiction of male genitalia.

Crane half-expected the main door to be locked when he pushed it, but it swung open freely and he stepped into a short passageway leading to another door. A hum of voices and laughter could be heard coming from the other side. Crane pushed through and walked into a bar that was just as dark and dingy inside as he'd expected, but it was certainly busier—nearly every table, chair, and barstool was occupied.

The noise level dropped as conversations paused and almost every pair of eyes turned to look at Crane. It was obviously a local pub for local people, the kind of place that made new faces feel about as welcome as a fart in a spacesuit. Crane ignored it and aimed for the bar. A low murmur of voices seemed to follow him, but by the time the barman approached to take his order, the volume of conversations had returned to full flow. He ordered a bottle of water because technically he was still working and it probably wasn't the best time to have something that could impair his judgement, reduce his reaction time, and affect his balance and motor skills.

When the barman placed the bottle on the bar in front of him, Crane leaned forward and said, "I'm looking for Steve Flockton."

The barman hesitated for a second, then his eyes darted over to a small round table in the corner with three men sitting around it. Two wore navy blue polo T-shirts and jeans, and one wore a dark grey pinstripe suit and a light blue shirt.

"The pinstripe?" asked Crane, handing the barman a ten-pound note to pay for his water.

The barman nodded.

Crane thanked him and instructed him to keep the change, then he picked up his bottle and headed towards the table in the corner. Steve Flockton was a short barrel-shaped man with dark slicked-back hair. The two men he was with were both bigger than him—probably around Crane's size—but it was difficult to judge with any precision with them both sitting down. One looked muscular, with a shaved head and a handlebar moustache. The other was probably a little wider but also a little softer around the edges, with messy blonde hair and a few days' worth of stubble. Judging from the empty glasses on their table, it looked as though they were already three pints deep into their afternoon drinking session.

"Good afternoon, gentlemen," said Crane as he stopped next to their table. Their conversation ended abruptly and they all looked up at him as though he'd just asked them if he could drop his trousers and take a dump on their table. Crane ignored their death stares and directed his words at Steve. "Any chance of a quick word, Mr Flockton?"

A few awkward moments passed, and then in his thick Cockney accent, Steve said, "If you've come here to try and sell me summin', you've gone about it the wrong way, son."

"I'm not here to sell you anything."

Steve's eyes narrowed. "Then, what the fuck do you want?"

"I want to talk to you about Michael Brookes."

Steve's brows shot up in surprise and he looked at his two buddies. "Well, well, well... now, this could be interesting, boys." He used a foot to push the unoccupied chair that was tucked under the table towards Crane. "Here, take a pew, son."

Crane pulled the wooden chair back from the table, sat down, and unscrewed the cap on his bottle of water. Unhurried, he took a sip, screwed the cap back on, and then set it down on the table amongst the empty pint glasses. He didn't need to look at the two big boys on either side of him to know that they were still glaring at him. But he didn't care; his attention was focused on the man sitting directly opposite him.

Steve leaned forward, resting a forearm across the edge of the table. "So then, why do you wanna talk to me about that slimy cunt?"

Crane cleared his throat. "I was told you recently accosted him while he was out having lunch with his wife."

"*Accosted*." Steve guffawed, and the two big boys joined in. "Now there's a word you don't hear every day, boys. *Accosted*."

Crane wasn't going to rise to the bait. Not yet anyway.

"Sorry," said Steve, raising a faux apologetic hand. "Go on. So, I *accosted* Michael while he was having lunch with his wife."

"And you threatened him," said Crane. His phone beeped and vibrated with a text message in his pocket. He ignored it.

"So what if I did? Don't tell me you've come here to warn me off."

"Warn you off?" repeated Crane, folding his arms across his chest. "Now, that's an interesting choice of words, Steve. Does that mean you haven't done anything to get back at him yet? You were just making idle threats, were you?"

Steve's eyebrows knitted together and his next words were spoken with a little venom. "Maybe I have, maybe I haven't. But more importantly, who the *fuck* are you, and what the *fuck* has it gotta do with you?"

Crane was about to respond when his phone began to ring and vibrate. Maintaining eye contact with Steve, he slipped his hand in his pocket and pressed the button on the side of the phone to mute it. "I'm someone that really doesn't care about your grudge with Michael Brookes, but I do need to know if you've done something to get back at him. And if you have done something, I need to know what you've done."

One corner of Steve's mouth curled up into a lopsided grin. "It sounds to me like Michael Brookes is getting a little scared and he's sent one of his dogs to come sniffing around." He glanced at the two big boys in turn before returning his attention to Crane. "Well, you can go and tell that little prick I've set some things into motion and he'll soon regret the day he chose to fuck with me."

Crane's phone started up again and he couldn't help but let out a frustrated sigh. He was tempted to mute the incoming call again, but whoever was trying to get hold of him was certainly being persistent and he felt obliged to at least see who it was. He pulled his phone out of his pocket and checked the screen. Crane immediately stood up. Not just because Ricky had tried to call him twice in the space of a few minutes, which was highly unusual in itself, but because there was also a text message preview at the top of the screen that read, "*Call me—urgently!*"

"I need to take this," said Crane, raising his phone briefly. "I'll be back to continue this conversation."

Crane turned and started to head towards the exit but stopped when he heard Steve's voice call out to him. "*Oi, son.*" Crane turned back to face him, now halfway between the table and the door. A hush descended over the entire bar. "I can't place your accent. Where abouts are you from?"

It wasn't an unusual question. Whether it was down to moving away and joining the army at a young age, the travelling he'd done while working close protection, or, more likely, a mixture of both, his Welsh accent had been somewhat diluted.

Wanting to keep his answer relatively vague, Crane replied, "On the other side of the Severn Bridge."

"Ahh... so you're a Welshman," declared Steve. "Is it true what they say about you Welshies? That you all like to shag sheep?" Steve and his two big boys broke into a chorus of chortles, and they were joined with a few sniggers on the nearby tables.

A part of Crane didn't want to sink to Steve's level, but a bigger part wouldn't let him allow Steve to have the last laugh. "Yeah, that's right," replied Crane, raising his voice to be heard clearly over the tittering. "We fuck 'em, then you eat 'em."

He waited long enough to see the smirk drop from Steve's face, then turned and walked out.

CHAPTER TWENTY-TWO

Crane hit redial as soon as his foot touched the pavement outside, and Ricky answered almost immediately.

"Sorry, did I interrupt anything?"

"Well, I have to admit, things were just starting to get interesting, but what's up?"

"I think I've found something worth looking into," said Ricky, his voice tinged with excitement. "Last night, when The Craftsman made the ransom call, didn't you say it sounded like Jacob was being kept in something metallic, like a shipping container?"

"Yeah, that's what it sounded like to me, why?"

"Well, I've just seen some satellite images of Steve Flockton's site, and it looks to me like he's got a big blue shipping container tucked around the back of the main building."

Crane was already striding along the pavement when he said, "Thanks for the heads up, Rick. I'll call you back once I've seen what's inside it."

He headed straight to the back of his truck, popped open the tailgate and the rear window, and climbed inside. Staying down on his hands and knees to duck below the hardtop canopy, he crawled all the way to the back, where a huge utility box was bolted to the truck bed. He unlatched it, raised the lid, and then pulled out a thirty-six-inch pair of heavy-duty bolt cutters, capable of cutting through over half an inch of hardened steel with ease. After closing the utility box lid, he jumped out of the truck, locked it, and then walked over to the gates for Steve Flockton's site.

The bolt cutters made light work of the chain, snipping through the steel as if it were made of plastic. Crane cut it in several places until the whole thing slid free from the gate and dropped to the ground of its own accord, then he pulled one of the gates open wide enough for himself to slip through.

The site was built on a substantial plot of land and evidently doubled as a headquarters and a depot. On the left, pallets of breeze blocks, roof tiles, and bricks were stacked and spread out with plenty of space for a forklift to manoeuvre between them. On the right, a crane-mounted truck and a scissor lift had both been abandoned for the weekend. Crane strode along the tarmac road that ran up the centre and led to a single-storey red-brick building with a flat roof. When he reached the halfway point, the pallets on his left ended and were replaced with stacks of drainage pipes and timber. On his right were large racks overflowing with scaffolding tubes.

The road curved around to the right and across the front of the building before veering to the left and disappearing down the side. Crane followed it, hoping that it would lead all the way around to the back of the building. It did, to an empty car park that, according to the white markings, could accommodate ten vehicles. Crane walked across it and stopped at the far end where the edge of the tarmac met a gravel-covered yard. There it was, tucked up against the rear perimeter fence, a dozen or so steps from where he was standing. The blue shipping container. *Could this be it? Could little Jacob really be inside?*

Crane imagined a car parked in the spot next to where he stood and then he visualised a dark, faceless figure of a man getting out of the car, with a phone held against his ear. The figure stepped off the tarmac and headed towards the container. Crane followed him. The gravel crunched beneath his feet with each step and sounded exactly as it had during the ransom call the previous night. Crane came to a stop in front of the container doors and, reaching out with his free hand, pressed his palm against the cold steel. It had taken him thirteen steps. The exact number of steps he'd heard The Craftsman take. *It could be nothing, but it could be something.*

He bent down to look inside the lock box, expecting to find a heavy-duty padlock behind the tamper-proof cover. But there was nothing there; the container wasn't locked. Admittedly, a padlock wasn't required to keep Jacob locked inside, as shipping containers can only be opened or closed from the outside. *But surely a padlock would have been used to stop someone else from inadvertently opening it.* His hopes of finding Jacob inside began to wane. But then another thought motivated him to get it open and take a look inside—*even if Jacob isn't in there now, it doesn't mean he never was. Maybe he's been moved.*

Crane placed the bolt cutters on the ground, then unlatched the two levers on the right-hand door before turning and pulling them towards him. There was a bit of resistance to start and the hinges complained with a piercing squeal, but once it had cracked open a few inches, it quietened down and started to move more freely. Crane didn't stop at the point where he knew he could fit through; instead, he kept going until he had opened it a little over ninety degrees to let some natural light inside. He dropped the levers, stepped around the open door, and peered in. But it was just a hollow metal shell.

Stepping inside, Crane pulled his phone out and switched on the torch. Then he slowly and painstakingly walked a full lap around the interior, sweeping the beam of light back and forth between each step, paying particular attention around the edges and in the corners. But he found nothing. There wasn't a shred of evidence that Jacob had been held captive inside. It wasn't just empty, it was spotless. He wondered if it had been cleaned out because Jacob *had* been held there.

Crane got out of the container and picked up his bolt cutters before retracing his steps across the gravel. He was planning on heading back to the pub to continue his conversation with Steve Flockton, but when he reached the edge of the small car park, he froze. He could hear something very faintly. For a couple of seconds, he struggled to work out what the sound was, but as it gradually became louder, it was obvious that it was the sound of multiple sets of footsteps on tarmac. *Maybe I won't need to go back to the pub after all.*

Three men came around the corner of the building and locked eyes with Crane.

"Well, well, well... look what we have here, boys. It looks like we've got ourselves a trespasser." They came to a halt around four or five yards from him. Steve took centre stage, with handlebar moustache on the left and blondie on the right. All three wore arrogant smirks, but Steve's was by far the most pronounced and his eyes looked almost gleeful. "And what do we do with trespassers, boys?"

"We teach 'em a lesson," said moustache, flashing a set of yellow gnashers.

Crane bent down and placed the bolt cutters on the ground. He'd certainly be quicker and probably do more damage without them. They were too awkward and cumbersome to be effective as a weapon in a fight, particularly when it was three against one. Although, if Crane were a betting man, he'd put his money on it being two on one. He suspected Steve was the kind of coward who would only get his hands dirty when there was no risk of getting a retaliatory punch in the face. When Crane straightened up, he rotated his torso a couple of times to loosen up his back and felt a couple of satisfactory pops in his spine. Then he tilted his head to one side, trying to get his ear down to touch his shoulder and stretch his neck out. He repeated the same move on the other side before finally turning his head to look left, then right, feeling a slight crunch in his cervical vertebrae when he twisted his neck to its limit.

The three arrogant smirks had disappeared and were now replaced with looks of confusion. They were likely wondering why he'd put what they deemed to be a useful weapon down. Crane inhaled deeply and felt a shot of adrenaline enter his system in preparation for what was coming.

"Come on, then," said Crane, holding his arms out to the side invitingly. "Which one of you bellends is gonna try and teach me a lesson first?"

Moustache was the first to accept his invitation and rushed forward swinging a wild right hand. He was going for the big Hollywood knockout and probably would have succeeded if it connected, but there was never any real danger of that happening. Moustache had power, but he lacked speed and accuracy. Crane squatted and rotated his shoulders to the left, winding up for his counter. He ducked his head and let moustache's fist sail harmlessly overhead, then he drove his bodyweight down into the soles of his feet before launching himself forward and up. At the same time, he torqued his shoulders around to the right and threw a vicious left hook. Moustache was overstretched from his air punch, which meant his right side was completely exposed; Crane had his eyes fixed on one particular target—his liver. He slammed his fist into Moustache's side, driving his knuckles up and under his tenth rib. He knew he'd hit the bullseye and it was confirmed by the noise that came out of Moustache, somewhere between a deep guttural grunt and the sound of his soul leaving his body. He crumpled to the tarmac clutching his side and gasping for air. His fight was over. It didn't matter how big or strong or tough you were, a decent liver shot was putting you down and keeping you down.

As expected, when Crane looked up to check where the other two were, Steve hadn't moved an inch, but Blondie had. He was charging towards Crane like a raging bull, with his head down and his arms starting to come around to rugby tackle him. Blondie was a big boy and definitely had the weight and the momentum to get Crane on the ground, but he was lacking in the same areas as Moustache. Against someone like Crane, he didn't stand a chance. Someone who trained every single day and concentrated on a combination of many disciplines. Strength, power, speed, agility, fighting techniques, balance, and flexibility. As far as Crane was concerned, all of those attributes were important and not a single one was prioritised over the others.

Crane sidestepped Blondie like a seasoned matador, then planted his feet and threw a solid straight right. Ideally, he would have targeted Blondie's jaw, but where his arms were outstretched for the tackle and his shoulders were hunched, it didn't leave much for him to aim for, so he went for the temple instead—the vulnerable juncture where four skull bones meet. He didn't put everything into the shot, but it connected well and Blondie was out cold before he hit the ground. His face skidded across the tarmac before he came to a stop flat on his stomach. Crane turned to look at Steve, who took a half-step back, his eyes wide with an equal mix of shock and fear. Watching his two big buddies getting floored by only two punches in almost as many seconds seemed to have robbed him of all his cockiness.

Crane almost laughed. "Isn't it funny how the big dick always seems to shrivel up without his balls?"

"Wh-who are you?"

Crane approached him and firmly placed his left hand on top of Steve's right shoulder. Steve visibly flinched and cowered down as though anticipating a hit. But it didn't come. Not yet anyway.

"I'm someone who wants to ask you some questions." Crane leaned in closer and lowered his voice to barely more than a whisper. "And if you don't answer them honestly and succinctly"—he used his thumb to point back over his shoulder—"I'm gonna get my bolt cutters from over there and I'm gonna start removing your fingers until you do."

Steve's Adam's apple bobbed up and down as he swallowed hard. "There's no need for that," he said, shaking his head vehemently. "What do you wanna know?"

"You said earlier that you've set some things in motion to get back at Michael. What have you done?"

Steve's eyes darted between Moustache, who was still writhing around on the ground and clutching his side in agony, and Blondie, who was snoozing face down on the tarmac.

"There's no point looking to them for help. If one of them does make it back to their feet, they'll be going straight back down."

Steve's shoulders sagged a little in Crane's grasp. "I paid off a few geezers at the council to delay Michael's planning permission."

Crane waited to see if Steve had anything else to add, but he just looked at Crane, wincing slightly, as though he was half-expecting to get hit. "Is that it?"

"What do you mean '*is that it?*'?" Steve frowned, appearing to be genuinely offended by the question. "It took a lot of time, effort, and money to set this up. It's gonna delay the building of his fancy new apartments by months."

Crane really couldn't care less about the apartments. "What's the empty shipping container used for?"

"What?"

Crane's glare turned icy. "Did I stutter?"

"No. It's just... one of our containers. We've got, like, five. They go on our sites for the lads to store all their tools and equipment securely. This one's the spare, but I think it's going to a new site next week."

"So, nothing's been stored in it over the last day or two?"

"No," Steve answered confidently but then hesitated before adding, "at least, I don't think so, why?"

"What do you mean you *'don't think so'*?"

"I'm the boss." Steve shrugged defensively. "I don't get involved in that kinda shit. The lads are meant to clean 'em out when they're 'ere so they're ready to be sent straight out to the next job. I don't physically check 'em myself. Anyway, what the hell's my shipping container got to do with Michael Brookes?"

Crane ignored the question and instead asked another of his own. "Is there anything else I should know about your grudge? Anything else you've set up or put into motion to get back at Michael?"

"No, nothing."

Crane had been studying Steve's reactions and responses the whole time they'd been talking, trying to spot any kind of tell that Steve may have been lying or hiding something, but he came up blank. Steve was certainly an arrogant arsehole, but Crane was confident he wasn't involved in Jacob's kidnapping.

"Do you want me to speak to the guys at the council to stop them from delaying the application?" asked Steve.

Crane released his grip on Steve's shoulder but ignored the question. He walked back to where he'd placed the bolt cutters on the ground, stepping over Moustache's legs on the way. Once he'd picked them up, he looked down at Moustache, who was glowering up at him and still grimacing in pain. Blondie was just beginning to stir and return to the land of the living.

As Crane walked back to where Steve was standing, he said, "I don't think it's fair for you to set your dogs on me to get hurt, while you, being the coward that you are, haven't got a scratch on you."

Steve's eyes flashed wide at the bolt cutters in Crane's left hand, but it was his right hand he should have been watching. Crane hit him with a stiff body shot. It wasn't a particularly hard shot, but it was enough to drop Steve to his knees and cause him to projectile vomit almost three pints' worth of beer onto the tarmac.

CHAPTER TWENTY-THREE

After leaving Steve Flockton and his boys to pick themselves up and dust themselves off, Crane headed back to Michael Brookes' home. He parked near the front door, just as he'd done the day before, but as he got out of his truck and closed the door, he stopped to listen. The faint sound of footsteps crunching on the shingle was coming from the side of the house and getting louder. Crane looked over to the front corner of the house just as the gardener, Geoff, came into view heading towards the vehicles parked in front of the garages. Geoff glanced across the drive and saw Crane, but instead of acknowledging him, he gave him a look that was dirtier than his soil-caked fingernails and turned away shaking his head, as though he disapproved of or was even irritated by his presence.

Crane watched him as he got into the old Land Rover Defender, reversed away from the garage, and drove off towards the front gate. He couldn't help but think the hostility Geoff was showing towards him was a tad over the top. Yes, he'd made an error of judgement with his apprentice yesterday, but he hadn't really hurt him and he'd apologised immediately. *Is there another reason for the animosity? Another reason why Geoff doesn't want me around?* Crane turned to the front door, not realising it was already open and Carol was standing in the doorway watching him.

"What's his problem?" asked Crane, heading up the steps.

Carol stretched her mouth wide in an awkward grimace. "Young Toby didn't show up for work today. His dad called Geoff and told him that Toby was traumatised by the man who chased him and threw him against a tree yesterday."

Crane, feeling a little lost for words as a wave of guilt and shittiness swept over him, just said, "Oh."

"Apparently, Toby's dad was talking as though he wouldn't be coming back. Geoff asked if he could call back to check on Toby in a couple of weeks. He's hoping that after some time away, he'll be able to convince him to come back." Carol raised her hand and crossed her fingers. "I hope he does come back; he seems like a lovely boy."

"I'll go around and see Toby and his dad, see if I can smooth things over."

"That's a good idea," said Carol, "but it's probably best to give it a couple of days to let the dust settle first."

Crane nodded in agreement.

"Anyway, are you hungry?"

He wasn't, but after sampling George's cooking the previous evening, Crane replied with, "Yeah, I could eat."

"Good." Carol beamed. "George has put a spread on for us in the kitchen." She gestured for him to follow her with a wave of her hand and told him to, "Come on."

Crane closed the front door and followed Carol through the foyer.

In the kitchen, George had indeed put on a spread. Cured meats, cheese, and freshly baked crusty rolls were the main ingredients of the impressive antipasti board he'd prepared on the kitchen island. Crane and Carol helped themselves to a plate before joining Michael, Lindsey, Eva, and George at the dining table.

The mood at the table seemed optimistic, even upbeat at times, with Michael and Lindsey describing how they couldn't wait to see Jacob and give him big hugs later. They spoke as though there were no doubt he would be coming home tonight; however, the food on their plates remained largely untouched, giving away the underlying apprehension they were sure to be feeling. Crane hoped with every fibre of his being that they were right, but he knew better than to trust the word of someone capable of abducting a small child.

When it got to around half six, Crane, Michael, and Lindsey retired to the library with a round of fresh coffees. Michael and Lindsey took one sofa and Crane took the other.

"So, I take it you didn't get much luck from 'shaking trees' as you put it last night?" asked Michael, placing the kidnapper's phone on the coffee table in front of him.

"Unfortunately, I didn't find any fruit, although, I suppose the lack of fruit coming from the particular trees I shook could be deemed as a positive thing."

Michael, frowning, opened his mouth to ask another question, but Lindsey cut in and beat him to it. "You went to see Christine, didn't you?"

Crane nodded.

"And..." Lindsey gestured with her hands for him to elaborate, eager to know what happened.

"And... she certainly wants to see you both suffer. But I don't think she would have used Jacob to achieve that."

Michael and Lindsey seemed to ponder his response for a moment or two, then Michael asked, "Did you tell her about Jacob?"

"I did, and I'm sorry. I know it wasn't my place to tell her, but I needed to see her reaction. The way she was talking about wanting something bad to have happened to you, I started to think that maybe she *was* involved. But then, after I told her what happened to Jacob and watched her reaction." Crane paused and took a sip of his coffee, then rested the cup back down on his knee and gave a slight shake of his head. "She seemed genuinely shocked and upset about it."

Michael and Lindsey looked down at their own coffees resting on their laps. They seemed to be processing what he'd just told them. Several seconds ticked by, then Michael looked up at Crane as though he'd just remembered something. "Did you speak to Steve Flockton, too?"

Lindsey scoffed at the mention of his name and turned her face away in disgust.

Crane nodded again.

"And did you tell *him* about Jacob, too?" asked Michael, a defensive edge creeping into his tone. Crane couldn't tell if it was because he didn't want Steve to know about Jacob or because just talking about Steve naturally brought the tone out of him.

"No, I didn't feel the need to. Steve wants to get one over on you, but not to this level." He took another sip of his coffee to give himself a moment to decide whether or not he wanted to get involved in Steve and Michael's tit for tat. He would have preferred not to, but what swayed him was the thought of public officers in the council accepting bribes from Steve Flockton. It wasn't right, and hopefully Michael had the resources to do something about it. "He's paid off some people in the council to delay the planning permission for your apartments."

Michael rolled his eyes as though he was only mildly annoyed by this information. "We'll see about th—"

Michael was interrupted by a loud, high-pitched ringing. All three of them snapped their gaze to the phone on the table. The screen illuminated, bright and sickly green, and as it started to vibrate on the hard surface of the mahogany coffee table, it began to glide slowly towards the edge, as though the table had suddenly turned to ice. Crane glanced down at his watch. The Craftsman wasn't due to call until seven; he was nine minutes early. Michael snatched up the phone to prevent it from falling onto the floor, but Crane held up a hand to signal for him to hold off answering it just yet. Ricky had given him very specific instructions that he wanted to recap with Michael first.

"He's going to give you a username and tell you to transfer the money to it," said Crane, shifting his weight forward so that he was now perched on the edge of the sofa. At the same time, he pulled his phone from his pocket. "When he gives the username to you, try and delay the transfer as long as you can. Tell him you've mistyped it or misheard him or the internet signal has dropped. Whatever it takes. We need to buy my associate as much time as possible to try and trace the money."

Michael gave a single, determined nod to show that he understood, then Crane pointed to the phone in Michael's hand to give him the go-ahead to answer it. Which he did.

"Hello." Michael pressed the button to activate the speakerphone and placed the phone back down on the table in front of him.

Lindsey shuffled across the sofa and lean-hugged into Michael's upper arm. Crane unlocked his phone and opened a blank message ready to type out The Craftsman's username to send to Ricky. Ricky had instructed Crane to text it to him rather than call for several reasons, but essentially it was the quickest and most accurate way of getting it to him. Especially if it consisted of uppercase and lowercase letters, numbers, and symbols—which was likely.

"Hello, Michael. I trust that you're ready?"

Michael leaned down closer to the phone. "I've done everything you asked me to, if that's what you mean."

"Fabulous." The Craftsman sounded almost chirpy. "Then let's get this party started."

"Can we speak to Jacob first?" blurted out Lindsey, then immediately brought her hand up to cover her mouth as though the question had popped out involuntarily.

"Hello, Lindsey." The Craftsman chuckled, seemingly unfazed by her outburst. "Unfortunately, he isn't with me at the moment. As I told you last night, when I have the money, I'll tell you where you can find him. Now, then, Michael, what's your username for EAPA?"

"It's umm..." Michael cleared his throat. "It's Brookes with a capital B, and instead of an E and S, I used the numbers three and five."

They heard computer keys being lightly tapped and then The Craftsman asked, "And what's your password?"

Shit. Crane jumped up from the sofa as though he'd been jabbed by an electric cattle prod. *Something is wrong. The Craftsman wasn't meant to ask for Michael's password.*

Lindsey and Michael flinched at Crane's sudden movement and stared at him with wide, questioning eyes. Crane's own eyes were fixed on the phone, but he wasn't really looking at it. His mind was rattling off questions and working through possibilities and options. He didn't know what to do. He was tempted to hang up the call to buy them some time, but if he did that and it resulted in something bad happening to Jacob, he would never be able to forgive himself.

"What's your password, Michael?" repeated The Craftsman.

"Uh... wh-what?" stammered Michael, upturning his hands to Crane.

The Craftsman's tone hardened with impatience. "Listen to me. If you ever want to see your little boy again, I suggest you give me your password *right fucking now.*"

Crane had no choice but to let it play out. He made a circular motion with one hand and mouthed the words "go on" to Michael, but at the same time, he hit an icon on his own phone to dial Ricky. He sidestepped out from between the table and sofa, hoping that maybe Ricky knew what was happening and could do something about it.

"What's wrong?" answered Ricky.

Crane didn't respond straight away, listening as Michael rattled off his password. He waited until he reached the corner of the library and was confident that his hushed voice couldn't be picked up by the other phone to speak. "He asked for Michael's username and password," Crane whispered into the phone.

There was a short pause, then Ricky said, "*Shit.*"

"What's he doing, Rick?"

"He's not transferring the money anywhere; he's just going to withdraw it straight out of Michael's account."

"I've got Michael's username and password if that would work?" asked Crane, speaking with so much urgency it was a struggle to keep his voice down.

"*Yes*," cried Ricky. "What's his username?"

Crane relayed the username as Ricky tapped it into his keyboard as quickly as he could say it. A glimmer of hope ignited inside him during the moment or two of silence that followed, but then a single word from Ricky instantly extinguished it. "*Shit.*"

"What?" urged Crane. "What is it?"

"It's too late." Ricky sighed. "He's already got in and changed his username. I can't even find him now. It's gone. I'm sorry, Crane, I should have anticipated this happening."

"It's not your fault, Rick," replied Crane, attempting to sound reassuring but coming across more direct than anything else. He didn't want Ricky to beat himself up over it; there was still a chance The Craftsman would stay true to his word and tell them where Jacob was being held. "I'll let you know what happens."

Crane ended the call and went back to Michael and Lindsey, who were perched on the edge of their sofa, staring at the phone on the table in front of them. Lindsey was still leaning into Michael and hugging his arm tight. Neither looked up or even seemed to notice Crane returning as they listened intently, waiting for the silent phone to make a noise. Around ten seconds or so ticked by before a clicking sound came out of the phone's speaker followed by The Craftsman's voice.

"Fantastic," he declared cheerily. "It's all in. Thank you, Michael. It's been an absolute pleasure doing business with you."

"Where's Jacob?"

"Oh yes," replied The Craftsman. "Little Jacob. I almost forgot."

Crane suddenly felt a sensation that most people described as a cold shiver running down their spine. He recognised it to be a hit of adrenaline and cortisol entering his system. Something was off. The way The Craftsman was talking, the tone of his voice. Crane didn't like it one little bit. Almost every muscle in his body seemed to tense up as he listened to the smug voice coming from the speaker.

"Now, I wish I had more time because I'd really love to play the hot and cold game with you. You know, the one where you hide something and then tell the people looking for it whether they're getting hotter or colder depending on how close they are to it."

"Will you just cut the bullshit and tell us where we need to go to get Jacob?" snapped Michael.

His outburst shocked everyone, including himself. It seemed to have come from nowhere, but Crane figured he must have been sensing something similar to himself. Michael's face had turned a shade of scarlet and the vein running up his forehead protruded and throbbed visibly. Lindsey turned to look at him, her mouth forming an O-shape and her brow crinkled. Michael's eyes were burning a hole in the phone on the table while waiting for The Craftsman's response.

A muffled sound came through the speaker that was difficult to decipher at first, but as the volume and intensity of it increased, it became clear. It was laughter. "That's the funny thing, Michael," he said between chortles. "You don't need to go anywhere. Jacob's already there with you."

Michael, Lindsey, and Crane all took turns looking at each other, their faces silently conveying the same question—*what the hell is he talking about?*

"Like I was saying," The Craftsman continued, "I wish I had more time to play the hot and cold game with you, but unfortunately, I don't. So, I'll leave you with this—he's somewhere very, very cold."

The line clicked dead and a dreadful silence fell over the library. Crane took off towards the door and almost ripped it off its hinges as he threw it open. A couple of strides into the adjoining sitting room and he was at a full sprint. *Please be wrong, please be wrong.*

He raced through the dining room and burst through the double doors and into the kitchen. George, Eva, and Carol jumped up and out of their seats at the kitchen table. Carol and Eva yelped in shock and raised their hands to cover their open mouths.

George gasped and then cried out, "What's going on?"

Crane barely even noticed them as he rushed around the kitchen island and crashed through the door to the utility room. He came to an abrupt stop in front of the overflow chest freezer and paused briefly before raising the lid. *Please be wrong.*

A blast of frigid air hit Crane in the face. But it wasn't the cold air that caused his breath to catch in his throat and made his heart turn to lead. It was the sight of a little boy dressed in space-themed pyjamas, lying on top of the joints of meat and plastic tubs that half-filled the chest freezer. He looked so serene, as though he was in a deep and peaceful sleep. But he wasn't sleeping. He was frozen solid.

CHAPTER TWENTY-FOUR

Crane slammed the chest freezer lid down when he heard footsteps approaching the doorway. He placed his hands flat down on top of it and leaned his weight forward, partly to stop whoever was coming from being able to open it but also because his legs suddenly felt weak and unsteady. Even though he'd seen more than his fair share of dead bodies in his time, this one... this one seemed to affect him more than any of the others. It was such a tragic and unnecessary waste of life.

Crane was no expert when it came to determining causes of death, especially from a glance and especially on a frozen body, but judging from Jacob's positioning—the way he was just lying on his back as though he were sleeping peacefully—he'd obviously been dead before being placed inside the freezer. The thought made Crane's stomach clench and almost forced its contents up to make a reappearance. He swallowed hard and inhaled deeply in an effort to regain some sort of composure.

Michael rushed into the utility room, stopping just inside the doorway. "What is it, Crane?"

Keeping his hands firmly on top of the freezer, Crane turned his head to look at Michael, but he couldn't bring himself to speak. Michael glanced down at the chest freezer, then looked back up at Crane. It was subtle, but his eyes widened ever so slightly, and in that moment, Crane knew he understood.

Lindsey trotted through the doorway behind him. "What?" she asked, her face scrunched up in confusion. "What's going on?"

"Please," uttered Michael, his bottom lip trembling and his voice shaking. "Please, no."

Lindsey's eyes flashed to the freezer and almost instantly popped open wide.

Crane knew there was nothing he could possibly say to help ease the pain they were about to experience. In the end, and in a voice that croaked more than he'd expected, he said the only words that seemed appropriate—"I'm so, so sorry."

Lindsey's legs instantly gave way and she dropped to her knees on the hard tiled floor. Her face twisted in pure anguish and her mouth stretched open in a silent scream. She wrapped her arms around her tummy, hugging herself tight, and folded over as if she were in excruciating physical pain. Crane knew all too well she really was in excruciating pain, but it was caused by something far worse than anything physical. Her sobs came now, forceful and desperate.

Michael took a step closer to Crane. His eyes were full of tears and his bottom lip trembled uncontrollably. "I... I need to see."

Crane looked into Michael's tearful, bloodshot eyes. The eyes of a broken man. "Trust me," said Crane, shaking his head, "you don't."

"Please. I need to see my boy."

Crane lifted his right hand off the freezer and turned to face Michael, but he kept his left hand firmly in place. "If you look inside, you'll never be able to unsee it."

"Please, Crane," sputtered Michael. The tears were now flowing and he could barely get his words out. "I... I have to."

Crane placed a consoling hand on Michael's shoulder. "I'm not going to stop you, but I think you should at least take some time first." He glanced over Michael's shoulder. Lindsey was rocking back and forth on her knees as she sobbed in utter despair. "Be with Lindsey. She needs you."

Michael hesitated, then turned away from Crane and dropped to his own knees in front of Lindsey. She looked up and they immediately wrapped their arms around each other in a tight, heartbreaking embrace.

Crane finally lifted his left hand off the freezer knowing he should leave to give them some space. They needed to be together and they certainly didn't need any spectators witnessing their grief. He quickly used the sleeve of his sweatshirt to wipe the parts of the freezer he'd touched. Although the camera footage showed The Craftsman had worn gloves, it was likely the police would still dust the lid for prints, and he would rather stay out of their investigation if he could help it.

When he walked into the kitchen, George, Eva, and Carol were standing near the doorway, each one of their faces filled with sheer terror. They'd obviously got the gist that something dreadful had happened, and to be fair, they'd shown a great deal of restraint and respect to have stayed out of the utility room.

"Please, take a seat at the kitchen table."

Crane followed them over. He remained standing as they took a seat, then he bent down and rested his elbows on the back of the chair opposite them. His legs still weren't back to their full strength and there was a big knot in his stomach.

"What is it, Crane?" asked Carol, the worry in her eyes magnified by her spectacles. "What's happened?"

Crane took a breath before answering. There was no easy way to tell them. "Jacob was never taken from the house. It appears as though the man who calls himself The Craftsman killed Jacob and then stored his body in the freezer before faking the kidnapping."

As expected, there was a chorus of gasps. Tears immediately started flowing for Carol and Eva, and George looked as though he would be following their lead soon.

"I can't believe it." George sniffed. "I almost went in the freezer this afternoon. I thought about roasting a joint but decided on a spread so everyone could help themselves." He lowered his head into his hands, elbows resting on the table. A single tear fell onto the oak tabletop.

"How often do you use the freezer?"

"Hardly ever. It's just an overflow. We usually only store joints of meat in there, maybe the occasional tub of leftovers that typically ends up in the bin anyway. We could probably manage without it."

The Craftsman must've been confident that Jacob wouldn't be discovered until after the fake kidnapping and money transfer had played out. *But how?*

"Look, Michael and Lindsey are going to need a lot of support. Don't do anything just yet, you need to wait until they're ready. But as soon as they are, call the police." Crane stood up straight. The knot in his belly ignited and began to burn. "Feel free to tell them everything; however, I'd appreciate it if you keep my name out of it."

"Wait," said George, wiping the final tears from his eyes with the back of his hand. "Where are *you* going?"

Crane's eyes passed over George, Carol, and Eva. His eyes were focused on them, but there was one vision burned into the back of his retinas—Jacob lying dead in the freezer.

"I'm gonna find The Craftsman," said Crane, his voice charged with grit and determination. "And I'm going to bury him and anyone who helped him."

CHAPTER TWENTY-FIVE

Crane turned his truck into Ricky's driveway and parked in his usual spot near the front door. He'd considered calling Ricky during the drive, but he couldn't bring himself to break the news over the phone. He jumped out of the truck, and as he took a step towards the front door, not only did the electric motorised locks clunk to disengage, but the door itself swung open.

Ricky stood to one side holding the door open for Crane. His forehead looked as though it had been freshly ploughed with rows of worry lines. "What happened?"

"I think you should put the kettle on," replied Crane, stepping into the barn.

While Ricky made the coffees, Crane told him exactly what had happened.

"*Jesus Christ*," exclaimed Ricky, handing Crane a steaming mug and blinking away tears of his own. "It's... It's just unimaginable. I mean, who would do something like that?"

"Scum," said Crane through gritted teeth as he sat down on one of the stools at the kitchen island. "Pure. Evil. Scum."

"Yeah, you're right," agreed Ricky, taking the stool opposite Crane. "I was thinking psychopath, but evil scum does fit better."

Crane stared at the steam rising from the coffee in his hand. "He killed an innocent little boy and dumped his body in a freezer and then extorted money out of the parents whose lives he just destroyed. There can't be a single shred of humanity in him. Whoever the hell he is, psychopath just doesn't seem to cut it. He's... he's something else." Crane looked up at Ricky with icy, resolute eyes. "We need to find him, Ricky. Justice. Vengeance. Retribution. Whatever you want to call it. I need it. I need to make him pay for what he's done."

"I'm with you," said Ricky. "One hundred per cent."

"The problem is, I don't even know where to start looking." Crane rubbed his tired eyes with the heels of his hands. "I feel like I can barely think straight at the minute."

"I'm not surprised. You look knackered."

"It's been a long day."

"Look, why don't you go home and get some rest." Ricky placed his mug on the island. "Come back here in the morning and we'll put together an action plan. We'll find him."

Crane clamped his lips together and nodded. It was the sensible thing to do. He wasn't going to achieve anything tonight, as his brain felt like mush. He picked up his mug and was about to take a sip of coffee when Ricky jumped up from his stool.

"*Stop.*"

Crane froze, the rim of the mug brushing against his lips and the aroma of fresh coffee filling his nostrils. Ricky scuttled around the island and snatched the mug out of his hand.

Crane frowned. "What the f—"

"This isn't going to help you rest, is it?" Ricky raised the mug in the air and pointed to it with his free hand.

"Are you being serious?"

"Yeah, deadly," said Ricky before wincing at his poor choice of words.

"Come on." Crane stood up from his stool. "Give it here."

Ricky took a step back.

Crane took a step forward.

Ricky spun around, rushed to the sink, and tipped it all down the plughole. "This is for your benefit," he called over his shoulder to Crane.

Crane reached over and picked up Ricky's mug, which was still sitting on the island, full and untouched. As Ricky turned around to face him, Crane raised his mug as though he were making a toast. "Cheers, Rick. I really appreciate you looking out for me." And with that, he downed Ricky's coffee in one.

When Crane arrived home, instead of going straight up to bed like he should have, he took a detour to the kitchen and went directly to his whisky cupboard. A vast array of bottles stared back at him when he opened it. Usually, he'd take his time and spend a minute or two considering his options, but not tonight; tonight, he just reached in and grabbed the first bottle he touched. Which happened to be an eighteen-year-old Scotch finished in a sherry cask—a selection he certainly wasn't disappointed with.

He placed the bottle on the kitchen worktop and retrieved an old-fashioned crystal tumbler from one of the other cupboards. After dropping two large ice cubes inside from the dispenser built into the fridge freezer, he half-filled the glass with whisky, then sidestepped back to the fridge and fetched a nicely chilled bottle of ginger wine to fill the rest of his glass. A whisky Mac. A very, very large whisky Mac—it had been a very, very long day.

The ice cubes clinked against the crystal as he raised his glass to take a sip, and he savoured the bold mix of complex flavours from the Scotch and the sweet and spicy notes of the wine, wondering how many whisky connoisseurs would be cursing him if they knew he was using an eighteen-year-old Scotch for his whisky Mac. Not that he cared. As far as he was concerned, a chef only used the best ingredients when producing a culinary masterpiece. Why shouldn't he use the best ingredients to make his favourite drink?

Crane returned the bottles to their rightful places before heading upstairs. By the time he reached his bedroom, over a quarter of his drink had disappeared. He savoured one more mouthful before placing his glass on the bedside table and sitting down heavily on the edge of his bed. While he sat there in the silence, his mind decided to play somewhat of a highlight reel of his day. He inhaled deeply and sagged a little as he let out a huge sigh. It really had been a long day, and a shit one at that.

He took another swig of whisky before pulling his phone out of his pocket and unlocking it with his thumbprint. Nothing. No messages. Even though Ella hadn't necessarily been at the forefront of his mind throughout the day, she had always been there somewhere in the background. He thought about their conversation that morning and how he'd left things with her. He thought about Jacob and The Craftsman. Then he tapped on Ella's name and typed out a message.

"My world is dark and unpleasant and dangerous, and you're right to not want to be a part of it.

But as dark as my world is, I can't turn my back on it. At least not yet, anyway. There are things I have done and things I'm going to do that I could never share with you. Not because I'm ashamed of them, but because you deserve to live in a world of light.

It was wrong and even selfish to think that someone like me could be with someone like you. You deserve so much more than me."

Crane's thumb hovered over the send button, but when it touched the screen, it landed on the delete button and remained there until the entire message had vanished. Then he typed out another one.

"You're right, our worlds are too far apart, but I'd like it if we could still be friends?"

Crane hit the send button and tossed the phone onto the bed beside him, then grabbed his glass and downed the rest of the whisky, finding solace in the burning sensation that flowed down his throat and into his stomach. Without waiting for the fire to dwindle, he stood up and stripped off before heading into the bathroom. After a long hot shower, he padded back into the bedroom and picked up his phone to put it on charge, but then he stopped when he noticed a message waiting for him from Ella. He tapped the screen to open it. It simply read:

"Of course x"

CHAPTER TWENTY-SIX

It wasn't unusual for Crane to have difficulty getting off to sleep, and after the day he'd had, he fully anticipated a battle. To give himself a fighting chance, he played a guided relaxation meditation through the Bluetooth speaker in his room, but when it came to an end an hour later, his eyes were wide open and his mind was still buzzing. In hindsight, he probably should've listened to Ricky and left the coffee alone.

He got out of bed, threw on a pair of shorts and a T-shirt, then went downstairs to his gym room, or more specifically, he went to his yoga mat. An hour of yin yoga later, his body felt open and relaxed and his turbulent mind seemed to have finally settled. He went back upstairs, but as soon as he got back into bed, the thoughts and questions began to creep back to the forefront of his mind causing it to buzz once again. One question in particular seemed to keep pushing itself to the front—*how are you going to find The Craftsman?*

As a last-ditch effort, he tried playing another guided meditation, but it was no use. The recording came to an end and sleep was still evading him. He didn't bother to replay it or try looking for another one; instead, he just lay there in the dark and accepted that he wasn't going to be getting any sleep tonight. He was just going to allow the thoughts and questions to come and go as they pleased. No more fighting. No more trying to push them away. Only acceptance. *It is what it is.*

And that was when he finally nodded off. But unfortunately for Crane, his slumber only lasted a few minutes. The sound of his phone vibrating and ringing dragged him back to full consciousness. He reached over and snatched his phone off the bedside table, ripping it free from the charging cable. He blinked at the screen a couple of times until the bright blur became decipherable to his tired eyes. The call was coming from a number he didn't recognise. He swiped the green symbol to answer it and took note of the time displayed at the top corner of the screen. Twenty-five past one.

Holding the phone against his ear, he said, "Hello?"

At first, there was nothing, but then he could hear sniffing and realised it was someone crying. He tried again. "Hello?"

"Crane."

It was a choked and weak female voice he immediately recognised. He sat himself up in bed. "Lindsey? Are you okay?" As soon as the words left his mouth, Crane winced and silently cursed himself. Of course she wasn't *okay*.

"The police are still here. They're downstairs with Michael. I... I just needed some time alone."

"I understand." Although, in truth, he was wondering why she'd decided to call him if she wanted to be alone.

"George told me that before you left, you said you're going to find the man that did this. The Craftsman." The line went quiet for a moment, as though just saying the name had taken something out of her. "Apparently, you said... you're going to bury him."

Crane didn't respond. Lindsey may have stopped speaking, but he got the impression she hadn't finished. He waited patiently, listening to her shaky breaths and a quiet rustling that he assumed was a tissue.

"Please promise me..." she started, but her voice croaked and faded away. She cleared her throat and tried again. "Promise me you'll find him... and you'll make him pay for what he did to our little boy."

Crane never made promises he didn't know if he could keep and he didn't intend to start now, which is why, with steely determination, he simply said, "I promise."

Lindsey must've been holding her breath waiting for his response because as soon as he answered, she audibly exhaled. "Thank you," she whispered breathlessly and then broke down in a fresh bout of heart-wrenching sobs before ending the call.

Crane lowered the phone from his ear and sat there in the dark for a couple of minutes. Even though he was surrounded by silence, the cautious part of his mind was anything but. *How can you promise her that? You have no idea who The Craftsman is or where he is. What if you can't find him?* Crane inhaled deeply through his nose, then exhaled slowly out of his mouth, and for once, he told the cautious part of his brain to go fuck itself. He was going to fulfil his promise one way or another, or he would certainly die trying.

Crane placed the phone back on the bedside table and was about to lie down when it started to ring and vibrate again. His eyes darted to the screen, expecting to see the same number calling. *Maybe she didn't mean to end the call.* But although the number displayed on the screen was one he didn't recognise, it wasn't the same one Lindsey had just called him on. Crane picked the phone up and used his thumb to swipe the green icon.

"Hello?"

"Oh, uh... hello. Sorry, I wasn't expecting it to be answered so quickly. Is that Mr Crane?"

It was another female voice, and once again, he believed it was a voice he recognised. "Christine?"

"Yes," she said, sounding surprised that he knew who it was.

Crane was about to ask her why she was calling him at half one in the morning when another, more pressing question popped into his head and caused his brow to furrow. "How did you get my number?" He hadn't given it to her or left her a card.

"Oh, umm... it was on the online booking form your assistant filled out for your appointment." She sounded jittery, not like the overly confident businesswoman he'd met the day before.

"What do you want, Christine?"

"I... I heard what happened." Her voice quivered as though she was on the verge of tears. "To Jacob."

Christ, news travels fast. Then he corrected himself. *No, only bad news travels this fast.*

"I need to speak to you."

Crane found himself pressing the phone tighter against his ear. "Okay."

"Not over the phone. Can you meet me?"

Curiosity instantly took over his desire for sleep and he simply asked, "Where?"

Her voice dropped in volume as though she'd pulled the phone away from her face. "I'm sending you my live location now."

Crane's phone beeped and vibrated against his ear. He lowered it and tapped on the notification from one of the messaging apps. A map of Bristol filled the screen, then it quickly zoomed into a red pin that represented Christine's live location.

"I'll be there in an hour," he said before ending the call and jumping out of bed.

CHAPTER TWENTY-SEVEN

Crane didn't need an hour. The roads were deserted at this time of night. He reached the point on the map where Christine's red pin had been displayed on his phone in a little over forty-five minutes. It was on a road that had a long row of four-storey townhouses on the left and a tree-lined park area on the right. There were vehicles parked on both sides of the road. Crane figured Christine would be sitting in one of them, especially in this weather. A persistent drizzle hadn't stopped falling since he'd left the house.

A gap in the parked cars came up on the right. Crane eased off the accelerator and coasted past it, then he stopped and parallel parked neatly into the space. He picked up his phone from the centre console, unlocked it, and refreshed Christine's live location. It took a second or two, then it showed him that he'd just passed her pin. Crane looked up and scanned his mirrors; according to the app, she should be right behind him. He searched for light or movement or any signs of life, but the street behind him appeared to be dark and deserted.

He was about to grab his waterproof jacket from the back seat to go for a wander when he caught sight of light and movement in his wing mirror. A car door around three cars back swung open, the interior light illuminating the back of the woman climbing out of it. She wore a long khaki-coloured rain jacket with the hood up and held a matching umbrella in her hand.

Crane couldn't see her face, but judging from the shape and size of her silhouette, it looked like Christine.

She popped open the umbrella before closing her car door, then steadily walked along the pavement towards his truck. Crane buzzed the window down as she approached his door. Christine stopped and looked at him. Her face was drawn and her eyes looked red and sore, as though she'd only just stopped crying. "Thank you for coming."

"Do you want to get in?"

She clamped her lips together and shook her head, a short burst of movement from side to side. "Will you walk with me?"

Crane looked at the water already dripping from the spokes of her umbrella, then he glanced up at the orange glow of the streetlamp in front of his truck. It may have only been drizzling, but it was still coming down in sheets. His preference would have been to stay in the truck, but he had a feeling this chat was going to be worth getting drenched for.

He buzzed the window back up, then reached behind and grabbed his waterproof jacket off the back seat. It was a bit of a challenge putting it on in the confined space of the cabin, but he was soon zipping it up and raising the hood over his head. Before getting out, he reached down into the rear footwell and felt around until his hand brushed against the umbrella he stored down there. He grabbed it and lifted it over the front seats. It was plain black, just like his waterproof jacket, and it was like new; in fact, he couldn't remember the last time he'd bothered to use it or even if he ever had.

Christine stepped back to give him space as he opened the door and jumped out. He locked up the truck, opened his umbrella, then looked at Christine and swept his free hand to the left, then to the right in a silent gesture to ask which way she wanted to walk. Without hesitation, she turned to the right, and Crane instantly knew exactly where they were heading. He also had a theory as to why.

They set off together, walking at a casual pace side-by-side along the pavement. Crane glanced across to Christine. Her gaze was fixed straight ahead and her lips were drawn into a fine line. She looked like someone who had something important to say but wasn't sure how to start.

"What have you done, Christine?"

She turned her head to look at him briefly, then returned her focus to the street ahead. "I need to start at the beginning if you don't mind."

"Please do."

"When you were in my office, I told you that I struggled after the separation between myself and Michael. But I don't think I made clear just how difficult it's really been for me. Over the last five years, I've been in and out of therapy more times than I can count. I've had counselling, NLP, and hypnotherapy, not to mention the ridiculous amount of antidepressants I've been on." She hesitated. "Although, if I'm completely honest, a lot of it was rendered useless due to the alcohol and recreational drugs I'd take just to get myself through some days." Another hesitation and a slight head tilt. "*Most* days."

They came to a side road that turned off to the right. Crane slowed slightly to allow Christine to lead the way. *Will she follow the road around to the right or cross over?* She crossed over and they continued walking along the main road, reaffirming Crane's suspicion of their destination. The row of townhouses on the left had come to an end and was now replaced with some greenery. Although, not much of the colour green was visible in the dark, only a little bit at the edges where it met the pavement directly below the puddle of light from the streetlamps.

"Anyway, the point I'm trying to make is I was suffering. And because I was suffering, I wanted Michael to suffer too. And the only way I could think of achieving that was to drag out the divorce and make it as hard as possible for him. For almost five years, I rejected every settlement his solicitors sent across. I was intentionally being the proverbial thorn in his side. You see, I knew there was one thing he would never let me have, so that's exactly what I kept insisting on."

"What was it?"

She suppressed a snigger. "The villa in the Algarve. He bloody loves playing golf out there. It's been his pride and joy ever since we bought it. Personally, I was never that keen on it and he knew that. Which is why *I knew* it would hurt him if I kept insisting on it as part of the divorce settlement."

"So, what happened for you to eventually agree to a settlement?" asked Crane, gently trying to nudge her towards the point she was leading up to.

Christine glanced at Crane with a knowing smile, making it clear she understood what he was doing. "Around three months ago, Michael called me out of the blue. It was the first time we'd spoken in years. He asked if I would be open to meeting up with him to discuss things with no solicitors, just the two of us. I was intrigued, so I agreed..."

CHAPTER TWENTY-EIGHT

Three months ago...

Christine pushed through the tall glass door and stepped into the swanky wine bar in the centre of Bristol. It had been her choice of venue when Michael had asked her where she wanted to meet. She liked it because it was expensive. It was the kind of place that priced out all the riff-raff to ensure it only attracted a more... classy clientele. Also, Michael had asked to meet her, so as far as she was concerned, he'd be the one picking up the bill.

His call had come as a real surprise and had also come at quite a good time for her. She'd been hitting the gym hard with her personal trainer recently and had lost over half a stone. And mentally, she was in a good place; or at least, she was in one of her "better spells" and thankfully not in one of her "dark" spells.

So today, in preparation for this evening, she'd spent most of the afternoon at the salon getting her hair, nails, and makeup done. Then she got dressed in her sexiest little black number and her best fuck-me boots. She kept telling herself that none of it was for Michael's benefit, she was doing it all for herself. Which was mostly true, but she'd be lying to herself if she didn't admit that she hoped to make him feel some remorse about what he'd done to her, even if it was only the faintest sliver of regret when he saw her. Although Christine knew she couldn't really compete with Lindsey—the youthful, skinny, beautiful, blonde, perfect... slut Lindsey. But even so, when she walked into the wine bar, she felt good. So damn good.

The inside of the bar was a modern and rustic blend of bare red-brick walls, clean whites, and solid oaks. Subdued lighting gave the place a warm, almost homely feel, and chillout music played at a level that made conversing easy. There was a long bar on the right, several tables and chairs spread out in the centre, and booths running down the full length of the left-hand wall. As always, it wasn't too busy. Half the tables and chairs were free, although all the booths were taken, one of which was occupied by a familiar face.

Michael must've sensed her eyes on him because he immediately looked up from his phone. Their eyes met, and Christine's breath caught in her throat. Michael raised a hand to acknowledge her. Christine gave a slight nod in return as she scolded herself internally for her reaction to seeing him. *You're pathetic. He's the dirty lying cheat who ruined your life.*

She casually walked over to his booth, ensuring to exaggerate the sway of her hips as she did. Michael slid out of his seat and stood up. *Ever the gentleman*, thought Christine as she approached him, then almost snort-laughed when she corrected herself—*ever the gentleman until he's shagging one of his employees.* As she reached him, there was an awkward moment where neither of them seemed to know how they should greet each other. Christine stopped a couple of steps away. There was no way, after everything that had happened, she was going to initiate any physical contact with him. She found herself wondering if she would let him give her a hug or a peck on the cheek if he tried, but she needn't have bothered; Michael made no attempt to close the gap between them.

"Thank you for coming," he said and gestured towards the booth with an open hand. "Please."

Christine slipped into the booth and sat down on the tan leather bench. A bottle of red wine and two large glasses were on the table between them.

"I hope you don't mind, but I ordered us a bottle," said Michael, sitting down opposite her. He picked up the bottle and tilted it in offering towards Christine. "I trust you still enjoy a Châteauneuf-du-Pape?"

Christine placed her immaculately manicured fingers onto the base of her empty wine glass and slid it forward a couple of inches. Michael obliged and poured her a glass before tending to his own. Christine took a sip and then placed her glass back down on the table, now with a fresh scarlet lipstick stain on the rim.

"So, Michael, to what do I owe the displeasure of this meeting?"

One corner of Michael's mouth upturned, amused by her little dig. "I've reached a point where I've had enough of the back and forth and getting absolutely nowhere. It's been almost five years, and the only thing we seem to have achieved in that time is line our solicitors' pockets."

"That's true."

"So, I thought it was worth a shot getting the two of us together, face to face, in the hope that we can finally hash it out and reach a mutually acceptable agreement."

If he thinks I'm going to roll over just because we're sharing a bottle of wine, he's got another thing coming. "From memory, I believe there's only one sticking point left in the negotiations."

"That's right," said Michael. "The villa."

Christine picked up her glass and took another sip of wine. "So, I take it you're ready to concede and give it up?"

"Not quite." Michael snorted. "It's on a golf resort, Christine. You bloody hate golf."

She smirked and gave a one-shoulder shrug. "I'm actually considering taking it up. Maybe when I have the villa, it'll give me the nudge I need to start playing."

"Come on, Christine, stop playing games. We both know you only want the villa to piss me off."

"And what if that's true?" she countered. "After what you did to me, I think I deserve to piss you off a bit."

"A bit?" asked Michael incredulously, his voice rising in volume. "You've been pissing me off for the last five years."

Christine's brows went up. "Have I now?"

Michael snatched up his glass and downed a big gulp of his wine, then he paused and took a deep breath to calm himself. When he began to speak again, his voice had returned to its normal volume and his tone had lost its edge. "Look, you're right. I was a coward. I should have asked for a divorce long before anything started between me and Lindsey."

"That's it?" asked Christine, a furious blaze seemed to ignite behind her eyes and there was more than a hint of disbelief in her voice. "Your only regret is not kicking me out and trying to divorce me sooner?"

Michael opened his mouth to respond but stopped himself and took another swig of wine. "I regret how things ended between us, but let's not pretend like everything was hunky-dory between us during the last few years we were together."

Christine's expression darkened. "What the hell is that supposed to mean?"

"Come on, Christine. You know exactly what I'm talking about. We didn't have a marriage towards the end; we were living like bloody housemates."

"Oh, right, I get it." She rolled her eyes. "Because we weren't having regular sex, we were just housemates."

"Regular sex?" Michael laughed contemptuously. "We hadn't had sex for over two years before I met Lindsey."

Over two years? Christine had to admit she hadn't realised it had been that long. Still, he couldn't put all that on her. "So because you weren't getting any from me, you went looking elsewhere."

"No. It wasn't like that at all. Sex wasn't even that big of a deal to me. It was the lack of..."

"Well, go on, spit it out."

"Affection. Connection. Love." Michael paused to emphasise each word. "Think back to the last couple of years we were together. Can you even remember giving me a kiss? Or a hug even? How about telling me that you loved me?"

"*Fuck you*," spat Christine. "Don't you dare try to make out like it was all my fault. *You* cheated on *me*." Several pairs of eyes on the tables nearby had turned towards them, she lowered her voice, but her tone remained venomous. "I knew it was only a matter of time. As soon as we found out that I couldn't conceive, I knew you'd start looking elsewhere."

"What?" Michael's jaw went slack for a moment. "Do you really believe that?"

"Believe it? It's *exactly* what happened. You traded me in for a younger and more fertile model as soon as you had the chance."

Michael averted his gaze to his hands, which were clasped together on the table in front of him. "That's just simply not true."

Christine snatched up her glass. "I think you'll find the evidence speaks for itself," she said before downing the rest of the wine in her glass.

"No, it doesn't." Michael's voice was low and his brow was furrowed. "When we found out you couldn't conceive, I didn't stop loving you. I accepted that I would never be a father and I remained fully committed to our marriage."

"Yeah, right," scoffed Christine, picking up the bottle of wine and pouring herself another serving that was double the measure Michael had poured for her first glass.

"Come to think of it, that's when *you* started to distance yourself and push me away. It's when *you* started to change from the woman I met and fell for. When *you* started to change into... whoever you are now."

"Stop it, Michael. Just... stop it," Christine snapped. "I know what you're doing. You're trying to manipulate me into thinking it was all my fault. Well, it's not going to work." She started jabbing her index finger at him. "*You* were the one who cheated. *You* were the one who kicked me out of my own home. *You* were the one who turned all our friends against me."

Michael calmly picked up his glass and drained the last two mouthfuls before gently placing it back on the table. "You know what, you can have it."

Christine flinched backwards in her seat. "What?"

"The villa," said Michael. "It's yours. I'll get my solicitor to draw up the contract and send it over next week."

Christine's lips parted slightly in shock. Knowing how much Michael loved the villa and how competitive he was, she'd never expected this outcome. She'd won. She'd finally beaten him.

"It seems as though you need it more than I do." Michael glared at her, his face reddening. "You see, I'm finally happy. I have a family. I have a woman I love and who loves me back. I have a little boy who means the world to me. And I have some great friends." Michael leaned forward and a harshness crept into his tone. "But sitting here, looking at you and listening to how bitter and twisted you are, it's obvious that your life is as barren as your *fucking womb*."

They may have only been words, but those particular words felt like a backhanded slap in the face. Her mouth opened and closed a couple of times, but as much as she wanted to respond and bite back, she couldn't seem to find her voice.

Michael slipped out of the booth and stood up. "Oh, and for the record, I never turned any of our friends against you. Maybe it's time you look in the mirror and take some responsibility for your situation instead of blaming everything on me." He leaned down so his face was only a foot or so from hers. "The truth is, nobody wants to be around you because you've turned into a nasty, horrible bitch." And with that, he turned and walked away.

Christine remained in the booth, desperately trying to hold back the tears that threatened to burst through the dam of her tough façade. She looked around and spotted several pairs of eyes quickly averting their gaze from her; they'd obviously put on quite a show for everyone. Christine inhaled deeply and vowed to not break down in public. Reaching out a shaky hand, she picked up her wine glass and gulped down a couple of mouthfuls before placing it back on the table.

A big part of her wanted to get up and leave, but another part, the stubborn part, wanted to save face and stay a little while longer to show everyone who'd witnessed their confrontation that she was strong and Michael hadn't upset her. Even if it was bullshit. Because he had. He really had.

There was also the small matter of a bottle of Châteauneuf-du-Pape that wasn't going to drink itself, and Christine knew finishing the bottle would help her feel a hell of a lot better than she did right now.

She picked up her small black clutch bag from the seat beside her and fished out her phone. She then spent the next five minutes or so aimlessly scrolling through social media to help distract her from having to deal with the hurtful things Michael had said. Without looking, she picked up her wine glass and drank the last mouthful, then placed the glass back on the table before reaching for the bottle with the same hand. As the tips of her fingers touched the bottle, a loud noise nearby demanded her attention.

An attractive young blonde girl, barely in her twenties, had abruptly stood up from the table for two next to Christine's booth. The loud noise had been the result of her chair legs scraping backwards across the stone floor. The girl glowered at the man opposite her.

"*You fucking arsehole,*" she hissed loud enough for everyone in the bar to hear. Then she spun on her heels and stormed out.

Christine watched her leave, then looked back to the table and at the man still sitting there. He was already looking at Christine, and she instantly felt herself flush slightly under his gaze. He was young. Not quite as young as his date had been, maybe mid-twenties. And he was Hollywood handsome. His dark hair was styled immaculately in a pompadour fade, his complexion was flawless, and his jawline was sharp. He looked as though he'd just come from a photoshoot for one of those fancy fashion magazines.

He held his arms out to the sides, shrugged, and grinned awkwardly at Christine. Then he said something to her, but she couldn't quite hear him. She raised a hand and pretended to cup her ear to let him know that she had no idea what he'd said. He laughed, picked up his wine glass, and stood up. Christine sat up a little taller in her seat as he approached.

"I said it looks like both of our dates didn't quite go to plan this evening." He smiled, revealing a perfect set of pearly whites.

Christine struggled to not get lost in his hazel eyes. "Oh, this," she said, pointing at the table. "This wasn't a date."

"Really? What was it, then?"

"It was a divorce negotiation."

The man's brows shot up. "Oh, right. I'm sorry."

"Don't be. Anyway, what happened with your date?"

"Oh, that." The man laughed. "She was a bit too... young for me." He paused to ensure he had her full attention, then added, "Personally, I prefer a more mature lady."

The line was one hundred per cent mature cheddar, but Christine still felt herself flush a little more under his gaze.

The man gestured with his free hand to the bench opposite her. "May I?"

"Be my guest." She smiled coyly.

The Craftsman was on a date with Kayla, or Kaylee, or was it Kaitlyn? He wasn't sure and he didn't really care. The truth was that it wasn't even meant to be a date. Not as far as he was concerned anyway. He'd made the mistake of messing around on one of those apps a couple of days ago. He'd swiped right, she'd swiped right, and they'd quickly agreed to meet. He was under the impression they were just going to find a cheap room somewhere and get straight to the good stuff; unfortunately, she'd had other ideas. She wanted to go somewhere for a drink first, and to top it off, her idea of "somewhere" turned out to be the most expensive bar in Bristol. The cheeky wench.

The Craftsman didn't usually do dates. He preferred to pay for a female's services. A straightforward transaction for him to get what he wanted without any of the bullshit or the baggage. Yet here he was, sitting opposite Kay... something, watching her mouth moving but not taking in a single word she was saying. So, while she continued to yap away at him, he started to pay more attention to the rich couple arguing in the booth next to them. He could tell straight away that they were loaded—designer clothes, his flash watch, her fancy jewellery, the three-hundred-and-fifty-pound bottle of Châteauneuf-du-Pape sitting on the table between them.

The Craftsman watched them closely as their heated exchange appeared to be reaching a climax. Suddenly, the man stood up, leaned down, and gave the woman a parting shot before walking out. He kept an eye on the woman afterwards. She looked hurt, devastated even. Whatever the man had said to her had really upset her, but she was doing her best to put on a brave face. Anyone else would have probably felt sorry for her, but not The Craftsman; he was incapable of a normal level of empathy. When he looked at the woman in the booth, the only thing he saw was an opportunity. But first, he needed to get rid of Kay-whatever-her-name-was.

Bringing his attention back to the table, he zoned in on what she was saying.

"...and there's just nothing worse than getting your nails done and then chipping one straight afterwards."

"Rape," he interjected.

She frowned at him. "Excuse me?"

"You said there's nothing worse than chipping a nail, but I think rape is probably a little bit worse." He shrugged. "I suppose I could be wrong, though, as I've never chipped a nail."

"Alright," she said, her frown deepening. "It's just a figure of speech. There's no need to be a dick about it."

The Craftsman smirked. She was a feisty one. He could use this to his advantage and create a scene. It would make a great icebreaker for him to introduce himself to the rich woman in the booth.

"You're right, I'm sorry," he said, raising an apologetic hand. But then as soon as her body language appeared to ease, he popped her with, "So, have you got anything more interesting to talk about other than chipping your fucking nails?"

Her mouth dropped open, seemingly more shocked than offended. He was going to have to take it up a notch if he was going to offend her enough to blow up and cause a scene.

"I mean, I've been sitting here for almost half an hour listening to you jabbering on and on, and all I keep thinking is, when are you gonna do something useful with those lips of yours and wrap them around my cock?"

Jackpot. Her entire face scrunched up as though she'd been hit with a potent whiff of raw sewage. The chair screeched across the stone floor as she pushed it back and sprung to her feet.

"*You fucking arsehole.*"

The Craftsman turned his attention to the rich woman in the booth before Kay-whatever-her-name-was had even reached the door. When the rich woman looked back at him, he did his best what-was-that-all-about? look and shrug, then intentionally mumbled to her, knowing full well she wouldn't be able to hear him. The rich woman cupped a hand to her ear to signal as such. And he was in.

A second bottle of red wine—which she paid for—and an hour of schmoozing and flirting later, he was ready to get down to business.

"Christine," he said, leaning forward and lowering his voice slightly. "I don't mean to pry, but your soon-to-be ex-husband doesn't seem like a very nice person. I mean, I couldn't hear what he said, but it certainly looked as though he was saying some truly awful things to you."

The smile left Christine's face as his words took her back to the confrontation.

"I'm sorry, I shouldn't have brought it up," said The Craftsman, his apology sounding a lot more genuine than it really was. "It's just... I got the impression he treated you very badly."

Christine lowered her gaze and began caressing the stem of her wine glass between her fingers. "He has."

The Craftsman allowed a few moments of silence to pass between them. "He *really* hurt you, didn't he?"

Christine nodded lethargically.

"Do you wanna hurt him back?"

Christine gave a short, half-suppressed laugh, borne from exasperation rather than amusement. "I tried, but it looks as though he still came out on top."

"I can help you."

Christine looked up at him and tilted her head to one side. "That's sweet," she said, almost as though he were a little boy offering to capture a shooting star for her.

"I'm serious." The Craftsman's tone now matched his words. "Whatever he's done to hurt you, I can make him regret it."

Christine's eyes narrowed slightly, but she didn't say anything. "For a price, of course."

Christine burst out laughing, but when she noticed he didn't join her and continued to look at her with a deadpan expression, she stopped. "Wait, you're being serious?"

"Deadly."

Christine stared at him sceptically, as though she was expecting him to crack up laughing any second and tell her he was just kidding. When he did no such thing, she asked, "So, what, you're like, some kind of hitman for hire?"

"I can be, for the right price. Is that what you want? Do you want him dead?"

Christine hesitated, but then her conscience seemed to kick in and she swiftly shook her head. "No, of course not."

The Craftsman sensed uncertainty in her tone and leaned over the table to get closer to her. "So, how would you like to hurt him?"

"I have no idea." Christine's mouth downturned and she shrugged animatedly. "What kind of options are there?"

"It really depends on how much you want to spend."

"Okay, then." One corner of Christine's mouth upturned in a lopsided grin. "So, what would five hundred pounds get me?"

Even The Craftsman cracked a smile at that. "A mild inconvenience. Like, maybe I'd break into his home and hide the remote control for the TV."

Christine raised a hand to stifle a laugh. It seemed as though she was beginning to enjoy herself or excited at the prospect of getting back at her ex. Probably a bit both. "What about five thousand?"

The Craftsman pursed his lips and looked up, as though the answer were scribbled somewhere on the ceiling. "I could assault him, maybe break his legs, or vandalise his home."

Christine ran her finger around the rim of her wine glass. "Okay," she said, nibbling one side of her bottom lip. "So, what would a hundred thousand get me?"

A hundred thousand pounds! He would've killed him for a quarter of that amount. This had the potential to be his biggest job so far by a country mile. Struggling to keep his voice level, he said, "Anything you want." And he meant it.

Christine chuckled. "It's a nice thought, but with all due respect, I'm not going to hand over a hundred thousand pounds to someone I've just met on a promise that they're going to do something."

"That's not how it works."

It was Christine's turn to lean a little closer. "How does it work, then?"

The Craftsman grinned, sensing her interest piquing. "We set up an account together on an anonymous payments app. You deposit the agreed funds into the account, but only you'll know the password and have access to the funds. Once I've completed the deed, you text the password to me and I'll be able to go in and withdraw the funds. You have complete control and don't pay a single penny until the deed is done."

Christine was quiet for a few moments, seemingly mulling it all over, then she asked, "But how would I know it's been done?"

"Oh, you'll know," said The Craftsman, with an arrogant glint in his eye. "I'll make sure to leave a calling card."

"A calling card?"

He nodded. "In my line of work, it pays to build a reputation. I use the name 'The Craftsman', so whatever it is you want me to do, I'll make sure they know it's been done by The Craftsman. As soon as you hear that name mentioned, you'll know I've done it."

"The Craftsman?"

"Yes. Someone who's skilled in a particular craft."

"And what craft would that be?"

There were a lot of words he could have used, but he decided to choose the one he thought may speak most to her. "Revenge."

Christine took a sip of her drink, then placed it back on the table. Her eyes were fixed on the red wine gently swaying and swirling inside her glass. The Craftsman recognised this as a moment for him to be quiet. She was in deep contemplation, possibly even replaying some of the things her ex had said or done to her. She remained in an almost trance-like state for almost two minutes, then she looked up and fixed him with a steely gaze.

"Okay, let's do it."

The Craftsman's grin widened. "What do you want me to do to him?"

Christine, still holding his gaze, said icily, "I want you to do to him what he's done to me... I want you to ruin his fucking life. I want you to mentally and emotionally destroy him."

CHAPTER TWENTY-NINE

Crane and Christine were more than two hundred and fifty feet above the water of the river Avon, standing on the Clifton Suspension Bridge. The bridge itself, with its illuminated suspension chains, looked majestic against the backdrop of the black night sky. And although neither of them were giving it their attention, the view looking down into the gorge and across the lights of North Somerset was truly stunning even in the dark and the drizzle. The pedestrian walkway they were standing on was completely deserted and only two cars had trundled past them the whole time they'd been there, which wasn't really a surprise considering the time of night.

"So, when you went on your phone while I was in your office yesterday, that was you sending him the password?"

Christine nodded. Her face was streaked with tears and mascara. "I had no idea what he'd done at that point. Then after I'd sent it to him, you told me about Jacob—" her voice broke and she had to take a couple of shaky breaths before trying to speak again. "When you left my office, I tried to call the number he'd given me, but it was already dead. So then I went into the payments app to see if the money was still there. I thought that maybe I could stop him from getting it, but the profile I'd created was gone. The whole thing had just... disappeared."

"How much did you pay him?"

Christine averted her gaze to the sliver of dark water below, evidently embarrassed by the answer she was about to give. "A hundred thousand," she mumbled.

Crane couldn't prevent a pained expression from appearing on his face. "You paid him a hundred thousand pounds and the only instruction you gave was to ruin Michael's life? Well, it looks like you got your money's worth. I mean, what were you expecting him to do?"

"I don't know," Christine sobbed, "but not... not *that*. I never thought for one second that he would hurt their little boy." She turned away from him as she broke down.

Crane waited patiently for her sobs to subside. "Is there anything else you haven't told me yet that could help me find him? Did he have any distinguishing features? An accent? Did he say anything that gave away where he was from? Anything at all?"

Christine frowned and bit down on her bottom lip while she considered, but then she slowly shook her head. "I was drunk and it was three months ago. My memory of it all is a little hazy. I've told you everything I can remember."

"And why have you told me?"

"Because... because I need to tell someone before..." She couldn't bring herself to finish the sentence. "You've probably guessed why I've brought us here." She glanced at the view before turning her attention back to Crane.

"I had my suspicions as soon as we started heading this way, although I think you're gonna struggle getting over that." Crane pointed up to the anti-suicide barrier. It consisted of five horizontal cables that ran across the top of the normal barrier, stacked on top of each other and arching towards them so that the highest one was well above their heads.

Christine unbuttoned and lifted the flap of material that covered her coat pocket. "I came prepared." She revealed two red plastic-looking lumps poking a half inch above the lip of her pocket. Judging from their thickness and how deep her coat pocket appeared to be, Crane figured they were handles for a pair of heavy-duty wire cutters. She released the flap before adding, "Please don't try to stop me."

"Try to stop you?" said Crane, arching a brow. "I was going to offer you the bolt cutters from my truck."

Christine recoiled and took a half step back, shocked by his response. Maybe a part of her had been hoping he would at least try to talk her out of it.

"Look," said Crane, "I understand you've been in a dark place for a long time and Michael certainly should have handled things better, but at the end of the day, it was your thirst for vengeance that started this chain of events."

"It was one stupid decision," she murmured, more to herself than to Crane.

"It was a reckless decision," he added. "A bitter, hate-filled decision that resulted in an innocent little boy being murdered by a psychopath."

"You're right." She sniffed. "I deserve to die."

"I didn't say that. You deserve to pay for what you've done. This"—he nodded to the barrier—"this is the easy option. Living with the guilt of what you've done would be harder."

"So what are you saying?"

"I'm saying you're going to suffer the consequences of your decision for the rest of your life. The guilt is going to eat you up every minute of every day, but I'll leave it up to you to decide how long you allow yourself to suffer for."

Christine stood and watched Crane walk away, fixed to the spot, his words still reverberating around inside her head. He was right. She'd been in a dark place for so long and she was no stranger to mental anguish, but this... this was something different. The guilt created an internal agony that was truly excruciating. She felt as though her entire being were filled with violent storm clouds threatening to tear her apart at any second.

She turned to face the barrier and looked out at the view. Hundreds of streetlights glowed brightly across the dark landscape. A handful of cars travelled along one of the main roads below. A whole world completely oblivious to her and her pain. Maybe she deserved to suffer for longer, but she knew deep down that she couldn't do it. The pain was too unbearable. She was a coward.

Christine lowered her umbrella and dropped it onto the ground beside her. The cool spray of drizzle immediately began to soak her face, but she couldn't really feel it; she was too numb. She slipped her hand into her coat pocket and grabbed the handle of the wire cutters. The same wire cutters she'd bought for this very task a couple of years ago during one of her dark patches. But this was the first time she'd actually brought them all the way here.

She opened the handles and clamped the jaws onto the lowest cable, then used both hands to squeeze them together. At first, nothing happened, but then as she applied more pressure, the cutting edges started to bite into the metal cable. Christine ground her teeth together and let out a strained grunt as she gave it everything she had. Suddenly, there was a satisfying snap as the cable gave way. Christine eased out a breath.

The original plan had been to cut two cables to make it easier to fit through, but after the first one, she knew she didn't have the strength to cut through another. Instead, she undid her coat, slipped it off her shoulders, and let it drop at her feet along with the wire cutters.

"*Hey,*" a man's voice called out. "*Wait.*"

She looked to where the sound was coming from, and even though the voice sounded nothing like his, a small part of her expected to see Crane coming back, but it wasn't him. It was an overweight middle-aged man dressed in what looked like a dark uniform. He appeared to be a security guard of some kind, possibly even a bridge attendant. He was around a hundred yards away, running towards her on the walkway.

"*Wait,*" he called. "*Please.*"

Christine ignored him and turned back to the barrier. If she was going to do it, she had to do it now. She leaned forward, ducking her head below the lowest intact cable, placed her hands on top of the barrier, then jumped up and squeezed through the gap. It was tight and the cable dragged across the top of her shoulders and down her back. She was halfway through. Her upper body hung over the edge looking down at the huge drop to the river below, and the hard edge of the barrier dug into the front of her hips. She couldn't see where the man was, but she knew he would be getting close now.

She desperately shuffled and shimmied and pushed herself through until she felt the equilibrium break and she started slipping. Gravity did the rest of the work for her. At the last second, just before her feet slid over the edge, a hand grabbed her left foot, but it was too late. Her shoe came off in the man's hand as she plummeted into the gorge. She didn't scream. She fell with only one thought in her head—*the storm will be over soon.*

CHAPTER THIRTY

After Crane had got home from his impromptu meeting with Christine, he dumped himself on the sofa in his living room, planning to relax, maybe watch a bit of TV while he waited for the hour to become more reasonable so that he could head over to Ricky's. He hadn't expected to fall asleep, but that's exactly what happened. He was unceremoniously woken by the shrill sound of his phone ringing in his pocket.

He pulled it out and squinted at the bright screen. His eyes burned and felt as though they were full of grit. Placing the chirping phone on his knee, he used the heels of his hands to rub his eyes free of sleep, then he picked his phone back up and tried again. Ricky's name came into focus first, but it was the time displayed in the top left corner that made him sit up—it was half eight. Crane swiped the green icon and tapped the speakerphone symbol.

"Morning," Crane half-said half-yawned.

"Have I just woken you up?"

"Yep."

"Really? What happened to Mr my-body-clock-always-wakes-me-up-at-six?"

Crane laughed. The problem with someone knowing you too well was they could use it against you. He got up from the sofa. "Well, I had an eventful night."

"Go on, what happened?"

Crane headed into the kitchen and fixed himself a coffee and a bowl of muesli while he gave Ricky the lowdown.

"*Holy shit*," exclaimed Ricky when he'd finished. "So, did she jump?"

"I didn't wait around to find out, but I'm ninety-nine per cent sure she would have."

The sound of computer keyboard keys being tapped rapidly came over the speaker. "Yeah, she did," confirmed Ricky. "There's already chatter online about it, although she hasn't been named yet."

Crane silently shovelled a spoonful of muesli into his mouth and noticed how indifferent he felt about this confirmation.

"So, did you learn anything else from her? Are you any closer to figuring out who The Craftsman is?"

"Not really," said Crane before taking a swig of his coffee. "She said he's around six feet tall, slim, probably mid-twenties, with dark hair and movie-star good looks."

"Movie-star good looks?"

"Yeah, she said he looked like a model and apparently he was very charming. I got the impression she fancied him."

"Maybe that's why she offered to pay him so much money. She wanted to show off to him."

"Maybe," agreed Crane before another spoonful of muesli went in.

The line went silent for a second, then Ricky dropped in with, "Well, I've found something."

Crane dropped his spoon, and it clanged loudly against the side of his bowl. "What? Why didn't you open with that when I answered?"

"Don't get too excited; I don't know how strong of a lead it is."

"*But* you've got a lead?"

"I think so."

"I'm all ears." Crane rested his elbows on the kitchen island and hunched over the phone.

"When I woke up this morning, I was about to crack on with digging into everyone's social media. I thought maybe I'd look at hacking into their phones again for a closer look, but then I found myself thinking what's the point? If anyone has been communicating with The Craftsman, it's highly unlikely they'd do it on any of their known devices and they certainly wouldn't contact him via social media."

"Okay," said Crane, hoping it would encourage him to skip to the good part.

Unfortunately, Ricky didn't get the message. "So, instead of looking at the devices themselves, I thought I'd take a look at the Wi-Fi routers. You know, just to see if there were any unknown devices connected. Also, the router would allow me to see browsing history that may have been deleted on the known—"

"Rick. You're a genius. I'm not. I don't need to know how you do what you do. Please, just tell me what you've found out, and preferably in layman's terms."

"Okay, sorry. I found a Wi-Fi router that was used to access EAPA at the same time Michael was on the phone to The Craftsman."

Crane sighed and drooped his head, fearing that Ricky's lead may not be a lead after all. "Yeah, that would have been Michael. He went into the app while he was on the phone to The Craftsman. He thought he was going to be transferring the money to him."

"I'm not talking about *that* particular Wi-Fi router," replied Ricky, a hint of smugness beginning to creep into his tone.

Crane frowned, and his thoughts went to the other people in the house at that time. "There's more than one router in Michael Brookes' home?"

"Yes, but I'm not talking about any of the routers in Michael's home. This particular Wi-Fi router is in a different property altogether. Another property you visited yesterday."

It took a second, but when the lightbulb finally illuminated, Crane's tired eyes popped open. "Darren Peterson's."

"That's right."

"So, let me get this straight. The Wi-Fi router in Darren's flat was used to access EAPA at the same time Michael was on the phone to The Craftsman, giving his username and password?"

"Yep." Then Ricky asked the obvious question. "Do you think Darren could be The Craftsman?"

It was the question Crane had already asked himself and was contemplating. "His height and build match Christine's description, but he has ginger hair."

"Could he have dyed it?"

"It's possible," agreed Crane. "But he certainly hasn't got movie-star good looks."

"Before you write him off, remember the description we've got is a three-month-old memory from an unstable drunk lady."

It was a fair point, but Crane just couldn't see it. "Well, regardless of whether or not I think he could be The Craftsman, it looks as though he's definitely more involved than he tried to make out yesterday. Do you know where he is now?"

"Well, his phone's still in the flat, so I would assume he's still there."

"Why does it sound like you want to add a 'but' to that?"

"Because he hasn't been active on his phone since yesterday afternoon, which is unusual for him judging from his historical screen time records."

"Okay, I'll head there now. Call me if you find anything else." Crane ended the call and downed the rest of his coffee.

CHAPTER THIRTY-ONE

Once again, Crane parked around the corner from Darren's flat so as not to spook him by parking his truck right outside. Before getting out, he grabbed his waterproof jacket from the back of the passenger seat headrest where he'd hung it to drip-dry. The drizzle was still falling persistently and there was no sign of it letting up anytime soon. After putting it on and zipping it up, he grabbed the handle to open the door, but he didn't pull on it. A scratching sensation at the back of his brain forced him to pause and take a breath.

Darren's Wi-Fi had been used to access EAPA during the ransom call. This fact alone could only mean one of two things: Crane's initial instincts had been wrong (they usually weren't), Darren had duped him and he was in fact The Craftsman, or at the very least, he was in cahoots with The Craftsman. Either way, knowing The Craftsman was a cold-blooded child killer, it was time to start taking precautions.

Crane reached over and popped open the glove box. He lowered the hidden compartment and pulled out the case containing his Heckler & Koch VP9 Match 9mm pistol. Placing it on the passenger seat, he opened it up and slipped the two spare magazines into his trouser pocket and the gun into his jacket pocket. He jumped out of the truck, raised the hood of his waterproof over his head, and shoved his hands into his pockets before setting off towards Darren's flat. The cool, solid grip of the pistol was firmly in his right hand.

Darren's van was still parked on the road outside and looked as though it hadn't moved since the day before. Crane crossed the road, keeping a watchful eye on the dark and seemingly empty upstairs windows. When he reached the front door, he glanced up and down the street. It was deserted. The miserable weather was likely deterring people from venturing outside. Keeping his hands tucked inside his pockets, Crane used his elbow to push down on the door handle just on the off chance it had been left unlocked. After an initial resistance, he was pleasantly surprised when the handle gave way and the front door opened.

Crane swiftly stepped inside and gently nudged the door closed with his shoulder. At the same time, he slipped his VP9 out of his jacket pocket and took aim at the top of the stairs. Then he waited for five breaths, listening intently for any sounds or movement coming from upstairs, but there was only silence and stillness. He edged towards the stairs and started up them, side-on to minimise the size of his own target, leading with his left foot, back to the wall but not touching. Stairs were generally creakier in the middle, so he planted his feet tight to the one side. He took slow deep breaths through his nose, although this became more challenging as the fusty stench of the flat became more intense the higher he rose.

As his eyeline cleared the top step, he could see the landing was clear, and there was still no sound or movement or any signs of life whatsoever. But he wasn't going to relax just yet; he knew from experience that situations like this could change in an instant.

Crane slowed his pace for the final few stairs, eager to make as little noise as possible. If Darren was up there hiding, waiting for him, he didn't want to give his exact position away. He silently placed his left foot onto the penultimate step, but as he transferred his weight onto it, the stair let out a resounding groan.

Crane froze. His eyes darted to each of the four open doorways in turn, but nothing happened. Nobody jumped out. Nobody shouted, "Who's there?". Nothing.

He stepped onto the landing with his right foot and allowed the penultimate stair to groan once again as his weight lifted off it. Still nothing. Crane held the VP9 in a two-handed grip, arms down, barrel lowered to the floor in front of him, but he was poised and ready to take aim at anything that moved. With his back still to the wall, he sidestepped until his left shoulder was in line with the bathroom door frame, then he craned his neck around it to peer through the gap between the door and the jamb. The bathroom was clear.

Crane brought his attention back to the landing and to the doorway for the lounge, which was opposite him. He crossed the landing in one big stride and turned so that his back was now against the other wall. Then he turned to peek around the door frame and scanned the lounge. Darren was there. He was sitting upright on the sofa with his head tilted back and his mouth gaping open as though he were fast asleep. But Darren wasn't asleep.

His skin had taken on a sickly pallor and his lips and ears were tinged bluey grey. It almost looked as though he were made of wax. A blatant clue to his cause of death sat next to him on the sofa—a clear polythene bag still moulded into the shape of his head with some blood smeared inside. The blood likely coming from the damaged nose Crane had inflicted on him yesterday. *How soon after I left was he murdered?* He guessed it was pretty soon, considering Darren was still shirtless and only wearing the same baggy shorts he'd had on when Crane left him.

Conscious that even though he'd found Darren, he still might not be alone in the flat, Crane moved on to the kitchen. It was long and narrow with nowhere for a grown adult to hide, so only a quick sweep was required to confirm it was clear. One thing he did notice though was the microwave was open and the envelope full of cash was missing.

Leading with the VP9, Crane crossed the landing and cautiously made his way into the final room, Darren's bedroom. A quick look between the door and the jamb confirmed there was no one waiting for him behind the door, which left only two possible hiding places—under the bed or inside the wardrobe. Crouching onto one knee, he leaned and tilted his head to get a good look under the bed. There was so much mess that it was difficult to decipher what was what: shoes, clothes, a rucksack, empty crisp packets. There were even a couple of dirty plates and empty beer bottles tossed under there.

When Crane was satisfied none of the lumps or shadows were a person hiding underneath, he stood up and approached the wardrobe at the foot of the bed. He went to the side, leaned his shoulder into it, and started to push. Essentially, he was analysing the weight of it. *Is someone in there?* As he gradually increased the pressure, one side of the wardrobe lifted and tilted away from him. It moved far too easily for someone to have been inside.

Suddenly, a man's voice came from somewhere within the flat. Crane spun around and trained the VP9 on the doorway. The wardrobe dropped back down heavily behind him.

"In here," they repeated.

Crane edged towards the doorway.

"Yoo-hoo," called the voice. "I'm in the lounge."

There was something strange about the voice; it sounded as if it was coming from the lounge, but it also sounded as though it was further away, too. Crane eased onto the landing, with the VP9 leading the way. His trigger finger was taking the slack. It would only take a small amount of pressure to fire a nine-millimetre piece of copper-coated lead, at a speed of over twelve hundred feet per second, into whatever he aimed at. Instead of heading for the lounge doorway, he sidestepped to the right to give himself an angle to look in.

Darren's body hadn't moved and there was no one else in the room, but something had changed. On the coffee table facing the doorway was an open laptop. Crane hadn't taken any notice of it when he first walked in, being more interested in the dead body and making sure he was alone in the flat. He thought back to when he'd first walked in. The screen must've been blank and therefore appeared to be turned off. If it had been displaying what it currently was—a big yellow smiley face emoji almost filling the screen—there was no way he would have missed it. It was on a black background and somehow looked sinister, with its toothy open-mouthed smile and big black eyes.

"There you are," declared the voice. "I knew you'd come back."

Now that he was closer and could hear it more clearly, Crane recognised the voice immediately—The Craftsman. Crane lowered the VP9 and walked into the lounge, stopping just in front of the laptop.

"I take it you're looking for me?"

Crane didn't respond.

"Well, good luck with that." The Craftsman sniggered.

Crane felt his jaw tighten, and his fists clenched. "It's only a matter of time."

"And what are you going to do to me if you do find me?" The Craftsman's tone was mischievous, seemingly enjoying himself.

"It's not an if, it's a when," replied Crane through gritted teeth. "And I'm gonna make you wish you never laid a finger on Jacob."

A noise came through the laptop speaker that was difficult to decipher at first, but then Crane realised he was pretending to cry.

"Awww... poor little Jacob," said The Craftsman, then followed it up with a few more fake whimpers. "Wait, you can't blame me for Jacob; I was just fulfilling my end of the contract. You should be blaming Christine." He snorted and paused. "Oh yeah, that's right, you can't. She threw herself off a bridge last night, didn't she?"

Crane's blood was beginning to boil and he was finding it difficult to remain composed. He opened his mouth to respond, but the sound of the doorbell ringing immediately followed by a firm knock on the front door downstairs grabbed his attention.

"What was that?"

Crane headed over to the window, slowing and ducking as he approached before risking a peek at the street below. *Shit!* A small white hatchback with a strip of blue lights across the roof was parked behind Darren's van—the police were outside. Crane quickly ducked out of sight below the windowsill as a female officer dressed in a high-visibility vest stepped back and looked up towards the windows. He didn't think she'd seen him, but there was no way of knowing for certain. Regardless, he needed to move, and he needed to move *now*.

"Don't tell me they're there already," exclaimed The Craftsman, his voice sounding louder than it had before. "I only tipped them off five minutes ag—"

Crane slammed the laptop closed and picked it up. The charging cable was still plugged in, but it soon popped out when Crane hurried towards the doorway. There was another knock on the front door, louder this time, and it was followed by the sound of the letterbox being pushed open.

A man's voice called out, "It's the police. Open up."

Crane rushed across the landing and went into the bedroom. He crouched down and grabbed the rucksack he'd spotted under the bed during his search. Tossing the laptop onto the bed, he unzipped the rucksack, turned it upside down, and shook the contents onto the floor. It was mostly clothes, but there was also a notebook, and surprisingly, a can of deodorant. He hadn't got the impression Darren knew what deodorant was let alone owned a can of it. Luckily, the contents from the rucksack blended in with the mess already there.

Picking up the laptop, he shoved it inside the rucksack and zipped it up before swinging it over his shoulders and making his way to the bedroom window. He tightened the straps to secure it to his back, then bent down and grabbed one of the many items of clothing strewn across the floor—a plain white cotton T-shirt. Not wanting to leave any fingerprints behind, he used it to unlock and push open the window before spreading it across the windowsill and climbing onto it. As he turned and lowered himself onto the glass roof of the conservatory below, he heard the front door open downstairs.

"It's the police," the male officer's voice boomed. "We're coming in."

Still holding most of his body weight on the windowsill outside, Crane tossed the T-shirt onto the bedroom floor and then silently pushed the window closed using his knuckles. He then spread his feet wide between the two rafter bars closest to him and tentatively began to transfer his weight down from the windowsill. He was fairly confident the roof would be able to take his weight, but the drizzle was still coming down and the glass was slick and greasy. It effectively turned the roof into a steep sheet of ice.

Unfortunately, time wasn't a luxury Crane possessed under the current circumstances; one of the officers could look out of the window at any moment. With one hand still holding the concrete windowsill, he reached out and grasped the furthest UPVC rafter bar. He took a deep breath to brace himself, then let go of the windowsill and grabbed the other rafter bar. As Crane had anticipated, his feet slid down, but he practically tensed every muscle in his body, particularly his core, and was able to control the descent somewhat. Still gripping the rafter bars tight, he lowered himself flat onto his stomach, his feet already overhanging the guttering. It was moments like this when his dedication to his physical training and his variety of training methods really paid off. Strength was great, but balance and coordination were equally important assets.

Loosening his grip on the rafter bars, Crane allowed himself to slide down the glass roof in a controlled manner until his legs were hanging over the edge and the guttering was digging into his stomach. It was the point of no return. He just hoped the ground below was clear and he wasn't going to land on anything that could make a noise, or worse, injure him. After another deep breath, he released one hand to help him twist, quickly followed by the release of his other hand.

He got lucky. The ground below was clear. He softened and bent his knees as he landed on the paving slabs, attempting to make as little noise as possible. So far so good, but he still wasn't in the clear. He raced down the side of the property and came to a closed and padlocked wooden garden gate, the same height and style as the wooden-panelled fence surrounding the garden.

Without missing a beat, Crane jumped up and planted one hand on top of the gatepost while using the opposite foot to kick off the top of the gate, propelling himself over it like a seasoned freerunner. He landed smoothly on the other side, raised the jacket hood up over his head, and started to walk away. Someone with something to hide would have run, which is exactly why Crane didn't. There was always the risk that a curtain twitcher had spotted him scaling the garden gate, but he didn't look around to check; instead, he kept his head lowered as though he were ducking slightly from the rain and casually strolled away.

CHAPTER THIRTY-TWO

Crane got back to his truck unscathed. He tossed the rucksack onto the passenger seat, started the engine, and drove away efficiently—not fast, but certainly not slow. The objective was to not attract any unwanted attention. He headed out of the estate and aimed for the M4 motorway. The plan was to go to Ricky's and get him to take a look at the laptop. Maybe there was a way he could use it to trace The Craftsman.

The traffic on the M4 was flowing smoothly and the drizzle had finally stopped, but twenty minutes into the drive, just as Crane was crossing the Prince of Wales Bridge over the River Severn, his eyes started to feel dry and heavy. The adrenaline from his narrow escape was wearing off, and that combined with the lack of sleep from the night before and the monotonous drive all resulted in him battling to stay awake. As tempting as it was to push through and keep going, he made the sensible decision to pull into Magor services in search of a strong coffee.

Once he'd squeezed his truck into one of the ever-shrinking parking spaces, he went into the service station and picked up a large takeout cup of coffee from one of the self-service machines. Then he immediately headed for the exit, eager to get back on the road as soon as possible.

He pushed through the main door to get out but stopped to hold it open for a young family who were heading inside. The mum, who was leading the way, smiled and thanked him as she walked past cradling a newborn baby wrapped in a fluffy pink blanket. The dad trailed behind with a little boy who looked to be around three or four years old. The dad was struggling to keep hold of his son's hand as the little boy tried to rush ahead and pull him along, like an excitable puppy on a leash dragging its owner. The boy was either a bit of a mummy's boy, or he was getting jealous of his baby sister getting all of Mummy's attention because he kept reaching out with his free hand, trying to grab the back of his mum's coat. As he went past Crane, he started to call out to her, "*Mummy, Mummy.*"

Crane frowned. The little boy's voice had triggered something in his mind, but he couldn't quite put his finger on what it was. He released his grip on the handle, and the glass door closed slowly on its hydraulic mechanism. Crane stood and watched the family through the glass until they disappeared from sight, then he hesitantly turned away and headed towards his truck. As he weaved his way between the rows of parked cars, his brow remained deeply furrowed in concentration. *What have I missed?* It wasn't until his hand touched the handle of his truck that the answer came to him.

He jumped into the truck, placed his coffee in the centre console, and pulled his phone out of his pocket. Opening up the media gallery, he tapped on the video of the first ransom call, which he'd recorded at Michael's kitchen table. He skipped to the part where Michael had just insisted on speaking to Jacob for proof of life, and then the sound of crunching footsteps started up. The steps were followed by two hollow bangs, then The Craftsman called out, "Say hello, Jacob."

Jacob's voice came through the phone, distant and muffled, "*Mummy. Mummy.*"

Crane paused the video just as Lindsey started to cry out to Jacob. He sat there for a few moments, frowning down at his phone, still trying to pinpoint exactly what it was that was bothering him. That part of the call had obviously been staged, as Jacob was already dead at that point. The Craftsman must've been playing a voice recording from a speaker placed inside a metal shed or a shipping container. The sound quality was so poor that any little boy's voice would have likely deceived the desperate parents of a missing child. *But what if it was a recording of Jacob's voice?*

Crane went into his call history and dialled the number Lindsey had called him from the previous night. It rang six times, then sent him to voicemail. He hung up and let out a frustrated sigh, but a second or two later, his phone started to ring and vibrate in his hand. The number he'd just tried calling was displayed on the screen. He answered.

Lindsey's voice came through. "Crane?"

"Hi, Lindsey. Look, I'm really sorry to bother you, but you know the video you showed me when we first met? Would you be able to send it through to me?"

"The video of... Jacob?" It sounded as though she'd had to brace herself before saying his name.

"Please."

There was a short pause, then Lindsey said, "Sure, but can I ask why?"

It was Crane's turn to hesitate. How was he going to answer that? He was just running with a hunch. "It's likely nothing, but there's something I want to check on it. If it turns out to be something, I promise I'll let you know."

There was another pause from Lindsey and Crane found himself hoping she wasn't going to follow up with another question. Thankfully, she didn't and just said, "I'll send it through to you now."

"Thank you," replied Crane before ending the call.

Less than thirty seconds later, his phone beeped with a notification. She'd sent it to him via a messaging app, but he had to wait another minute for the video to fully download. When it had, he used the timeline bar across the bottom of the screen to skip to the final video clip and pressed play.

Michael and Jacob were playing football in the garden. Michael was playfully keeping the ball from Jacob and having him chase after it. Jacob, seemingly tired of all the chasing, wrapped his arms around his dad's legs and tackled him to the ground. Michael was laughing, and Lindsey, who must have been the one filming the video, could be heard laughing in the background, too. Jacob stood up and belly-flopped on top of his daddy, then he looked up and spotted that he was being filmed.

Jacob screeched, "*Mummy, Mummy, no.*" He jumped up, started to giggle, and ran up to the camera. He grabbed it, pulled it close to his face, and with a mischievous glint in his eye, he blew a raspberry into it.

Crane tapped the screen to pause the clip. There was obviously a big difference in sound quality between the two video clips, and although he couldn't be one hundred per cent certain, he was sure the voices were the same; in fact, it sounded identical to the recording used by The Craftsman for the ransom call.

He dragged the timeline back and played the clip again. When it reached the part where Jacob spotted the camera, he raised the phone slightly to get a closer look and studied the screen intently. His eyes narrowed at a point where he thought he saw something. He dragged the timeline back once again, but only by a couple of seconds this time, then he hit play. In the clip, when little Jacob got up and started running towards the camera to blow a raspberry into it, Lindsey's grip on the phone wobbled, likely from where she was laughing so hard. For a split second, the camera turned to the left, but Lindsey quickly corrected it and returned the focus to Jacob.

Crane dragged the clip back but didn't press play this time. He held it at the moment when the camera had turned to the left. The frozen image on his screen was blurred and unfocused, but in the background, about ten to fifteen yards away, there was clearly the silhouette of a man. He was dressed in dark clothes, standing next to a bush, and holding what appeared to be gardening shears. The peach-coloured oval shape of his face looked as though it was turned towards Jacob, Lindsey, and Michael. The image was too blurred to see any details or facial features. It was impossible to tell who the man was and the picture would most certainly have been deemed inadmissible as evidence in every courtroom in the country. But Crane knew. Crane knew exactly who it was.

CHAPTER THIRTY-THREE

Crane buzzed his window down as he pulled up to Michael Brookes' front gate and pushed the call button on the intercom. He sat patiently while he waited almost a full minute until it was eventually answered.

Carol's voice came out of the small speaker loud and clear. "Hello?"

"Hi, Carol, it's Crane."

There was a short pause and then when Carol spoke again, her voice came through slightly hushed. "There's still a couple of police officers 'ere."

"Where?"

"In the sitting room, with Michael and Lindsey. Most of 'em left about an hour ago, but these ones seem to be planning on sticking around for a while. I think they said they were family liaison officers, or summin' like that."

"That's fine. I'm not planning on coming into the house. Do you know if Geoff's in the garden?"

"I'm sure he'll be out there somewhere. I think he said he was planning on doing some work in the orangery today. Why's that?"

"I just want to have a quick chat with him. Is there any chance you could buzz me in, please, lovely?"

"Right you are."

There was a beep and then the gates began to open smoothly. Crane waited until the gap was wide enough, then he drove his truck through and made his way down the long driveway. A marked police car was parked in his usual spot by the front steps, so to make sure his truck didn't stand out if the police decided to leave anytime soon, he went right and parked alongside Geoff's old Defender in front of the garages. It was the closest he'd been to it and it was the first time he'd taken any notice of the white stickers in the rear and side windows. They appeared to be almost as old as the truck itself. The black writing on them had faded to grey and read, "Geoff the Gardener". His landline telephone number was printed underneath.

Crane jumped out of his truck and made his way down the side of the property. As he approached the window to the utility room, he tried to avoid looking in, as he didn't want to be reminded of the awful moment he'd discovered Jacob's body, but his eyes were drawn to it, like a driver passing an accident on the motorway. Thankfully, the blinds had been closed tight, so he couldn't see inside anyway.

He continued around the back and walked past the swimming pool, which was currently being protected and insulated with a thick blue cover. Five steps descended to a perfectly trimmed and healthy-looking lawn with a wide path running up the centre. The path led to a large circular pond with a quadruple lotus bowl water fountain sitting in the middle of it. The water trickled down each of the bowls before reaching the pond, producing a calm and tranquil sound. Although, under the circumstances, the effect was wasted on Crane. To anyone looking on, he may have appeared calm and composed, but under the surface, he felt anything but.

The pond was situated in the centre of the lawn, with four identical paths leading from it in the shape of a cross. Crane circumnavigated the pond, ignoring the path to the left, which led to a fenced tennis court, and instead continued on the path that led straight ahead and up to the orangery.

The orangery was a large stone building with enormous arched windows running along its full length. The roof appeared to be mostly flat, but Crane counted three huge glass roof lanterns spaced evenly apart. Five steps led to the main door, which had been left wide open. Crane walked straight through and into the warm and humid atmosphere inside. He immediately came face to face with another pond, but this one was filled with a mix of koi and goldfish.

Crane stopped a yard from the water's edge and looked around. He couldn't see Geoff, but that didn't mean he wasn't in there somewhere. The vast array of tropical plants appeared to cover every square inch of the orangery, and it looked as though there were plenty of places to hide even if you weren't intending to hide.

Almost right on cue, Crane heard shuffling coming from the far-right corner of the orangery followed by footsteps heading his way, then Geoff appeared from behind a giant cycad to Crane's right. He was wearing his usual brown trousers and tweed flat cap, but today his shirt had a red and black check on it. His eyes widened with surprise when he saw Crane, but he quickly dropped his bushy grey eyebrows and turned his expression into an unfriendly scowl.

"Uh oh, look out," Geoff announced to nobody. "Who are you here to beat up this time?"

"If you don't answer my questions honestly and succinctly"—Crane gave a pronounced nod in Geoff's direction—"you."

Geoff's frown deepened, but his voice went up in pitch. "Wh-what?"

Crane felt a little bad for threatening an older man, but he wanted information from him and didn't have the patience to put up with his cantankerous attitude.

"Who is Toby?"

"What? What do you mean *who is Toby*?"

"Exactly that. Who is he? Where did he come from? How did he become your apprentice? How long has he been your apprentice?" Crane could have kept going, but he figured that should be enough to get the ball rolling.

Geoff's bushy brows shot up as the realisation of what Crane was asking him hit home. "Wait, surely you don't think Toby had anything to do with what happened to Jacob? There's just no way."

"Just answer my questions."

"Okay, okay," said Geoff, briefly raising both hands submissively. "His dad called me about three months ago. He told me that his son had learning difficulties and he'd been struggling with his confidence recently. He said Toby loved doing bits in the garden, so he was trying to find a local gardener who would be willing to let him help them out. Like a kind of apprenticeship, you know, to get him out working and help build up his confidence. He said that I wasn't to pay him, I'd be doing enough just by letting him help me out."

"His dad called you? So, you know his dad?"

Geoff shook his head. "No, not at all. He just called me out of the blue one night. He said he'd been behind me at some traffic lights and had made a note of my number from the sticker on the back of my truck."

"Have you ever met his dad?"

Geoff shook his head again. Crane could tell by the look in Geoff's eyes that it was suddenly dawning on him that the man on the phone could have been anyone.

"So, you agreed to take Toby on, allowing him access to Michael's grounds and home without really knowing who he was or where he was from?"

"I thought I was doing a good deed."

Crane snorted. "No, you thought you were being clever by taking advantage of him to get a bit of free manual labour."

Geoff looked down to avoid Crane's glare and mumbled, "It wasn't like that."

Crane took a calming breath. He was taking his frustration out on Geoff, which was probably a little unfair. "So, you agreed to take him on, then what happened?"

"The next morning, Toby was at the front gate, just standing there next to his push bike, waiting for me. He used to cycle here every day."

"So, he lives locally, then?"

"Yeah, just over in Bradley Stoke."

"Where exactly?"

Geoff hesitated. "I... I don't have an *exact* address for him."

Crane glared at Geoff for few awkward moments. "What?"

"I know, I know." Geoff's cheeks reddened slightly with embarrassment. "It's just, when he started, I wondered what I'd let myself in for. He wouldn't give any eye contact and barely spoke a word. He struggled to complete even the simplest of tasks. It didn't even cross my mind to get any of his details. To be honest, I wasn't sure if he was going to come back the following day. But he did. He came back and he kept coming back, every single day, at nine o'clock on the button. And with each day that passed, he became more and more useful, he came out of his shell, and..." Geoff's voice trailed off and his gaze wandered to the fish gliding around the water inside the pond. When he continued speaking, it was as though he were verbalising his thoughts rather than speaking to Crane. "And he... he became my friend."

Crane had been wondering how much Geoff knew, but in that moment, he saw him for what he truly was—a lonely man who had been duped and manipulated. "You said that he's from Bradley Stoke," said Crane, hauling Geoff back to the present moment and attempting to get his interrogation back on track.

"How do you know he lives in Bradley Stoke if you haven't got a record of his address?"

"A few weeks ago, it started pissing it down just as we were finishing up for the day. I offered to give him a lift home, but he declined. I insisted, but he kept refusing. In the end, I locked his bike in the back of my truck, so he had no choice but to let me drop him home."

"Where exactly did you drop him off?"

Geoff's mouth downturned and he shrugged. "Outside one of the houses on the estate. They all look the bloody same to me, to be honest."

"Was it a flat in an end-of-terrace house?"

"Yeah," said Geoff, as his bushy eyebrows shot up towards the peak of his flat cap. "How do you know that?"

Crane ignored the question and asked another of his own. "Did he go into the ground-floor or the first-floor flat?"

"I don't know. How am I meant to know that?"

"Did he go in the front door or the side door?"

Geoff frowned as he tried to remember. "Side. He went in the door on the side. In fact"—he raised an index finger as though an important thought had just come to him—"it must've been the first-floor flat because I remember a sign on the front lawn saying that the ground floor was up for let."

Crane just nodded. He knew Geoff's assumption was wrong, but he had no inclination to correct him. Toby had been living on the ground floor, in the flat directly below Darren Peterson.

The sound of a man clearing his throat suddenly demanded their attention. Crane turned to find Michael standing in the doorway. He looked between them in turn a couple of times before his gaze finally settled on Crane.

"What's going on?"

Before Crane had a chance to open his mouth to respond, Geoff piped up behind him, "He thinks Toby was somehow involved with... what happened."

Michael's brows knitted together as his eyes flicked back to Crane. "Is this true?"

"Not quite," replied Crane. "I don't think he was *somehow* involved, I believe it was all him. I believe Toby *is* The Craftsman."

"What?" exclaimed Geoff. His voice reaching a pitch that was almost only audible to dogs. "There's just no way."

Crane ignored Geoff and took a step towards Michael, whose jaw had gone slack with shock. "Walk with me."

It took a second for Michael to register what Crane had said, but when he did, he blinked a couple of times and gave a single nod before stepping back to allow Crane through the doorway.

They descended the steps together, and Michael turned to look at Crane. "Are you sure? I mean, Toby, really?"

"It was him," said Crane, his tone conveying the absolute certainty he felt.

"What about Geoff? Did he know?" The pain on Michael's face evident at the thought. "Do you think he was involved, too?"

"If I thought Geoff was involved, he wouldn't still be breathing."

Michael went quiet for a few steps as they approached the pond at the centre of the pristine lawn. Then he asked, "So, what happens now?"

"I hunt him down and make him pay for what he did to Jacob."

"Thank you," said Michael, sounding a little choked, as though he was finding it a challenge to maintain his composure. He swallowed the lump in his throat. "I'll make it worth your while. You know, financially."

"I'm not doing any of this for your money."

"I know. You're doing it for Jacob. And you're doing it because you're a good man." Michael stopped and turned to face Crane at the bottom of the steps leading up to the pool. "But I don't think you quite understand. I *need* to feel like I'm doing something.

I need to feel like I'm contributing in some way. And money... money is the only way I know how. Look, whatever resources you need, however much it costs to track him down, whatever you need, please, just let me know."

"I will."

Michael offered his hand, and Crane shook it without hesitation.

CHAPTER THIRTY-FOUR

Crane slid the rucksack containing the laptop he'd taken from Darren's across the kitchen island towards Ricky.

"So, you're one hundred per cent that Geoff wasn't involved?"

Crane nodded. He'd already given the full rundown of what had happened the last few hours.

Ricky unzipped the rucksack and pulled out the laptop, leaving the empty rucksack to fall to the floor. He turned the laptop over in his hands and verbalised his thoughts as he inspected it. "Okay, so there's no sim card slot and there's nothing plugged into any of the USB ports, which means it's currently offline. It must've been connected to Darren's Wi-Fi." He looked up and gestured for Crane to follow him with a wave of his hand. "Come on."

Ricky hurried over to his workstation and took a seat in his usual chair. Crane followed and stood behind him to observe. Ricky placed the laptop on the desk in front of him, then bent down and pulled out another laptop from a black case under the desk and placed it next to the one from Darren's flat. Next, he opened the drawer under his desk and fished out a short cable and something that looked like a big blue USB stick.

"What are you doing?"

"So far, we've underestimated this guy at every turn. I'm not doing it again." Ricky plugged one end of the cable into Darren's laptop and the other end into his own. "I can't afford to let him gain access to my network here, so I'm going to use this"—he raised the blue stick—"to reconnect it to the internet."

"You really think he could hack into your network?"

"No, but I'm not willing to risk it to find out."

Ricky plugged the dongle into his own laptop and started tapping away. The screen was plain black with small white writing that seemed to dance across it. A couple of minutes later, Ricky smashed the enter key and declared, "Okay, let's do this."

He opened Darren's laptop and pressed the on button. The screen immediately turned blue and seemed to start its booting-up procedure, but as soon as the login screen popped up requesting a password, it went completely black, as though it had died.

"What happened?"

"I'm not sure," replied Ricky. "Did you notice if the battery had much charge when you took it?"

"I pulled it from the charger when I grabbed it."

Ricky stroked his beard and frowned. "Then it should still be fully charged."

He reached out and tapped the spacebar. Suddenly, a high-pitched laughing sound came out of the speaker and a huge laughing face emoji appeared on the black screen. Crane and Ricky glanced at each other with what-the-fuck? expressions on their faces. The laughing face emoji then disappeared and was replaced with the words "*Nice Try!*" written in a bright yellow font above a big middle finger emoji. It stayed like that for a few seconds and then, just as abruptly as the whole thing had started, the laughing stopped and the screen went blank.

"*Shit*," declared Crane, fearing the worst.

"Don't speak too soon," replied Ricky, already tapping away at the keyboard on his laptop.

"What do you mean?"

Ricky was too engrossed doing whatever it was he was doing on his laptop to answer. Eventually, he stopped and swivelled around on his chair, with a smug grin spreading across his face and a cocky glint in his eye.

Crane arched a curious brow. "What have you done?"

Ricky swivelled back ninety degrees so that he was side-on to Crane and the desk. "I created a worm-like virus a few months ago on this." He pointed at his laptop. "And I've just unleashed it on this." He pointed at the laptop from Darren's flat. "And now it's currently finding a way into whatever device The Craftsman used to connect to it."

"What if the device he used was a burner?"

"It's a possibility, but I don't think he would have gone to all that effort to protect a device he was just going to throw away." Ricky waved his hand over the screen almost as though he were pretending to wipe it clean. "All that wasn't just for show. It was a distraction for him to strengthen his firewall and protect his device."

"But your worm thing got through?"

"Not yet, but it will."

"When?"

Ricky winced and shrugged, seeing Crane's impatience. "I don't know. I mean, I'm hoping it'll just take a couple of hours, but it could take a couple of days. We just need to sit back and let it do its thing."

Crane checked his watch. "I'm meant to be meeting up with Chloe for pizza soon."

"That's fine, you go." Ricky shooed him away with a sweep of his hand. "I'll call you if anything happens."

"You sure?"

"Of course. There's no point in both of us sitting here and waiting around."

CHAPTER THIRTY-FIVE

Being a Saturday evening, the pizza place in Cardiff Bay was heaving. And in truth, Crane could've done without being there. The last couple of days had taken their toll and he was exhausted. But he didn't want to let Chloe down, especially at the last minute. As his sister-in-law kept reminding him, he was the only responsible male role model in her life; which she used to say even before his brother Dylan went AWOL. Regardless of what his sister-in-law said, Crane had always been a man of his word. And he didn't want Chloe growing up thinking flakiness was an acceptable trait. It was just one of the many values he hoped to instil in her as she continued to mature into a young lady.

They were sitting at a small table for two tucked up against the left-hand wall. Crane had his back to the kitchen door but had a view of the main entrance. Not ideal, but it was certainly the lesser of two evils. They'd both skipped starters and had opted for pizzas as their main. Crane hadn't realised how hungry he was; he'd finished off his meat feast before Chloe was even halfway through her classic margarita.

As usual, Chloe's long dark hair was tied up in a high ponytail and she wore little makeup, which Crane thought was probably quite unusual for a fourteen-year-old. She wore a pink tracksuit over a white crop top that revealed a sliver of her tummy. Crane wasn't a fan, but then who was he to judge anyone's fashion sense?

He watched Chloe as she picked up another slice of pizza from her plate. A particularly stubborn piece of mozzarella stretched up from the next slice and refused to snap. She raised it higher, almost getting it above her head before it finally broke free, leaving a long string of mozzarella dangling from the slice in her hand. Chloe tilted her head to one side and opened her mouth wide in an effort to catch it, but the cheese swayed as she went to go for the bite and it bounced off her nose. It then swung away from her before it came back and bounced against her chin. Chloe's eyes refocused and spotted Crane watching her, grinning with amusement.

"Did you just see that?" She asked even though she already knew the answer.

"It was a smooth move," replied Crane, with a chuckle.

"Shut up," said Chloe playfully before laughing at herself.

She wiped the cheese grease off her nose and chin with the back of her hand before having another go. This time, she caught the string of mozzarella with her teeth and chewed on it whilst looking very pleased with herself.

"So, when can I start my apprenticeship with Ricky?" she asked between bites.

"What makes you think you're doing an apprenticeship with Ricky?"

"You said I could on the phone, remember?" There was a cheeky glint in her eye as she said it, and she quickly took a bite of her pizza slice before she could start giggling. She was a trier, Crane had to give her that.

"I certainly did not," he replied, jesting a stern tone.

Chloe swallowed her mouthful, then shrugged and said, "Okay, I guess plan B it is, then."

Crane leaned forward and rested his elbows on the table. "What's plan B?"

She dropped the remaining crust of her slice down on her plate and sat up a little taller. "Oh, I watched a video online the other day and this ad came on. There was this guy who was saying he'd found an easy way to make loads of money. He didn't say what it was, I think you have to sign up and pay for a course or something, but his house looked massive and he had a Ferrari, just like you. He said he makes ten grand a week and only works for like ten minutes a day." Chloe abruptly stopped speaking and crossed her arms. "What's that look for?"

"What look?"

"You rolled your eyes."

"Did I?"

"Yeah, you did. You think it's a con, don't you?"

Crane hadn't registered whether or not he'd rolled his eyes, but what Chloe had been describing certainly warranted an eye-roll. He took a second to consider how to respond diplomatically. "A wise person once said bees don't waste their time explaining to flies that honey is better than shit."

With her brow furrowed, Chloe said, "What's that supposed to mean?"

"It can be interpreted in different ways, but I'm using it in this context to get you to think more critically about this guy and whatever it is he's trying to sell."

Chloe looked at him blankly.

"If this guy has found an easy and quick way to make lots of money, why is he not just doing more of that? Why is he spending more time, money, and effort trying to sell the secret of making money to other people?"

Chloe didn't respond, but her brow gradually unfurrowed as the cogs began to turn behind her eyes.

"Look, all I'm trying to say is, if it sounds too good to be true, it probably is. You should think critically and question everything. I've worked with a lot of wealthy and successful people, and do you know what they all have in common?" He paused to give Chloe an opportunity to take a guess, but she just shrugged at him. "They all made it by working extremely hard and making lots of sacrifices. If it ever comes to you too easily, it's likely going to cost you more in the long run."

Chloe's gaze lowered. "What about people who inherit lots of money or win the lottery?"

Crane smiled. "They're wealthy and very fortunate, but not necessarily successful."

Chloe nodded, then took a sip of lemonade through her straw. "So, I guess that leaves me with plan C, then."

Crane could tell by the look in her eye and the way the corners of her mouth were turning up slightly that a joke was incoming. Even though he knew he was walking into it, he entertained her. "Go on, then. What's plan C?"

"I'm going to have to find myself a rich man to marry." She struggled to get her words out before snorting and starting a fit of giggles.

"Now I know you're winding me up. You make sure you don't need to rely on any man."

"I know, I know." Chloe finished giggling and raised a brow. "If I was a super hacker like Ricky, I wouldn't need to rely on anyone."

This time, Crane knew full well he'd rolled his eyes.

"Please, Uncle Tom." Chloe clasped her hands together beneath her chin. "You know how much I like computers and technology. It's what I really want to do." She widened her eyes and tilted her head down to put on her best puppy dog face, which she'd evidently mastered over the years.

"Nail your GCSEs and then we'll have a conversation about it." It wasn't a yes, but it also wasn't a no.

Chloe certainly took it as a yes and pumped her fist in victory before picking up another slice of her pizza.

It was too loud in the pizza place for Crane to hear his phone ring, but he immediately felt it as it started to vibrate inside his pocket. He eagerly pulled it out, and when he saw the caller ID displayed Ricky's name, he raised his phone as though he were making a toast with it to get Chloe's attention.

"Sorry, I need to take this," he said, getting up from the table. "I'll just be a couple of minutes."

Crane headed towards the main entrance, weaving and sidestepping between the tables and chairs. A waiter kindly tucked into a gap to let him through, and Crane thanked him as he went past. He pushed through the glass door and stepped out into the cool evening air as he tapped the green icon on his phone. Dusk had well and truly set over Cardiff Bay, but there were plenty of lights covering the walkway outside, giving it an almost daytime feel. The walkway was busy with pedestrians, but even so, it was a lot quieter outside than it had been inside.

Crane brought the phone to his ear and stepped to the side so that he wasn't blocking the entrance. "What's the news?"

There was a short pause, then Ricky said the three words he was hoping to hear. "We've got him."

Crane stopped in his tracks at the side of the front window. "Are you sure?"

"Yep, one hundred per cent. I'm inside his phone as we speak. I can see exactly where he is and I already know his real name. I'm about to run a background check on him now."

Crane didn't really care who he was, where he was from, or what had even turned him into the sick and twisted monster he was. At this moment, he only wanted to know the answer to one question. "Where is he?"

There was another slight pause, then Ricky said, "He's in Turkey."

"Where?" Crane frowned, pressing the phone more firmly against his ear. "It sounded like you said Turkey."

"I did. Specifically, Bodrum. It looks as though he's treating himself to a little holiday with some of the money he got from Michael and Christine."

"In that case, I'd better start looking at flights to Turkey."

"I can do that for you. Shall I look at the next available ones from Cardiff?"

Crane didn't respond straight away. On the brickwork next to the window of the pizza place, someone had put up a poster that had grabbed his attention. It was a picture of a fish trapped inside a plastic bottle. The words "Stop ocean plastic pollution" were written above it, sending a clear message to raise awareness. But it wasn't the message of the poster that grabbed Crane's attention, it was something about the fish. The way the artist had vividly drawn the eye gazing out at him, perfectly capturing the anguish and despair of being trapped.

"Don't do anything just yet," said Crane. "I've just had a thought and need to make a couple of calls to see if it's even viable. I'll pop around and see you after I've dropped Chloe home."

"Oookay," said Ricky, curiously dragging the word out. "I'll look forward to hearing all about it when you get here, then."

Crane ended the call and went into the contacts on his phone. He searched for the name of an old client from when he'd worked close protection. A client who had a particular area of expertise he was hoping to utilise. It didn't take him long to find the name he was looking for. He hit the dial button and raised the phone back to his ear, wondering if they would even answer. It had been several years since they'd spoken last and he was conscious it was Saturday night; however, he was pleasantly surprised when a breathy female voice answered on the third ring.

"Crane, to what do I owe this pleasure?"

"Sorry to bother you out of the blue, but I have a proposition that may interest you."

"A proposition from Tom Crane?" she purred. "I'm all ears."

CHAPTER THIRTY-SIX

The Craftsman walked the three-quarters of a mile from the small apartment he was renting down to Bodrum Harbour, just as he'd done every morning since he'd arrived in Turkey. He found it funny that even though his brain wasn't programmed the same as "normal people", he still found some level of comfort in routine, just like "normal people" did.

There wasn't a single cloud in the bright blue sky, and although it was only half eight, the sun was already starting to heat up and feel warm against his skin. His flip flops gently slapped against his heels as he strolled along the waterfront, admiring the boats and small yachts moored along the harbour from behind his oversized aviator sunglasses. The thought that he wasn't far off being able to afford one of his own, especially after the wedge he'd just made from his latest job, made him smile.

The cafe he'd visited every morning since he'd been there came up on the left, set just a few metres back from the water's edge. There was a large patio area out the front filled with tables and chairs beneath a huge red and white striped canopy, ready to protect the customers and waiters from the inevitable blazing sun that would beat down on them throughout the day. The Craftsman gradually altered his course and sauntered towards it.

His usual waiter, a slender young man in his late teens with short dark hair, was outside standing up menus on the tables. He happened to glance up and did a double take when he spotted The Craftsman approaching, then waved enthusiastically. "Do you want the usual, boss?" He called out in great English.

The Craftsman gave a single nod, and the waiter immediately dropped the remaining menus in his hand down on the table in front of him before hurrying off inside. The Craftsman headed straight over to the same table and sat down on the exact same chair that he'd occupied every morning so far. It was in the front corner, with his back to the cafe, and a view overlooking the harbour. As far as he was concerned, it was his table and his chair.

He sat back and inhaled the salty sea air that was tinged with the lingering scent of seafood, and he listened to the calming sound of the water lapping against the harbour wall and on the hulls of the vessels moored in it. Only the occasional squawk from the resident seagulls disturbed the peace. He sat there knowing that this would all change dramatically over the next thirty minutes or so. The harbour would gradually wake up and transform into a bustling area filled with tourists. Most would be heading out on boat trips and excursions, but some would come for the shops, sightseeing, and the food and drink.

Pulling his phone out of his shorts pocket, he checked the time as he unlocked it. The waiter was taking a little longer than usual to fetch his order. But then, *Speak of the devil*, he immediately thought as the waiter appeared over his shoulder and placed his espresso on the table.

The waiter bowed his head and said, "Enjoy, boss." He dropped a single sachet of brown sugar next to the tiny cup and saucer, then retreated to the table where he'd left the menus and continued to distribute them onto the other tables on the patio area.

The Craftsman didn't thank him or even acknowledge him. He had a rule of never thanking anyone he believed was below him, which was practically everyone. He placed his phone on the table next to his saucer, then picked up the sachet and tore off one corner before pouring the contents into his coffee. Then he opened up the internet on his phone with his left hand while stirring his espresso with the little demitasse spoon with his right.

Over the last couple of days, he'd been deciding where he should go next. He knew he had to get away from Bristol, and to be on the safe side, he should probably stay away from the whole South West of England. He'd been considering heading North, maybe near one of the affluent suburbs of Manchester, like Bowdon or Hale. There were sure to be plenty of potential clients around there.

He slowly swiped up on the screen using his index finger, browsing the rental properties that were currently available in and around the Altrincham area. He was looking for something small, preferably furnished, not too expensive, and somewhere with good transport links. But most importantly, he was looking for something that was being rented out by a private landlord and had ideally been on the market for a while. From his experience, landlords who were struggling to find tenants for their properties were often open to letting him stay in them short-term and off the record for cash in hand.

With his eyes still fixed on his phone, he picked up his espresso and downed it in one, almost as though he were drinking a shot in a nightclub. But something wasn't right. He wrinkled his nose, removed his sunglasses, and slammed the cup back down on the saucer before twisting around in his chair to search for the waiter. The sound and movement immediately caught the waiter's attention, and he hurried over.

"What the fuck is that?" spat The Craftsman.

The waiter's forehead crinkled with concern. "What's the matter, boss?"

"It was cold," he fumed.

"Sorry, boss. I make you fresh." The young waiter bowed his head and picked up the cup and saucer from the table. "I make you fresh," he repeated before rushing back inside.

It hadn't really been cold, it just hadn't been as hot as he normally liked it. The fucking moron had obviously let it sit on the side cooling down before bringing it out.

The Craftsman huffed with frustration and shook his head as he placed his sunglasses on the table. His morning routine had been ruined. He snatched up his phone and was about to start scrolling again when a fresh espresso was placed on the table in front of him, but the man who put it there wasn't the waiter. The man was dressed in stone-coloured linen trousers and a white short-sleeved shirt.

"Good morning, Toby." The man sat in the chair opposite and placed his own coffee on the table. "Or would you prefer me to call you by your self-proclaimed nickname—the man raised his hands and made an air quote hand gesture as he said it—'The Craftsman'? Or, better still, why don't I use your real name?" He paused for emphasis. "Robert Campbell."

The Craftsman recognised the man immediately. He'd been the one snooping around during his last job, the man they called Crane.

As he stared into Crane's icy blue eyes, an uncomfortable sensation began to churn inside his stomach. He'd experienced the sensation before, although for him, it was an extremely rare occurrence. And it was especially rare for him to experience the sensation to this magnitude. He experienced almost all emotions at a far lower intensity than "normal people". The only emotion that seemed to come easily to him, particularly growing up, was anger.

Outwardly, he tried to remain impassive and look relaxed. *How the fuck did he find me?*

CHAPTER THIRTY-SEVEN

Crane had been patiently waiting for this very moment. Although, he had to admit, it had been a struggle at times. For instance, yesterday morning when he saw Toby for the first time. Crane had been watching the apartment from a distance waiting for him to leave, ready to track his movements and observe his routine. But when Toby, or rather Robert, eventually appeared and Crane laid eyes on him, he was almost overwhelmed with the urge to take him out there and then and only just managed to restrain himself. He tracked Robert down to the harbour during his morning stroll, having to suppress the urge to wrap his hands around his throat and squeeze the life out of him the whole way.

Then last night, Crane hadn't slept well. The temptation to break into Robert's apartment and smother him with a pillow, just like he'd done to little Jacob, had been almost unbearable. But now, sitting opposite Robert, looking into his eyes, Crane was glad he'd persevered and his willpower had withstood the tests. This moment was going to be worth it.

It was remarkable how different Robert looked. He no longer had an underbite, which had obviously been something he'd put on for the character of Toby. His greasy fringe, which had been stuck to his forehead, was gone, and instead, his dark hair was styled immaculately. And noticeably, he wasn't avoiding eye contact anymore; in fact, he was staring directly into Crane's eyes and seemed completely unfazed by his sudden appearance.

"Are you enjoying your holiday?" asked Crane, pouring a single sachet of sugar into his own coffee and stirring it.

"I was."

Crane couldn't help but smile at his response as he sat back in his chair and folded his left ankle over his right knee. "You don't seem very surprised to see me, but I suppose surprise would be a bit of a stretch, you know, for someone who doesn't experience emotions to the same intensity as they should." Crane frowned, feigning deep concentration. "What was it you were diagnosed with as a kid?" He paused for a second, then snapped his fingers as though the answer had just come to him. "That's it, alexithymia. Although, we both know that was a misdiagnosis, don't we? You don't suffer from alexithymia. You don't suffer from anything. The world suffers from you being in it. You're a psychopath. An evil, child-murdering psychopath."

Robert smirked. "Somebody's been doing their research."

"A little. I guess curiosity got the better of me and I wanted to find out what created the monster."

Robert leaned forward and rested his elbows on the table, intrigued. "And what did you find out?"

"Not what I was expecting," said Crane. "It's funny because we all know we shouldn't make assumptions about people, but we all do. For instance, I fully expected to see a history of neglect, trauma, and abuse. I thought maybe you'd been brought up in the care system and got damaged along the way. But no, you were raised by both parents in a middle-class home and privately educated." Crane picked up his coffee and took a sip before resting the cup on his left knee. "At the very least, I thought you must have been a spoiled only child, but again, no. You have a younger sister who, by the way, is doing great. In fact, she's just qualified as a midwife."

"Good, I'm really happy for her," said Robert without a shred of sincerity in his voice.

"Of course you are." Crane grinned. "To be fair, it's remarkable how well she's turned out considering she had you as a big brother. How many times did you put her in the hospital growing up?"

Robert's stare was gradually turning into a glare.

"It's probably difficult to know the exact number. I mean, she was very accident-prone and seemed to be in and out of hospital all the time, so it was probably impossible to keep track of which times were caused by you." Crane frowned again, feigning contemplation. "And then coincidentally, as you got older and bigger, your parents seemed to become more accident-prone, too. Your whole family seemed to be constantly walking into things and falling over. All of them except you, of course." Crane stroked his chin with his free hand. "I don't want to point fingers, but since you left home and disappeared out of their lives, your whole family has been doing great. No accidents or injuries whatsoever."

"Good for them." Robert's words were devoid of any emotion.

"It is, although it's not been so good for the people you've hurt since, has it? Like, Jacob."

A malicious grin spread across Robert's face at the mention of Jacob's name, and Crane immediately felt his jaw tighten. To distract himself from the urge to get up and knock Robert's teeth out, he lifted his cup and drained his coffee.

"Are you not going to drink yours?" asked Crane, tilting his empty cup towards the one that was still sitting untouched on the table in front of Robert.

"I'm not thirsty."

"Fair enough." Crane placed his cup on the table. "You know, when I came out, I half expected you to do a runner like you did the first time we met."

For the first time since Crane had sat down, Robert broke eye contact and looked around. There were a lot more people walking along the harbour now and two other tables were occupied nearby. The waiter was currently taking an elderly couple's order a few tables over and three middle-aged men appeared to be nursing hangovers at a table towards the back.

Robert held his arms out to the side. "I figure this is probably the safest place for me at the moment. I don't think you'll lay a finger on me somewhere so public." One corner of his mouth curled up in a cocky grin.

Crane returned a grin of his own. "What if I told you I don't need to lay a finger on you at all?"

Robert's grin remained, but his eyes narrowed slightly.

"So far, it's been all you, you, you. Now, let me tell you a little bit about myself," offered Crane. "Before doing what I do now, I spent several years providing close protection. I mostly worked with celebrities and businesspeople, but occasionally I'd look after government officials and representatives, typically when they were going on a trip which the government wanted to keep hush-hush. One of those particular clients happened to be quite a brilliant toxicologist. I used to look after her when she went collecting samples from some of the most obscure and remote places on the planet."

Robert gazed down at the coffee cup in front of him, then slowly looked back up at Crane. His eyebrows pinched together as he put two and two together. "You've poisoned me?"

"I have. It's why your coffee wasn't as hot as usual; I didn't want to risk the heat affecting the spores."

Crane expected to at least see a glimmer of panic in Robert's eyes. He thought that maybe he'd try shoving his fingers down his throat in an effort to vomit his coffee up—even though his efforts would have been futile if he did. But there was nothing. He just stared back at Crane blankly for a few seconds, then his mouth downturned and he shrugged. "I'm not afraid of dying." He said it as though he were casually telling someone he wasn't afraid of heights or spiders.

"Dying?" said Crane. "Who said anything about dying?"

Now Robert reacted—his brow furrowed with confusion.

"Death would be too good for you," Crane continued. "It would be too much of an easy way out, and you don't deserve an easy way out. No, you're not going to die. At least, not yet anyway. You see, my old client specialises in neurotoxins. She works with and has access to substances the likes of you and I have never even heard of. It took a little convincing, but when I told her what you did to little Jacob, she soon opened up to the idea of helping me. Although, I must admit, even though she was willing to help, her services aren't cheap." Crane held up a hand and rubbed the tips of his index and middle fingers over his thumb. "However, as you well know, the man whose son you murdered has very deep pockets indeed, and when I told him what I had planned for you, he was more than willing to pick up the bill."

Crane unfolded his legs and sat up in his seat. He was getting to the good bit. "The substance you've ingested is extremely potent and the dosage needed to be fairly accurate for it to achieve the desired result without killing you. Luckily, when I picked you up and held you against the tree in Michael Brookes' garden, it gave me a good opportunity to figure out your height and weight." Crane glanced down at his watch. "In fact, we'll soon see if my estimation was right because the effects should be starting to kick in any second now."

Crane leaned forward and placed his elbows on the table so that his face was merely a foot away from Robert's. "The toxin is going to destroy part of your brain stem and cause you to suffer from a condition called locked-in syndrome. If you've not heard of it before, it's where your entire body becomes completely paralysed, even down to your facial muscles. At the very most, you may retain vertical eye movement and the ability to blink, but you certainly won't be able to voluntarily move anything else or have the ability to verbally communicate." Crane leaned even closer to him. He wanted to look into his eyes and watch as the realisation of what was going to happen to him sank in. "And here's the best part—your consciousness and cognition will be unimpaired. You're effectively going to be locked inside your own head, unable to move or communicate for the rest of your life, unable to hurt anyone else. And bearing in mind you're only twenty-six now, that's potentially a long time to be trapped inside a shell. You're going to have plenty of time to think about what you've done."

Robert's eyes were now wide with panic and tiny beads of sweat seemed to appear from nowhere across his brow. His eyes darted around as though he was searching for something, then they stopped and became fixed on a point over Crane's shoulder. He tried to push himself and his chair back from the table, but he was already weakening. His flip-flops slid forward on the patio floor and he remained seated in his chair.

Crane sat back in his chair and watched Robert as he tried again. This time, he used his hands on the table to haul himself to his feet. He was up, but his legs were trembling and he couldn't seem to straighten them fully. It looked as though he were tentatively standing on a sheet of ice that could give way at any second.

He made a guttural grunt as he took a sideways step away from the table, then it seemed to take a great deal of concentration and effort for him to change direction and take a forward step. With his eyes still fixed on a point behind Crane, he let out another grunt and took another step forward. The harbour was much busier now. A few couples strolled past casually, some of them hand in hand, some not. A group of four ladies walked by with a little more purpose in their gait, probably heading out for a trip on one of the boats. Some of them glanced at Robert but immediately looked away, seemingly afraid to cause offence by staring at him.

Crane remained seated. He knew what Robert was planning to do, but he figured at this pace he had plenty of time to stop him before he reached the water. He turned in his seat and looked on as Robert took another laborious step forward. He was now sucking in rapid shallow breaths through clenched teeth and was moving as though his feet had suddenly turned into giant cannonballs.

As he staggered to the halfway point between their table and the water's edge, more passers-by began to take notice of him and their glances were turning into worried stares. Crane decided it was time. He stood up and approached Robert. To anyone looking on, he appeared to place a supportive arm across Robert's shoulders, but the purpose of Crane's grip was to prevent him from taking another step closer to the water. Another step closer to ending his nightmare.

Crane leaned into Robert and tutted in his ear. "Now, now, Robert, I told you I'm not letting you take the easy way out."

Robert whimpered and dropped to his knees. Both of his arms were now completely limp and hung uselessly at his sides. He made a high-pitched, almost inhuman mewling sound as his entire body shuddered and began to topple forward. Crane used his free arm to catch him and gently lowered him face down to the ground, more for the benefit of the spectators who were beginning to gather around than any real desire to help soften Robert's fall.

Crane went down on one knee and lowered his head to make it look as though he were checking on him. Robert was still breathing rapidly through gritted teeth. Specks of spittle were being ejected from his mouth with each forceful exhale and his eyes bulged with panic and despair. Robert then let out one final desperate wail. It was an animal-like cry that seemed to originate from deep within him. Several of the people in the crowd surrounding them gasped at the sound, but it quickly faded away along with all the tension within his body. His teeth gradually unclenched, his breathing began to slow down, and his entire body seemed to melt onto the concrete. He appeared to be at peace, but when Crane bent down a little lower to look into his eyes, he could see the anguish that remained within them.

"*Help*," called Crane, straightening up and looking around at the faces in the crowd. "I think he's having a stroke."

A grey-haired man in a khaki-coloured shirt stepped forward, "I'm a doctor."

"Please, help him." Crane got to his feet. "I'll go and call for an ambulance."

The doctor sidestepped around Robert and knelt beside him. At the same time, Crane slipped through a gap in the crowd and started to walk away along the harbour. Not a single person seemed to take a blind bit of notice of him; everyone's attention was on the sick man lying on the ground.

CHAPTER THIRTY-EIGHT

The overcast sky was drab and grey, but at least the rain was holding off so far. Crane, dressed in a black suit and tie, stood amongst the crowd of mourners as the vicar rattled off the order for the burial of the dead, just as he had no doubt done countless times before. The bearers standing on either side of the small grave gradually released the webbing hand over hand to gently lower the tiny coffin into its final resting place.

"We therefore commit his body to the ground; earth to earth, ashes to ashes, dust to dust; in sure and certain hope of the resurrection to eternal life..."

Michael and Lindsey were on the opposite side of the grave to Crane. They were both tearful, but as soon as the coffin disappeared below the surface, Lindsey broke down and turned away. Michael pulled her into him and wrapped his arms tightly around her, although his eyes never left the open grave. He appeared to be in an almost trance-like state, as though he was desperately trying to hold himself together.

Crane cast his eyes over the other faces in the crowd. Understandably, there was barely a dry eye in sight. Nobody ever wanted to say goodbye to their loved ones, no matter how long or full their lives had been. But there was something particularly heavy that weighed on people when they were saying goodbye to the life of a child. A life that hadn't been allowed to flourish.

This particular one taken under such horrific circumstances. It was truly heartbreaking and felt wholly unfair.

Crane had been to enough funerals to know that it was moments like this when people seemed to pause and consider the brief and finite nature of life. It's so easy to get caught up in the day-to-day rigours of life and allow ourselves to become stressed and frustrated at minor misdemeanours that won't matter tomorrow, never mind next week and certainly not next year. Trapped in our own little bubbles, forgetting what's most important in life.

He noticed his thoughts wandering to the important people in his life. He thought about Chloe, his niece. Such a sweet and bright young girl with bags of potential, a little bit of a smartarse at times, but overall a great kid.

Then there was Ricky. His business partner and best friend. One of the very few people in this world he trusted with his life. He thought about how he was becoming increasingly concerned about him and how he needed to do something to help him with his social anxiety and agoraphobia. Maybe he would bite the bullet and book a therapist to visit him soon; after all, it was easier to ask for forgiveness than permission.

His mind then inevitably drifted to Ella. Such a kind and gentle soul. Beautiful inside and out. Certainly too good for someone like him. Too pure. If she knew half the things he'd done, regardless of how righteous or just the cause, she would likely never want to see him again, let alone be with him. His mind played back some of the last things she'd said to him. *Would you give it up? Fixing, or whatever it is you call it. Would you give it up?* Could he? Could he go back to a "normal" life? Even if he did give it up, it didn't change who he was or erase the things he'd done.

When the committal service came to an end, the crowd began to disperse sporadically. Some people wanted to head off at the earliest opportunity, others preferred to stay and stand in silence a little longer to pay their respects in their own way. Crane stayed for another minute or so before turning away and starting up the path towards the car park, still partially lost in his thoughts.

"*Crane.*"

A man's voice called out his name and brought him back to the moment. He looked back over his shoulder and saw Michael hurrying to catch up to him. Crane stopped and turned around to face him.

"I just wanted to thank you for coming," said Michael before glancing around to make sure nobody could overhear them, then he leaned in a little closer and lowered his voice. "I also wanted to thank you in person for... you know... what you did for us."

"Don't mention it," replied Crane. "You've already thanked me enough."

When Crane had returned from Turkey, Michael transferred a substantial sum to his and Ricky's business account to show his gratitude to them.

Fresh tears began to well in Michael's eyes. "You know, after you did what you did, I thought I'd feel a little bit better, but all I feel is pain."

"Vengeance is not a cure for grief; the only cure for grief is to grieve." As composed as Crane looked in this moment, he'd experienced his fair share of grief. He had been forced to live beneath its crushing weight for almost five years after losing his wife.

Michael nodded almost imperceptibly. "I guess."

A moment of silence passed between them, then Michael lifted his head and his brow furrowed slightly. "I also had a thought earlier. You haven't asked me for the name of my friend. You know, the one that I called on for help."

"I didn't fulfil my part of our agreement, so I don't expect you to fulfil yours."

"You *couldn't* fulfil your part of the agreement," corrected Michael.

"A deal is a deal."

Silence fell between them once again. Crane watched as a gust of wind took hold of a few leaves, then twirled them up into feeble mini tornado before it discarded them on the grass.

"You're a good man, Crane. A man of principle, and I really respect that," said Michael, holding his gaze. "Look, for what it's worth, I've spoken to my friend about you, and he wanted me to assure you that he doesn't know the real identity of the man you've been seeking. He did, however, give me this." Michael reached into his inside jacket pocket and pulled out a small slip of paper. "It's the nickname he goes by, which I'm sure you already know. But he also gave me the phone number he uses to contact him."

Crane looked down at the slip of paper Michael held out for him. He could see the word *Chief* written across the top, but Michael's thumb covered most of the number. Only the final three digits were visible: *two-zero-six*.

"Thank you." Crane gave a brief smile as he pocketed it. He didn't want to seem ungrateful by telling Michael he already knew the nickname and the number.

"I'd better get back to Lindsey." Michael held his hand out between them. "Look after yourself, Crane."

Crane gave Michael's hand a firm shake. "Same to you." Then with a mutual nod of respect, they both turned and went their separate ways.

When Crane reached the car park, he pulled out the slip of paper Michael had given him, looked at it one last time, then squeezed it into a tight ball and flicked it into a bin as he walked past. It seemed as though every time he thought he had a route to find out who Chief was, he ran into another dead end.

A queue of cars was snaking its way around the car park, heading to the exit, nose to tail, inching forward. Other people were sitting in their cars and looking frustrated as they waited for a gap to pull out into. As expected, there had been quite the turnout for the funeral, and Crane had been fully anticipating a long wait to get out. So when he got into his new car, he didn't bother to push the power button.

He'd finally got around to trading in the Maserati, although his intention of getting something a little more low-key hadn't gone entirely to plan. He'd bought himself a Porsche Taycan Turbo S but justified his decision because it was jet black and electric. Admittedly, it wasn't exactly low-key, but it certainly wasn't as brash and loud as the red Maserati. *Baby steps*, thought Crane as he inhaled the new car smell and sat back to get comfortable.

While he waited for the car park to clear, he slipped his phone out of his pocket and unlocked it. There were three missed calls waiting for him. All from the same number he didn't recognise and all within the last thirty minutes. Crane took his phone off silent mode and then tapped to return the call. It rang twice, then a woman answered.

"Hello? Is that Mr Crane?"

"Just Crane's fine, who's this?"

"Thank you for calling me back," said the lady. There was a hint of relief in her tone. "My name's Bridget Everhart and I really need to speak to you about something."

"I'm listening."

"I believe you were the last person to see my husband before he died."

Crane frowned. "I'm sorry, but you're going to have to be a little more specific than that."

There was a slight pause, as though she was surprised by his response, which to be fair, was completely understandable. "Um... he shot himself in front of you in a cafe in Cardiff."

Oh...

"He handed a phone to you before he did it. I want to know who was on the phone and I want to know what they said to you."

Now it was Crane's turn to hesitate. He hadn't given the man much thought since it happened. Especially after what Chief had said about him. But now his mind went into overdrive. *How did she know that her husband gave the phone to me? And how did she get my number?* "I don't know who the man on the phone was, but he told me your husband was a convicted paedophile."

"*A what?*" she practically shouted down the phone, her tone containing an equal mixture of shock and outrage. "That is a complete and utter lie."

"Is it?" Asked Crane in a way that really said, "*Are you sure? Maybe you don't know him as well as you think.*"

"Of course it is," she snapped. "I'll have you know my husband was a good man. A great man. He certainly wasn't a..." it sounded as if she removed the phone from her face to make an "*ugh*" noise, as though she was too disgusted to say the word. "Did the man on the phone happen to call himself Chief?"

Crane immediately sat up and pressed the phone more firmly against his ear. "What do you know about this Chief?"

He heard movement on the other end of the phone, as though maybe she'd done the same, then she said, "What do *you* know about Chief?"

"I asked you first."

This time, the pause was longer. Almost ten full seconds of complete silence ticked by, then Bridget said, "I know he's the head of a criminal syndicate involved in everything from drugs and prostitution to arms dealing and people smuggling." It sounded as though she wanted to say more but stopped herself. "Now it's your turn. What do you know?"

"You pretty much just summed up everything I know about him," replied Crane. "Well, that and it seems to be practically impossible to find out his real identity."

"You're telling me," scoffed Bridget.

"But I don't understand. How do you know about him?"

"Jeff, my husband, was looking into him."

"Looking into him?" Crane's eyes narrowed. "Was your husband a policeman?"

"No. He's... he *was* an investigative journalist. He'd heard a rumour about Chief and his organisation a few months ago and had been looking into him. On the morning he..." Her voice cracked for the first time and she had to take a shaky breath before clearing her throat and trying again. "On the morning he died, he told me he was meeting up with a lead. He said he felt like he was getting close."

"Did he tell you who he was meeting?"

"No. I asked him, but he wouldn't tell me. He said it was for my safety."

"Have you told the police all this?"

"I haven't told anyone."

"Why not?"

"Because just before my husband took his own life, he sent me two text messages. The first one said 'run' and the second one said 'trust no one'. So, I—" Bridget stopped talking abruptly, and then after a moment of silence, she blurted out, "In fact, I've already said too much to you."

"You can trust me," urged Crane.

"I hope so."

"Can we meet up?"

"I'll be in touch."

"*Wait.* What else do you know about..." He stopped when he heard the line cut off and immediately tapped redial on his phone, but the call didn't connect, as the number was already dead.

Shit.

He opened an internet tab and typed '*man suicide Cardiff cafe*' into the search engine. Several news reports instantly popped up, and he quickly scanned over them. They all detailed Jeffrey Everhart, an investigative journalist from Cardiff, as the man who took his own life, but it was the subheading on the fifth article that really grabbed his attention. It said Jeffrey's wife, Bridget Everhart, was currently missing.

Acknowledgements

With special thanks to:

You. The reader. Thank you for taking the time to read my work - without you, this is just a bunch of black lines on white paper - you are the ones who really bring these stories to life. And in return, I hope that I entertained you for a few hours and helped you to escape the rigors of "real life".

My publisher Cassandra of Cahill Davis Publishing for your support.

My editor Lauren, for your wisdom and guidance in helping me smooth out all the rough edges.

My wife Jo and daughters, Holly and Summer. For surrounding me with love and being my world.

All my family and friends for your unwavering support.

Writing can be a very challenging and solitary experience, so I would also like to say a HUGE thank you to everyone who supports me by leaving reviews and following me across the different social media and retail platforms. Your support and words of encouragement mean the world and motivate me to keep going.

About the author

Keith lives in Wales with his wife, two young daughters and a cockapoo that looks more like a teddy bear than a dog.

Before he began writing thrillers, Keith served in the British Army and actively engaged in operational duties in Iraq, Kosovo and Bosnia. He then pursued careers in a multitude of industries until he finally decided to follow his true passion - writing.

When he isn't writing you can usually find Keith up one of the many mountains or on one of the many beaches of Wales, probably with a teddy bear in tow that's desperate for him to throw the ball again and again and again.

You can also connect with Keith on X (formerly Twitter) @kjdandoauthor or on Instagram @K.J.Dando

Milton Keynes UK
Ingram Content Group UK Ltd.
UKHW040846181124
2919UKWH00020B/71